A BEAUTIFUL
SATAN

BY

RJ CHAMP

❖Prairie State College

Back to
Books

Purchased with
Library Services
and Technology Act
funds provided by
the Illinois State
Library.

FY 2013

Published by DC Bookdiva Publications
Copyright © 2011 by RJ Champ

ISBN-10: 0-9846110-1-0
ISBN-13: 978-0-9846110-1-0
Library of Congress Control Number: 2011933083

Paperback Edition, September 2011

Publisher's Note

Edited by: Jenell Talley

DC Bookdiva Publications
#245 4401-A Connecticut Ave
NW, Washington, DC 20008
www.dcbookdiva.com
facebook.com/dcbfanpage

twitter.com/dcbookdiva

By
RJ CHAMP

" Beware of DC's charming
men, you never know whose
path you may cross."
-DC Bookdiva

A
BEAUTIFUL
SATAN

A NOVEL

DC BOOKDIVA PUBLICATIONS

Acknowledgements

First and foremost I would like to thank the following: Tiah Short- DC Bookdiva and The Official DC Reviewer Michelle Rawls, for recognizing talent and giving me the opportunity to express such words to the masses.

To My Family:

My loving mother, for my existence on this plain, and for giving me the initiative to pursue my dreams. My ex-wife, Sharon, for blessing me with a wealth of life experience that has shaped me into the man I am today. My grandmother Adelaide Champ – Van Buren, for all your prayers and blessing in my quest to become a better man. My aunt, Valarie, for believing in me and providing me with the tools to make this all possible: I told you, Val, I was gonna make it happen. My lil' sister, Karentha: Baby girl you held the fort down for your brother the entire way through. I got nothing but love for you, Big Head...you kept it trill!!! My little brother, Darryl: Yeah, I did it brother! My step-daughters, Dominque & Dawne, and my step-son; Man Man; I told you anything is possible...Stay focused, have patience and perseverance. And to my favorite cousins, Shayla & George: Keep reaching for the sky...My one and only favorite nephew: Kaulin: Be good and stay good.

For My Dawgz:

To my main road-dawg, Carlos Umanzor: I ain't forget about you...you one of the realest niggaz to ever touch my life- I got U! Oscar-Hollar at your boy...Central America ain't far baby! Raymond "Big Pimpin'" Church: Don't look surprised...I told you I was gonna make it happen! Brian & Herman Mayfield, and my road dawg Lefty: Pop them bottles! You know what time it is! Casper and Tony Purnell: What up! Leonard "Charlie" Cunningham: Keep bustin' heads. Curtis and Tye: Don't stop now. Uptown Jefro: You know how we do…it's party time! Dude, Rome, Stink, Red Man and Duck- Morton Street Mob: I comin' your way! First & O Crew (88); One of us had to make it! West B-More- My niggaz Getty, Wesley, Abdula, Cuzo and Fats…Stay on your grind! Getty-Get at me! My Youngstown, Ohio soldier, Sean…Keep it trill! Anthony Rowley- Barber To The Stars…I still got your back! Riggs Park- Elmo, Blue, Steve, HB and Sean. Ledroit Park- Red D and the crew. Carlton "Spook" Stewart, Chim-Chim and Bernard. Michael "Super Fly" Dorsey. Big Dex, Manny and Big Dave: Keep pushin' those Macks! Lee Gardner & Robert "Go-Go" Perry: See you at my next book signing!

For My Brothers On Lockdown:

My young soldier for Life, Harold "Six" Short-Bey: I got your back, baby boy…you put a brother on…Whatever you need, holler! My Eastern Shore Hustlaz-Black and Avery: y'all brothers kept my game tight, kept me focused and kept me bangin' out pages, non-stop..Big Up's! Y'all were my motivation. My DC soldier, "South-East RB" (you sat outside my cell and couldn't wait to get the next page hot off the press)…What I tell you youngin'…can't stop the hustle! Davon Henderson-Southside Hustlaz: Keep stackin' paper and mackin' honeys! My Frederick, MD Soldier-Trotez "Juice" Leonard: Slow your roll youngin'…Life too short! Joe "Heavy" Smith: Tell moms I said what's up. My Southeast youngin' Freddy G: Keep pushing that pen…you can make it happen. My brother Toke: What you though I was fakin'? Lavoir "Swamp" Johnson-cherry Hill, B-more…Represent! Benny "old School" Thorpe: Tighten up your game…you too old for the bullshit. Floyd Nash: Get uptown, leave them gats alone, and take care of your fam, brother. Lil b: Get them movie scripts together. Marques 'Lil Turk" Davis: Walk the walk youngin! Clarence "CJ" Jones- Triumph Productions:

Stay strong soldier. I'm looking for you to touch down...This is only the beginning!

And to anyone else I may have missed...I got love for ya.

Most of all, I would like to thank everyone that purchases this book. There's plenty more where this came from...Enjoy the story.

Preface

The Breaking Point ...

The bluish glass window shimmered in the afternoon sun, casting rays of dancing sunlight upon Angel as she slept. Warm sunbeams flickering across her eyelids began to awaken her. Slowly, Angel emerged from her sleep. She rolled over in bed. A tired frown was etched in her face, and long black tresses fell over her eye. Angel felt fuzzy, like she hadn't gotten a wink of sleep.

"What's this?" she said. Her hazel eyes focused on a crumpled piece of paper on the pillow beside her. The name Natasha was scribbled at the top.

The note was a letter from her husband, Rafael.

Will I ever see you again? Angel wondered as she reflected over the recent loss of Rafael.

"Why, Lord? Why would you allow me to fall so deep in love with a man, then allow Satan to intervene in our lives? Father, you let Satan take my love away. Why??!!" Angel cried out, tears of pain swelling in her eyes.

As if all her energy had just been sucked right out of her, Angel's head collapsed onto the pillow. Dazed, Angel stared at the ceiling, spellbound dozing.

Suddenly the sound of a smooth jazz melody drifted into the room. Startled, Angel turned and gazed tiredly at the door.

Where's the music coming from? she silently mused. Shivering, Angel pulled herself to her feet. As she stood, she felt a cold chill go through her entire body.

Kenny G's "Songbird" floated from the open doorway into the master bedroom as if it were trying to drown out the pleasurable moans of a woman in some kind of synthetic coup.

Angel lingered in the hallway; a concoction in whipped cream–fragranced candles saturated the air outside the master bedroom. Angel's trembling fingers moved along the wall as she reached for the door.

The blonde with crystal-blue eyes, Natasha, was inside the master suite on her hands and knees, doggy-style. She was getting her world rocked by Angel's cheating-ass husband, Rafael.

Gripping Natasha firmly around her waist, Rafael pounded her insides, pushing all 12 inches of his throbbing organ to the hilt.

"Yeah, that's it, bitch," Rafael hissed through clenched teeth. "Who's your daddy now, huh, bitch?" A smug grin spread on his lips. Rafael got off watching Natasha's rump jiggle every time he gave that ass a slap.

Angel stood in the doorway-pure rage simmering in her eyes, grinding her teeth as a icy chill ran down the back of her neck. She screamed out at the top of her lungs then lunged across like a woman who had totally lost her mind.

"You dirty-dick bitch!" Angel leaped on Rafael's back like a panther with the intent to kill. She hissed, bearing a

perfect set of pearly whites, and sank her teeth deep inside the huge muscle bulging from his shoulder.

Total shock and fear exploded on Rafael's face. He yelled from the pain and stumbled backward-twisting and turning with Angel strapped to his back. It took Rafael all the strength he could summon to pry his crazy wife's arms from around his throat. Rafael spun around and slung Angel toward the bed.

Angel hit the king-size bed poised on all fours when she landed; she resembled a feline preparing to attack. Operating on sheer impulse, Angel licked her lips and pounced on the frightened woman. Natasha, scared to death, tried to leap across the bed to escape the clutches of Angel. Moving to slow, her attempts were unsuccessful.

"On no, bitch!" Angel shouted aggressively, "You ain't going nowhere!" Angel tore into Natasha with death in her eyes. She mounted a vicious assault-fist, teeth, and nails-exerted pain and punishment on Natasha's nude body. The attack was so severe; Natasha swore she was being attacked by more than one woman.

Rafael rushed to Natasha's rescue. "Let her go!" Rafael stammered, locked in a heated struggle-wrestling and tussling to save his battered and bruised lover from the death grip of his enraged wife.

Angel's uncontrollable rage had her adrenaline pumping in overdrive, her strength was uncanny. Rafael had to use all 220-pounds of his muscular frame to hoist Angel in the air. He was stretched to the limit, all six feet of Rafael stood erect. Rafael let out a lout roar and tried one last time to muster the strength needed to release Angel's hold on Natasha. Gasping for air and in pain the wind was knocked out of him from the full impact of Angel's weight crashing on him.

Immediately, Angel bounced to her feet when she realized he was hurt. She stood over him, glaring. "Ha! You like fucking around on me?" she spewed, "You dirt dick *bitch!" Angel cocked her right foot back and kicked him right in his nuts. She leaned over him and coughed up a snotty blob of phlegm, and hawk spit right in his damn face. "You and your bitch can meet in hell!"*

Angel took a step inside the bathroom and was surprised at how chilly the air was inside. With caution in her every step, she walked to the mirror and gazed at herself. She looked discombobulated when she noticed a bright white T-shirt covering her torso. She couldn't remember putting on the shirt. Angel looked down at the white tee, her fingers trembling as they brushed against the wet cotton. "NATASHA" was finger painted across the front in large crimson letters—fresh blood. Angel froze, utter horror and disbelief radiating in her expression. She looked toward the mirror and cringed. An ice-cold sensation pierced her to the core when she saw the inverted reflection of Natasha's name in the mirror. Spelled in fresh blood, "AH-SATAN" seemed to leap off the shirt. The painted letters were all Angel could see. She stared at herself in the looking glass and realized the woman looking back was a total stranger.

Suddenly the fog lifted from Angel's eyes and she was brought back to reality. She realized she was still on the bed, gazing up at the ceiling. Shaken, Angel sat upright and reached out to yank open the top drawer of the nightstand. She pulled out a prescription pill bottle with the narcotic Oxyline printed on the label.

Angel popped two pills in her mouth, tossed the pill bottle back in the drawer and then closed her eyes tightly, exhaling deeply.

"Father-God, I pray for you to vanquish the bad dreams, the bad feelings and the bad demons that I feel surrounding me and taunting me. Please, oh Lord, I know that I am nothing without you, so please have mercy on me. I put no other above you. I'm begging you, Lord, please bless me with a real man so I can move forward with my life and forget

A Beautiful Satan

Rafael. Help me purge my husband's unclean spirit from my soul. Help me, Father-God. I need you. Please!"

Chapter 1

There was a full moon shimmering in the clear, star-filled sky over D.C. on this warm, summery night.

Tonight was a very special night: Jovan and Angel Rising were in the midst of celebrating their new union as husband and wife.

They were inside the elegant Rosewood Manor, a bed and breakfast located in Southern Maryland. The smooth mesmerizing sounds of Corinne Bailey's Rae's "Like A Star" were serenading the happy couple as they shared their first dance. This was their wedding song, their love song.

Mrs. Angel Rising was living her dream at this moment. She was the center of attention, dancing in the arms of the man she worshipped and to whom now she was married. *I'm Mrs. Jovan Rising!* she thought happily, emotions overflowing.

Angel looked like a fairy-tale princess brought to life. She was Angelic in her glowing white gown and sparking tiara. Her warm caramel eyes twinkled and seemed to melt men's souls. With her curvaceous hour-glass figure and soft, butterscotch complexion, Angel Rising was the epitome of beauty.

As she melted in her husband's arms, Angel said to herself, *This has to be what they mean when people say a nigga got a bitch sprung 'cause I'm in heaven!*

Jovan gazed into her tearful eyes. "Everything alright, baby?" he asked with a soft smile. She nodded and wiped her eyes. "Aww," he cooed. "Are those tears of joy I see?" He looked dashing in his tailored pearl-gray tuxedo.

Angel looked up into his eyes and whispered, "Yes. I'm so happy to be your wife." Their lips touched as they embraced.

"Aww, baby," he cooed again with a devilish grin. "I love you so much." Jovan kissed her gently on the forehead. His piercing gray eyes swept the crowd and paused when he made eye contact with one of his nympho sex partners. Her name was Tara. Shorty had the bangin' hooker body with all the trimmings. She attended the ceremony to bid him farewell—and hopefully slide off somewhere and get broke off. Tara winked at Jovan. She had a sleazy "come fuck me look" in her eye.

Jovan Rising had a lethal reputation as a mack. Angel's girlfriends were blown by her decision to marry him. They couldn't believe for one minute that Angel would be crazy enough to marry his wild ass. But she was head over heels in love with him, and she really believed she could change his ways.

However, some brothers just aren't marriage material. That was a fact of life. Jovan Rising topped that list. The nigga was fine! That was a given. He was 6'1", and 220 pounds of chiseled muscle. He had a smooth, light-mocha complexion, killer dimpled smile and piercing gray bedroom eyes, and his short, curly hair and mustache was always tight. And the nigga's dick game was legendary. Her friends could see why her head was all up in the clouds over the brother.

A Beautiful Satan

But their girl needed to weigh out her options. Were his manly attributes (good looks and bomb sex) worth a life of heartbreak and turmoil? Because this brother was offering a heavy dose of misery. All of her close friends could see it just as plain as day. Not Angel. She had on blinders when it came to this man.

Jovan Rising was fling material. He was the nigga you kept on the side and let beat up the pussy when you needed that thang beat. Her girlfriends begged her not to marry him, but their words fell on deaf ears. Angel was a freak for pain, her girls reasoned. Either that or she was one crazy-ass bitch. How surprised they would all be when they found out she was both.

After the storybook wedding, Jovan whisked his new wife off to Honolulu, Hawaii. The newlyweds spent 10 glorious, sun-filled days basking on the white, sandy beaches. They sipped on Mai-Tais and Cristal while enjoying the sight and sound of the picturesque blue Pacific Ocean crash upon the shore.

The lovely couple spent romantic evenings together—engaging candlelight dinners on the beach under moonlit skies with soft Polynesian music playing in the background.

Angel's smiling eyes twinkled softly as the candlelight danced in them. "Baby," Jovan said in his sexy Barry White tone, "You are the most beautiful lady on the island. You know that?"

Angel blushed. "Thank you, Da," she replied softly, swirling her spoon in a tasty sea-urchin soup.

"I really mean that, baby," Jovan added, looking deeply into her eyes while caressing her cheek. "You are truly mine now." His earnest demeanor touched her. "You are my lady, my wife, my life. This is what you wanted. We're one now, husband and wife." Jovan smiled. "I'm married," he said, his tone holding a hint of uncertainty that went clear over Angel's head. She hadn't come down off her high from the wedding yet. "You're Mrs. Rising now, baby," he said while turning up a glass of straight Hennessy. "You better represent too!" he said with a playful smirk as he slammed the empty glass on the table.

Angel smacked her lips and waved him off. "What are you talking about?"

He shot her a sly look. "You know what I'm talkin' 'bout. "I'm steppin' our game up. Stepping my game up: bigger house, tighter whip. You know, time to make some sound investments."

Angel looked uncertain. "Okay. We'll sit down and talk about it."

"Nah, baby girl," he interrupted. "You let me make all the financial maneuvering. You just lay back and chill," Jovan directed smoothly. He winked and blew his wife a kiss.

She was momentarily taken aback by her hubby's remark but also felt secure knowing that she had married the right man.

The Risings' romantic, whirlwind honeymoon ended far too soon for Angel. She was living her fantasy and never wanted it to end. Nothing else mattered to her. Nothing else could compare to the way she was feeling. Angel was in love! She had her man, and she was loving life.

♛♛♛♛

The couple was two days removed from their exotic Hawaiian honeymoon. Back in Clarksville, Maryland. Angel was standing on the rear deck of their beautiful estate. She looked lovely, even this early in the morning. She was wrapped snugly in a delicate gold silk gown. Angel was sipping her morning java, staring off into the wilderness and listening to the sounds of the birds chirping in the distance.

This was the second morning she had awakened to an empty house. Her foot was tapping incessantly as thoughts coursed through her mind. The crease in her brow grew more intense the more she thought. "We need to have a serious talk when he gets home. I'm not having this," Angel told herself adamantly. She needed to do something to quell her anger.

Upstairs in the spacious master bathroom, which was her sanctuary, she produced one of her favorite wedding photos from her Marc Jacobs bag. "Oh, I love the shit out of this man," she admitted to herself, quietly smiling. Jovan was her life now. She peered into the body-length vanity mirror.

Angel loved this man unconditionally with all of her heart and soul. She placed the wedding photo against her chest. Thinking of Jovan made her heart flutter. She watched herself in the mirror. She couldn't get enough of seeing herself in her glamorous wedding gown. "I'm willing to do whatever it takes to be in your life," she remembered telling Jovan one blissful night as her head lay against his thick chest. "I'm willing to kill—even die— for you," Angel had told him, swearing her allegiance. She knew Jovan didn't take her seriously. But in Angel's mind that shit was real. This man was her soul mate, and now they were joined in a holy union in the eyes of the Lord.

She pranced in front of the mirror, ecstatic. Angel loved how the gown accentuated her figure. The sound of the phone ringing irritated her slightly, as she didn't like for anything or anyone distracting her when she got into a blissful state.

Angel slowly walked across the zebra-skin rug that lay in the center of their exotic tropical-themed love nest. She flopped on the edge of their canopy bed, hoping the person on the other end of the phone would hang up before she answered. No such luck.

"Hey, ma," the caller said. "Jo-Jo."

"Jo-Jo, girl what in the hell do you want this early in the morning? How you know I was home anyway?"

"Well Miss Thang," she replied smartly, "for your info, I didn't know your ass was back. I thought that I was your girl. Why you keeping me in the dark about your whereabouts? That's where we at now?"

"Now, Miss Blackness," Angel replied jokingly, "I know you did not go there."

Jo-Jo laughed. "Well, bitch, you gonna meet me at Starbucks in a hour or what?"

Jo-Jo was Angel's Nigerian homegirl. The two had been inseparable since high school. Jo-Jo was a dark-chocolate stallion, thick in all the right places. She was an entrepreneur. She owned a fly-ass hair salon in N.E. Washington. It was rumored that Jo-Jo got the money to start her business by getting this Nigerian drug dealer's house hit. She would have you believe that her father purchased the business for her as a gift.

Angel was seated at one of the outside tables when Jo-Jo's silver Cadillac CTS coupe pulled into an empty parking space in the front of the Starbucks. Angel looked beautiful sitting at the table in jeans and stilettos. She seemed to glow under the bright sun as she waved with excitement the moment Jo-Jo arrived.

Jo-Jo hopped from the Caddy, a hot piece of dark chocolate draped in a white midriff and tight white cropped pants, a stark contrast to her swarthy skin tone. Jo-Jo was outgoing and effervescent, which was obvious as she rushed over to greet Angel.

"Girl, look at you!" Jo-Jo gushed gleefully when Angel stood to greet her. They embraced one another happily. "Girl you got that glow! Damn! What the hell happened in Hawaii?" She took her seat and leaned across the small round table as if they were exchanging top-secret information. "How that nigga treating you, girl?" You all glowy and shit. Jovan must be tearing that thang up!" The envy was evident in Jo-Jo's expression.

Angel was silent, her eyes sparkling. "Ain't this some shit," huffed Jo-Jo, straightening up in her seat. "Where's my latte, freak?" The remark prompted a laugh from Angel.

A Beautiful Satan

"What's the matter, blackness?" she inquired with a chuckle. "Youngin' not handling his business at home?"

"Don't get sassy with me, ho," Angel warned jokingly. "I ain't the one holding out on you. You have to take that up with dude," she teased, referring to the college senior Jo-Jo was fucking around with.

When she first hooked up with the college boy, she referred to him as her toy. That was six months ago. Now the youngin' had turned the tables. Jo-Jo had caught feelings, but the college boy didn't want any part of that. Jo-Jo was feeling the sting from her young toy.

"Where's your hubby right now?" she asked. "I know that nigga ain't change his spots overnight. You better keep a close eye on him. Y'all married now, so don't take no shit off of him," she said. "I know that nigga might be a little crazy, but you get crazy right along with his ass!"

The soulful voice of Raheem began to emanate from Angel's bag. The ring tone for the song "My Wife" brought a smile to her face. It was Jovan. Angel quickly fished the cell from her bag. There was a new text alert: "Just thinking of U Precious...Just wanted to say I Luv U –XOXO."

"Aww, he is so sweet," she sighed. "Look what my daddy left for me." Angel passed Jo-Jo her cell.

"I'm gonna be sick," said Jo-Jo as she leaned over acting like she wanted to puke.

Chapter 2

A black Mercedes SL 550 drove on the outside lane on I-95 Northbound. The vehicle went ballin' past a forest-green Porsche like the car wasn't even moving. Inside the dark tinted Mercedes the sounds of 50 Cent's "Baby By Me" filled the airwaves.

Jovan was slouched in the driver's seat, gripping the wheel with a stern look. "Oh fuck, baby!" he gasped suddenly. A female's head popped up from his lap.

"What's the matter?" she whispered, her voice sounding sultry as she used the back of her hand to wipe saliva from her lips. It was Tara, the blonde red-bone from the wedding reception.

"Nah, everything good, ma," he assured quickly, stroking her long hair. "I felt you tryin' to deep-throat my joint, and I was feelin' that shit. Damn!"

Tara smacked her lips. "What, you want me to stop?" she pouted.

"What?" he frowned. "Nah, shorty, I want you to finish handling you business. I just told you I was feelin' that shit you was doing." Jovan palmed her plump ass and flashed his killer dimpled smile.

A wave of relief and eagerness spilled across Tara's face. "Mmm," she moaned, "that's what I like." She looked at him lustfully. "Oooh!" she sighed. "Are we almost there? I can't wait to ride this big ole thang you got here. Mmmph!" Tara's head suddenly did a swan dive onto Jovan's throbbing dick.

He had to grip the wheel tightly with both hands. Jovan's right leg went into an epileptic seizure, suddenly jamming on the accelerator. "Oh my God!" he said as he tried to gather his composure. Baby girl was handling her business; she was putting in work with a vicious head game.

Damn, I'm having a good day, Jovan thought silently, pushing the Ferragamo shades down over his eyes as he settled back in the seat. He was enjoying the feel of the road under his wheels, the feel of his dick massaging Tara's tonsils and the warmth of the sun's rays cascading through the windshield. *It's still early*, Jovan thought. *Could this day get any better?*

ⓊⓊⓊⓊ

Later that evening, reggae music drifted throughout the basement of the Rising home. Jovan sat shirtless on the edge of his weight bench, sweat flowing profusely down his forehead as he bobbed in rhythm to Bob Marley's "Three Little Birds."

This my last set, he said to himself before stretching out on the bench. Jovan got into position under a 320-pound barbell. He inhaled deeply, his black-gloved hands gripped the iron bar tightly, his eyes focused intensely on an invisible spot on the ceiling. Jovan pushed the bar from the rack and allowed it to descend onto his chest. Then with a powerful thrust, the 320 pounds blasted off his chest as he locked out his arms and let out a low growl that seemed to reverberate off the walls and ceiling. Jovan completed ten reps before placing the bar back onto the rack.

Jovan felt nice and tight after his 90-minute chest routine. He went up to the kitchen and dined on his usual after-workout snack: a bowl of granola cereal in soy milk and a super-sized vanilla-flavored whey protein shake.

Suddenly the sound of a car engine humming inside the garage grabbed his attention. Jovan polished off his shake then bounded up the stairs seconds before Angel emerged from the garage.

Upon entering their posh and impeccably furnished home, her eyes quickly scanned the first floor in search of her hubby. She placed her shopping bags at the bottom of the stairs when she noticed the basement door was open.

"Da," Angel called out, pulling back the door. "Da, are you down there?" She closed the door when there was no reply.

Angel could hear the shower running when she walked into the bedroom. She stepped into the walk-in closet and stashed her expensive clothing purchases in her secret hiding spot.

Jovan strolled into the bedroom with a gold bath towel wrapped around his waist, beads of water glistening from his hard, buffed frame. "Hey babe, "he said, looking surprised. "How long have you been here?"

"Damn!" she gasped, slightly startled by his sudden emergence from the bathroom. He had just missed her goody stash. Angel quickly scooted out of the closet.

"I just got home," she answered. Lust jumped on her face when she caught a glimpse of her man's wet body gift wrapped in terry cloth *just for her*, she fantasized. "How long have you been home, Mr. Street Runner?"

"Mr. Street Runner?" He eyed her. "What's that supposed to mean?" he inquired while rubbing his chin. Jovan then rounded the bed and planted himself in his tan contemporary recliner by the window. "What, you gotta problem with something?"

He then reached for the remote and the 55-inch plasma mounted on the wall flashed to life. "You got something you need to get off your chest?" There was a tinge of indifference in his tone.

Angel looked at him skeptically. He was so busy channel surfing, he didn't notice—or didn't care to notice—her watching him. Angel wasn't feeling this vibe one bit.

"Well, as a matter of fact," she began, taking a seat on the edge of the bed across from him, "I'm feeling lonely. Since we got home from our honeymoon, you haven't spent any time with me."

Jovan turned around with an agitated look. "What?? I ain't spend no time with you? We live together. How in the hell can you fix your mouth to say that shit?!"

Her eyes fell to the floor. "What I'm talking about is quality time. We haven't spent any time together alone as a couple."

"I can't believe you," Jovan exploded. "We just had a big-ass wedding! We spent almost two fucking weeks in Hawaii! Shit, we got our fuck on in so many damn spots on the island, anytime you hear the word Hawaii, your pussy should get soaking wet."

Their honeymoon in Hawaii *did* leave an indelible mark on Angel's mind, body and soul. Memories of their romantic excursion suddenly put a warm smile on her face.

"You right," she admitted softly. Her eyes moved from the carpeted floor to her husband's bare legs. She was surprised to find him watching her with intensity when their eyes met.

A devious smile began to unfurl on his lips. "You find something you like?" As he stood, his towel fell to the floor.

Jovan strolled over to Angel, bent down, moved her hair out of the way and softly bit her neck. Although it hurt a little, she loved it. She shuddered as Jovan climbed on top of her. He could tell she wanted him, but he took his time. The couple's sexual affinity for one another was extremely intense; this couple was attracted to each other like magnets, their souls seemed to become one. Jovan spread Angel's legs and slid his dick into her hot, wet pussy. His body suddenly crashed into hers and he began ramming his long, thick penis deep into her. Angel was in heaven, experiencing orgasms at a phenomenal rate, sounding off each minute as the pressure became almost unbearable. Angel lay in the middle of the bed, exhausted, in a complete state of bliss. To Angel, sex with this man was an adventure that totally wowed her body each time. Jovan's dick game was addictive, and Angel was his number one fiend. She was hooked, and the thought of another bitch getting a taste of her golden dick made her cringe.

ΨΨΨΨ

Angel watched as Jovan moved to the edge of the bed. She reached for him.

"Da," she silently whispered. She had to look him in the eyes and show him her contentment. Then she lay there in the middle of the bed, still in a state of complete bliss.

The sound of a door closing woke Angel from her nap. Her eyelids opened gradually to see Jovan standing in front of the dark oak armoire impeccably dressed in a Dolce & Gabbana linen ensemble.

Her eyes blinked. She was wide awake now. "Where you going? Angel asked, surprised and suspicious at the same time.

"I dunno," he said, flashing her an evil glare as he slipped his D&G shades over his eyes.

Angel bolted upright. "You fuck the hell out of me and then get all dressed up to go out? You think that's fair? What about me? I thought we were going to spend the evening together. You *know* I have to go back to work soon. I miss you," she said, "Can you stay home with me tonight? Please."

A Beautiful Satan

Jovan was unmoved. "Not tonight, babe, I got some things I need to, uh, take care of, you know?"

Angel's head twisted to the side. "Things like what?" she retorted. "Some other bitch?"

Jovan mugged her with a harsh stare. "You questioning me?" he said, "I told you when we first hooked up—what I tell you, huh? I told you I was a wild nigga! You fuck with me, you had to be ready for my wildness! You said you was ready. You said you could hang! So don't start no bullshit," he warned, pointing his finger. "Don't try to put no shit in the game. This is me," he yelled pounding his chest. "I do what I do, I am what I am, and it is what it is, baby. Take it or leave it. I'm not changing for no damn body!" Jovan said and walked out.

In his wake a dark cloud seemed to hover above the spot where he stood. The harsh words he spoke struck a bad chord in Angel. *Have I made a grave mistake?* she thought. This is not how she pictured herself being treated by her husband.

Angel was a spiritually endowed woman who was raised with Christian virtues. "The man who finds a wife, finds a good thing," she said, quoting one of her much-used Bible verses out loud enough for her husband to hear. She could hear Jovan snicker as he descended the stairs.

The Bible speaks of how a sharp tongue can crush a soul. Jovan's words literally crushed Angel's heart. His words had ripped open her soul, and she could feel a dark rage starting to brew inside.

Angel's eyes brimmed with tears as she made her way to the closet. Maybe trying on her newly purchased apparel might give her some form of solace from her asshole husband.

ⓌⓌⓌⓌ

Angel was a savvy, smart young woman. In the eyes of her many female associates, she was an accomplished woman in many regards. However, this was Angel's second

13

marriage. Her first husband was a D.C. drug lord who had left her very well off just before his untimely death, thus enabling Angel's independence. Angel loved her career as a nursing manager for N.I.H's Oncology Department. She had a prestigious position, and she was blessed with a heart of gold. She was kind and caring. Angel would give the shirt off her back if a person was in need. Some people might say she was too loving, too trusting. Some would even go so far as to say that Angel's loving heart would cause her great hardship one day.

As she kneeled in the closet pulling her prizes from her secret stash, she began to smile. She pulled a pair of gold Manolo Blahnik boots out of her Neiman Marcus shopping bag. She held one boot in the air, admiring its form and color. Suddenly, out the side of her eye, she noticed a long blonde strand of hair dangling from the bottom of Jovan's Ferragamo shirt that was hanging in the closet. Her nose scrunched as she carefully plucked the hair from the shirt and studied it.

Suddenly Angel's breathing became labored, her chest rising and falling with distress. Her warm eyes frosted over with sheer hatred as she rose to her feet. Snatching the beige linen shirt off the hanger, she quickly rifled through the pockets and was stunned when she stumbled across a hotel receipt from the Capitol Hyatt. Rage erupted in her eyes, and all she could see was a crimson tide rolling slowly through her mind.

Chapter 3

Angel emerged from an exclusive day spa in Georgetown. She looked sophisticated and sexy in her periwinkle Gucci suit, which accentuated her hour-glass figure superbly. With her new platinum-blonde wig and blue contacts, she bore a striking resemblance to a tan Christina Aguilera.

The warm afternoon sun felt invigorating as Angel strutted across the parking lot to a Mercedes CLK. A minute later, Tara, the ho Angel suspected was fucking her husband popped up on the passenger side. "I'm riding with you, right?" Tara asked, looking like a ditzy airhead.

The white Mercedes gleamed like crystal under the blazing afternoon sun as it cruised to the edge of the lot and paused momentarily before merging into the oncoming traffic.

ॐॐॐॐ

Three days was the timeline Angel gave herself to put her plan into effect.

Right after stumbling across the blonde strand of hair and hotel receipt, Angel was hot on Tara's trail, like a bloodhound hunting down a fox.

It just so happens that Angel's girlfriend, Ronnie, worked part time at that very hotel. Angel phoned Ronnie at work and gave her the receipt information. In no time, Angel had the ho's full government name, home address and home and cell phone numbers.

Acquiring Tara's personal information was the easy part. Now it was time for the real work—how to arrange a face-to-face meeting with the ho without raising any suspicions.

Then it hit Angel–there wasn't a woman alive who would turn down the chance for a day of relaxation and pampering at one of D.C.'s hottest day spas, free of charge.

With Tara's personal information in hand, Angel phoned one of her favorite spas in Georgetown. She reserved spaces for two appointments for the same time and same day (using an alias for her name) and paid in advance for the Ultimate Platinum Spa Treatment. Angel had the spa fax her two separate reservations. She placed Tara's inside one of those extra-fancy silk-latent fuchsia-colored envelopes and labeled the front "Compliments – Georgetown Day Spa." Angel hand delivered the envelope to Tara's home address, discreetly slipping the envelope under her apartment door.

On the day of the appointment, Angel made a point to arrive at the spa 30-minutes early. She wanted to be there to see the tramp walk through the door.

Angel was so in tuned to Jovan's taste in women, the moment Tara walked in, she knew without a doubt she was the ho.

"Dirty bitch," Angel sneered under her breath before standing. She glared at Tara as she stood at the counter talking to the receptionist. Angel approached from behind. *This the dirty ho that's fuckin' my husband!* she said to herself, raging.

A Beautiful Satan

The urge to reach out and strangle the bitch was growing stronger with each step Angel took. Out of nowhere a disturbing image popped in Angel's head—it was the blonde with the crystal-blue eyes. But this time it wasn't Rafael fucking her; Jovan was smashin' that ass! The image in her head changed suddenly, as if a page had turned in her head. Now Angel could see herself standing in a dark bathroom gazing at her own reflection in the mirror. She could see there was something scribbled on the mirror. When she moved closer, Angel felt her heart go ice cold in her chest. The name Natasha was finger painted on the mirror in fresh blood.

"Damn, girlfriend, you killin' 'em in that bad-as-shit suit! You gotta put a bitch down. Where you cop that joint?" Angel heard Tara say as a cloud of haze seemed to lift from her eyes.

It took Angel a second to gather herself. When she realized what was going on, she found herself standing at the counter face-to-face with the ho! She was momentarily stunned.

"Pardon me?" Angel smirked drily.

Tara giggled slightly and apologized. "Oh, excuse my bad manners, girlfriend. You know how us hood chicks can be sometime." She hesitated briefly, then announced, "My name's Tara." She offered her hand in greeting. "And your name is?"

Angel looked her straight in the eye, gave a firm handshake and coolly responded, "My name's Natasha. Nice to meet you, hood chick."

Both women shared a laugh at how Angel put a verbal twist on the term hood chick; she pronounced it "ho chic."

After spending a few hours in the spa chit-chatting and getting to know one another, they decided after the spa they would hang out together and make a day of it.

Angel was more than satisfied. Her plan was moving along without a hitch.

The women were driving north on Connecticut Avenue en route to Houlihan's restaurant for lunch and drinks. About halfway into the trip, Tara asked if Angel could swing past her crib, which was close by, because she needed to grab some extra cash.

This was playing out better than Angel could've hoped. She had already been past the bitch's apartment building, which wasn't much to look at. Now she could take inventory of how that bitch really lived.

Tara lived in a modest one-bedroom, garden-style apartment, just off Connecticut Avenue and a stone's throw away from the UDC college campus.

Tara switched on the light to her apartment and invited Angel inside. A big gray tabby cat sauntered up to greet them. "Hey, Snooky," she cooed while kneeling to the pet the purring cat. "This my baby," said Tara, smiling up at Angel who was busy surveying the cramped little apartment.

"What?" Angel asked and glared down at the woman and her creepy-looking Chia-Pet. "I'm not too fond of cats," she said while side-stepping the cozy duo. "Nice little place you have here," Angel said as she stepped into the small, shabby-looking living room. She was glad Tara was busy with her cat because it took her a moment to gather her composure and wipe the disgusted expression off her face.

This bitch can't shine my damn shoes, Angel said to herself. She wondered if her husband had been here and had gotten a whiff of how this bitch was living. *This bitch is so far beneath me,* she thought as her anger started to boil. The crummy crib assaulted her emotions. *How dare him!* she thought. She was seething now.

"Can I get you a drink, girl?" Tara asked, suddenly appearing at her side. Angel nodded.

"Yea, I can use a drink." She had to fight off the urge to reach out and strangle this bitch. "What do you have to drink?" Angel asked. Tara walked towards the kitchen, totally unaware of the threat lurking in the midst of her home.

A Beautiful Satan

"I got some Grey Goose. You fuck with the Goose?" She pushed away from the counter holding up the bottle with a dumb grin plastered on her lips.

Not long after, both women were seated at the dining room table talking and drinking Grey Goose.

"What do you do for a living, Natasha?" Tara asked. The effects of the alcohol were starting to show in her tone and demeanor. "Girl, that suit you rocking is saying something!"

Angel regarded her with a steady look. "I'm in the medical field," she replied.

"What? A doctor?" she blurted. "That's how you got that pretty-ass Benz?"

Tara suddenly reached out and grabbed Angel's left hand. "Damn! Girl, that's a big-ass rock!" she exclaimed with wide eyes. "Who the hell you marry? Tara's speech was starting to slur.

Angel jerked loose, startling Tara. "What's that all about?" Tara retorted, tossing her hands in the air defensively.

Daggers were flying from Angel's eyes. "You know a nigga named Jovan?" she asked in a deceptive voice.

"Jovan," Tara stuttered. "That's my boo. You talking about that fine nigga who just got married?" Tara's words suddenly froze in her throat. A threatening aura seemed to explode into the atmosphere and then linger. A cold chill ran down Tara's neck.

"OMG, you're his wife!" a stunned Tara said.

Angel had a crazed look in her eyes. "You were at my wedding," she raged. "You nasty bitch!" Angel snatched the bottle of vodka off the table and wacked Tara across the nose with the butt of the bottle. She cried out and fell to the floor, blood gushing from both nostrils.

A wicked look played itself across Angel's face as she rose from her seat. She crouched beside Tara and snatched her head back. "Get the fuck off me!" Tara shouted as she struggled against Angel's grip.

"Shut up, bitch!" Angel smacked her. "You fuckin' my man!" She then slammed Tara's face into the wooden table leg with such force the leg snapped.

"Bitch, you gonna pay for this shit," Tara stammered drunkenly as she fought off the urge to pass out. Her arms flailed about wildly in a futile attempt to defend herself.

Fury ignited Angel's soul. She hovered over the woman who had been fucking her husband. She was full of rage. "You like fucking married men, bitch!" Angel spat viciously and disappeared into the kitchen.

Tara staggered down the hallway, trying to make it to the front door.

"Oh, no, bitch," Angel yelled, wielding a claw hammer firmly in her grip as she charged across the room like a madwoman with a score to settle.

The chilling voice made the hairs stand up on the back of Tara's neck. She dared not stop or look back.

Angel swung the hammer. She watched Tara's legs buckle under the force of the blow. She stumbled but didn't fall. Angel kept coming.

"You fucking, ho!" she shrieked. "Bitches like you don't deserve life!" She hit her once more in the back of the head with the claw end of the hammer. Tara's body crumpled to the floor with the claw imbedded in the back of her skull. Angel stood over her and watched her twitch. She looked like a beast hovering God-like over her fallen prey. Suddenly the gravity of the situation was like a slap in the face.

She had just committed murder, the ultimate taboo. However, slaying that ho gave her a feeling like a bitch having an orgasm while getting her twat licked for the first time. The powerful allure of death spawned a spirit of pure evil that ignited Angel's core. Suddenly a dark mental space opened inside her mind. Angel could feel a dangerous presence surge and take control of her mind. She could actually feel her mind being pulled apart, splitting in two. She sensed her conscious slip away as the soul of Natasha invaded her body.

Natasha took a knee beside Tara's corpse, ripped the hammer from her skull, and twisted her head around face up. Natasha proceeded to gouge out her eyes with the claw end of the hammer. When she finished, she stood up, grabbed Tara's corpse by the left ankle and dragged it into the bedroom.

Chapter 4

Jovan's eyes fluttered open. He saw he couldn't move his hands and legs. Peering down, he noticed what seemed to be a giant web. "What the fuck!" he stammered and froze when a giant tarantula suddenly appeared from the shadows. "Oh, God! Help me!" he screamed, struggling to get free as the tarantula descended upon him.

The spider closed the distance, and Jovan could see its face. He was petrified when he recognized the face of Tara who grinned, exposing a grotesque mix of sharp jagged fangs. "Somebody help, please!!!"

Out of the blue, another giant tarantula appeared. This one charged into Tara with killer speed. The spider ripped Tara's head clean from her torso. Jovan stared in disbelief when the spider whipped around with the head of Tara dangling grotesquely from its mouth.

The whites of Jovan's eyes went wide, the horrible sight before him was enough to bust his heart. Watching Tara's head swing from the mouth of Angel made him cringe and he cried out, "Lord! Help me!!!"

A Beautiful Satan

Jovan was awakened suddenly by a loud pounding on the front door. "Son of a bitch!" he snapped. Relief flooded his senses when he realized it was all just a dream. He snatched his Cartier off the nightstand and saw it was 9:30 a.m. Way too early for him to be up. He dove back into the pillow, hoping whoever it was would leave. No such luck; they were persistent. "Alright! Hold the fuck up!" he shouted.

Standing on his front porch and greeting him with a broad, happy-go-lucky grin stuck on his face was his road dawg, Ray.

"Dude, what the hell are you doing banging on my goddamn door this early in the morning?" Jovan rubbed the sleep from his eyes. "You must've bumped your damn head," he said, pulling the belt tight on his robe while heading for the kitchen. "You want some coffee? Whatever you got to tell me better be some good shit," he muttered over his shoulder.

Ray tossed his gray blazer over the back of the kitchen chair and grabbed a seat on one of the bar stools at the granite isle in the center of the kitchen. "Wifey gone?" Ray asked.

"Yeah, nigga," Jovan grunted. "She rolled out a couple hours ago. Why?"

"Man, I got this wild-ass e-mail early this morning from one of my hos, right."

"And? What the hell she got to do with me? What, she heard about this super dick, and she trying to sample the goods, huh, man?" he chuckled lightheartedly.

"Your new pussy got slumped the other night. Somebody bashed her head in with a hammer," Ray said flatly. He slid his BlackBerry across the granite. "Check out that e-mail."

Jovan was shaken. "What the fuck? Somebody killed Tara. What kind of sick fuck would do some crazy-ass shit like that?!" Jovan stared at the BlackBerry, dazed.

"Sounds like a jealous psycho boyfriend got hold of her to me," offered Ray casually. "He might've got wind of those secret rendezvous y'all been having lately." He eyed

Jovan with a raised brow and cautioned, "You might need to watch your back, cuz. With a nut like that on the loose you best be prepared for anything. Ya feel me?"

Jovan agreed with his road dawg. There was a profoundly inquisitive gleam in his eye as both men eyed one another in silence. "Damn ... shorty dead," he mumbled under his breath. "That's fucked up!" he said shaking his head. "I was just starting to feel shorty too. Damn, she gone."

Jovan silently recalled his dream. *What the hell was that all about? How could I have dreamed of Tara's death before knowing anything about it?* He thought that was some creepy shit he best keep to himself. A psycho boyfriend on the loose? *What the fuck is going on?* Jovan wondered silently. He got a sick feeling in the pit of his stomach, and he knew his instincts were sending him a vital warning. Jovan felt both wary and baffled as he rolled the question around in his head as he asked himself why this happened.

Chapter 5

Days earlier a Mexican maintenance worker entered Tara's apartment to inspect the air conditioning unit. He knocked three times on the front door. When there was no answer he pulled his huge key ring off his hip (at least 50 keys) and proceeded to unlock the door.

He opened the door halfway, stopped abruptly and sniffed the air inside.

"What the hell?" he murmured when he detected a foul odor circulating in the air. "Her cat must've kicked the fuckin' bucket," he quickly concluded and stepped inside the dimly lit hallway. The light from the building hallway spilled across the carpet just inside the door. The Mexican's eyes went wide in surprise when he saw streaks of blood smeared on the carpet.

"What the fuck?" he stammered as he stepped in and pushed the door closed. "No way." He shook his head. "The cat ain't die; somebody killed the cat," he calmly surmised.

He slowly moved along the hall, his eyes wide, alert and focused on the trail of blood.

"Hola, senorita!" the Mexican called out as he stepped in the living room and froze. His eyes locked on the overturned dining room table with the broken leg.

"Oh, shit," he said, shifting his eyes from the dining table to the trail of blood leading from the spot where he stood, clear across the living room carpet, right into the bedroom. He stood there for a moment, his heart pounding. The thought of a dead cat totally had been wiped clean from his mind.

"There's a dead body in that room," he said softly. The Mexican stood up straight, took a deep breath of courage, pulled the brim on his red Washington Nats baseball cap to the left and forged ahead. He could feel an eerie vibe in the air as he moved through the vacant living room and closed in on the bedroom.

The maintenance worker stepped in the bedroom unprepared for what was inside. Utter shock leapt from his face and his hand flew over his mouth in a horror-stricken jerk when he laid eyes on the nude corpse sprawled across a bare Serta mattress.

He gagged when he recognized the face of the attractive women who always had a kind word to say to him whenever they crossed paths.

"Her eyes!" he gasped in horror, hyperventilating. He grabbed his stomach, doubled over and stumbled backwards out the room. "Someone stole her eyes!" he stuttered breathlessly and then stumbled toward the front door.

ⓌⓌⓌⓌ

D.C. homicide detectives and a team of forensic specialists converged on the apartment not long after the call from the hysterical maintenance man was dispatched over the wire.

Homicide detectives Louis and Clark, dubbed the Dynamic Duo of D.C.'s homicide squad, were greeted by a grisly scene of carnage inside Tara's apartment. The forensic specialist, Tony Woo, a classic super geek, had his one-inch-thick pop-bottle wire-rimmed glasses glued to the bridge of his nose like a hood ornament. He was down on his knees intent on collecting specimen samples.

Detective Rich Louis originated from the Canadian law enforcement and was touted as one of the top constables on the Canadian task force. When asked, Louis was quick to tell you that he relocated to Washington for the city's prominence and prestige. His co-workers were quick to dispute that. At first glance it was obvious to see this man was looking for the big-city crime and the excitement. Louis was the swashbuckler type: tall, dark haired and tan with a uniquely styled handlebar mustache. He was quite a character.

"So how's it going, Tony?" When Louis spoke the deep baritone in his voice seemed to vibrate in the air.

"Not good, detective," Tony answered without looking up from Tara's bloody, eyeless corpse. Tony Woo was consumed with the meticulous task of examining the body and the surrounding vicinity.

"Well, I can see that," Louis grunted, peering over Tony's shoulder. "Have you come across anything substantial yet? Anything me and my partner—"

Tony cut him off with an agitated huff. He paused for a second before climbing to his feet. Tony Woo was a short, stout fellow who was well respected in his field of forensic science.

"Detective Louis," Tony began. The firm, steely tone of his voice was in total contrast with his super-geeky persona. He faced the detective and ripped the latex gloves off his pudgy hands. "It's going to take some time to sift through this very messy crime scene. If you haven't noticed, detective, the bedroom isn't the kill zone. The hallway just inside the front door is. And, yes, the hallway has been thoroughly inspected and examined by yours truly. All we can do right now is let me finish collecting my specimen samples and play the wait-and-hope game. Wait and hope that we get a vital DNA match." Woo lingered for a moment, then stared the detective in the face and said, "There is one vital aspect of this case that does jump out at me." Tony flashed him a shrewd look, reached into his leather evidence bag and pulled out a fresh set of latex gloves.

Louis' brow shot up. He was anxious and hopeful. "Well, Woo, what'cha got?"

Tony Woo pressed his index finger against his hairless chin with one hand and straightened his glasses with the other. He exhaled and said, "Well, detective, I'm led to believe our perpetrator in this extremely violent crime is very skilled in some aspect of the medical field. Skilled with an extremely twisted nature."

"What brought you to that conclusion? The missing eyeballs?"

"The eyes," Tony said, nodding slowly, "along with my very strong gut feeling," he said. A poignant gleam shone deep in his eyes. "True to form, detective, what we're looking for here is a real sicko. Sicko with a capital S."

Well that's fucking dandy," Detective Will Clark interrupted scornfully. Clark had adopted the whole Isaac Hayes look: the beard trim, the shades, the demeanor, the whole nine. With his hands clasped behind his back, he strolled over to the men authoritatively. "Our victim's eyes were gouged out," he said with a frustrated look. "What kind of psycho are we dealing with here?"

Louis responded, "A sick degenerate ass for the summer."

Clark hissed, "Kiss my black ass! That's just what the fuck we don't need with the damn chief and mayor already breathing down our damn backs!"

"Gentlemen," Tony spoke up suddenly. "What we're dealing with here is an extremely savvy and sadistic predator. We need to track this individual down pronto. This type of predator will strike again." He hesitated and looked at Louis then Clark. He went on, "The question is, gentlemen, when and where? Take it from me, detectives, our victim here is the first of many. Believe me when I say our eyeless corpse here is this asshole's calling card." Tony Woo's eyes were intense.

The Dynamic Duo shot each other knowing looks. Both men were getting that dreadful feeling that this was the beginning of a journey that was bound to lead to some hellish, unforeseen conclusion.

Chapter 6

A severe thunderstorm rolled through the D.C. area. Long, leafy tree branches swayed to and fro under the assault of strong winds and rain that dotted the landscape around the Rising home.

Inside the Rising household, the smooth jazz of Boney James and Nona Gaye's "When Your Life Was Low" wafted through the dimly lit rooms on the first level and drifted up the dark staircase.

Upstairs in the master bedroom dark shadows danced about ominously on the walls and ceiling. Angel sat on the floor in the midst of the noiseless performance in front of the burning fireplace. Her hubby insisted that she not touch the thermostat, which remained at 65 degrees throughout the summer. Angel wouldn't say anything; instead she would activate both gas fireplaces, the one in their bedroom and the one downstairs in the family room, whenever Jovan was away from the house.

Angel sat with her back leaning against the tan leather ottoman. In her right hand she nursed a glass of red Chardonnay; her left hand clutched their cell phone bill.

A Beautiful Satan

She stared into the dancing flames. Suddenly she heard the sound of the automatic garage door opening. Angel folded up the phone bill, then slipped the paper underneath the zebra-skin rug.

By the time Jovan had parked the car in the garage, made his usual pit stop in the kitchen, climbed the stairs and pushed through the double entrance leading into their bedroom, Angel did a subtle transformation.

"Baby, it's hot as hell up in this joint," Jovan complained as he walked into the bedroom. "C'mon now, do you really need to have the fireplace going?" He disappeared into the closet.

Angel followed him with her eyes from the moment he stepped foot into the room, but said nothing.

"So how's my precious girl doing tonight?" he said, taking a seat on the ottoman beside her. Tenderly, Jovan started to stroke his wife's flowing hair. "You okay, babe? What's on your mind?" he asked, studying her.

She glanced up. *OMG!* Angel gasped silently. *My husband's one sexy-ass nigga in a wife-beater!* Angel kept her composure and shrugged. "Oh, it's nothing. I was just sitting here."

For some reason, Jovan wasn't buying that. He was getting another kind of vibe from his wife. Her words seemed to contradict her true feelings. "You've been sitting here waiting for me?" he asked skeptically. "How did you know I would be home so early?" His hand moved down to the back of her neck; he began to massage her neck and shoulders.

"I kind of figured you would," she answered casually, enjoying his touch. "With the weather being as nasty as it is, I know my man." Angel stopped short, then got on her knees and turned to face Jovan. "And my man," she continued with a cunning grin, "doesn't like to drive around in nasty weather like this." She paused, her hands moved to his belt, where she methodically began to unloosen his pants. "Now does he?" she whispered, her tone sultry.

Jovan was beaming with a wide, expectant smile. His head bobbed up and down. "Yeah," he agreed without hesitation, "You right 'bout that, baby." He exhaled when she finally unleashed his now erected manhood.

"Damn," Angel sighed, looking pleasantly surprised. "Is all of that surprise to see little ole me?" She watched him, licking her lips provocatively. She pursed her lips and placed a wet kiss on the tip of his head. "I smell Dial soap," she said, crinkling up her nose. "We don't have any Dial, We don't use Dial," her words catching in her throat. She stared up at Jovan with a blank look. "Why does your penis smell like Dial soap?"

He smacked his lips and waved her off with his hand. "I went to the gym today," Jovan told her matter-of-factly. "Go 'head with that. Now you tryin' to fuck up the mood. C'mon now." He started stroking himself. "You got my joint jumping, don't stop now. C'mon baby," he urged playfully.

It was a heavy moment for Angel. She stifled her emotions and choked off the words that were itching to fly from her mouth. Instead, she took her husband's penis between her lips. Her eyes watered as she watched Jovan arch his head back, feeling her. *I love this man.* Angel repeated this over and over in her mind as she allowed her heated sensuality to overcome her senses.

The following day, the storm had passed through the area and the sun was shining bright in a clear blue sky.

Angel had phoned her job earlier, notifying them she wouldn't be in today. The contents of their phone bill were nagging at her the whole night, causing a case of insomnia. Angel never thought that she would say she couldn't wait for her husband to leave the house.

She smiled when she heard the sound of the garage door closing. Angel hopped out the bed. She was so full of energy this morning. She walked right over to the zebra rug, where she had stashed the phone bill, then grabbed the cordless phone and plopped her ass in her husband's recliner. Angel was in detective mode today. The anticipation of what she might uncover gave her an unexpected rush.

She unraveled the phone bill and skimmed down the list. *Here we go*, Angel said to herself as she eyed the strange phone number. "Let's see whose number this is. Probably one of your slutty hos," she commented drily. Her palms sweated rivers with anticipation while she was dialing. That was odd, she thought, then immediately forgot about it when a woman answered. "Hello. Oh, I'm sorry," said Angel politely, "I must have the wrong number. You're not affiliated Life Time Fitness, are you?"

"No," responded the woman.

"Oh, okay. I found this number in my phone. What's your name?"

"Ariel," the caller replied.

"I'm sorry to have bothered you, Ariel. I must have misdialed you. Pardon me. What's my name? My name is Natasha," she pronounced with a twisted grin. "Oh, okay, I'm so sorry to bother you." Angel giggled lightly as she felt this eerie sensation invade her senses.

"Well, it's so nice to have made your acquaintance, Ariel. Maybe we can talk again some time, you know, seeing how hard it is to meet new friends around D.C. What you think about that?"

ⓦⓦⓦⓦ

Although Jovan had arrived at Ibiza nightclub awhile ago, he wasn't his normal social self tonight. He just sat in the VIP tossing back $150 shots of Remy while texting on his BlackBerry.

Jovan was in a different mood, Ray thought, while moving his way through the crowd, ready to check his partner. Suddenly Ray's attention was caught by a stunning Beyoncé double by the name of Monica.

"Hey, bad boy," she said, throwing her arms around his neck. "Where's my man? I know you know. That nigga got my ass sprung, and now he don't wanna answer my calls," she expressed with attitude.

"Whoa, baby," Ray said, prying her arms loose. He took a step back, gave his tailored black pin-striped suit a quick visual inspection and smoothed out the wrinkles with his hand.

Monica leaned back and eyed Ray with a gassed look, like the nigga was off his rocker. But in retrospect, she really couldn't blame him because she really didn't know this man.

She had met Ray only once, when Jovan brought her past his crib one late night on the creep tip.

Jovan had rocked her world so viciously that night. From the way she was hollering and climbing the walls, Ray thought he was in there killing the bitch. After they were gone, he discovered embedded teeth marks in his expensive Scandinavian bed frame. Ray couldn't for the life of him figure out what Jovan was doing to her ass to drive her out of her mind like that.

Ray was what the ballers called a "playa from the Himalayas." He was vanity in motion, an exact replica of pretty-boy actor Shemar Moore. Ray's entire style and mannerisms were patterned after the celeb—so much so that at times Ray actually thought he was Shemar.

He adjusted the dark Fendi frames shielding his eyes from view. With a smug look, he said, "Check this out, ma—don't ever greet me like that again. Not ever," he stressed with a pointed finger. "Now why don't you press rewind, and let's take this from the top."

Jovan sat with his back against the bar, peering over the top of his platinum Gucci tints. His hawk-like eyes panned across the rainbow sea of faces moving in waves on the dance floor to the flaming hot sounds of Drake's "Successful."

He caught a glimpse of Ray approaching and noticed he was being tailed by this chick. Jovan smiled devilishly when he recognized who the chick was. Mmph! Shorty had that sweet-sugar sex! The mere thought of it made salacious visions of their sexual rendezvous reeled through his mind. He had to let that thang cool off for a minute. Monica's nectar was a little too sweet, and she knew it. He had her sprung, so he wasn't about to let her turn the tables.

"Look what the cat dragged in," Jovan said, softening his demeanor.

"Oooh, baby!" Monica gasped, flashing a wide grin as she pranced over to the bar. She stood in front of him attempting to look sassy with her hands on her hips. "You're looking very handsome tonight, as always," she complimented, checking him out from head to toe.

Jovan responded with an arrogant smirk. "Baby girl," he began, his tone calm and collected. "Tell me something I don't know." He looked her off and shot his man a quick knowing wink while adjusting his silvery Prada sports blazer. "Come here, girl," he directed, spreading his arms. "Come show Big Daddy some love. I know you miss me. Don't say a word. I'm a mind reader, girl. I know what you want."

Monica smiled warmly, and her pretty green eyes twinkled with excitement. It was obvious to anyone paying attention, this broad was content just being in this man's arms. One could only imagine what it would be like if she got the chance to get her swerve on with Jovan again. Monica was ready to put it on him; she couldn't conceal the heated lust radiating from her body.

The trio moved over to one of the VIP's coveted sofas.

"So what went down today, playboy?" asked Ray, as he popped a bottle of Dom Pérignon and filled up the three champagne flutes. "You and the wife have a falling out?"

Jovan was lounging beside him with Monica cradled snugly under his right arm. "What?" he frowned. "What the hell you getting at, Ray?"

"When you came in earlier, I was here," Ray answered evenly. "You come straight over to the bar, ain't holler at nobody. You was caught up in your own world," he told Jovan, shoving the bubbly down in the ice. "C'mon, cuz," Ray said, offering up his glass to toast. "We've been road dawgs for years. Don't you think by now I can tell when something's fucking with you?"

Jovan nodded with a thoughtful look and toasted. "I went to Tara's funeral today," he muttered, and took a gulp of champagne. He then shook his head and added, "She had a closed casket ... that was some fucked up shit, fo' real."

"I feel ya, cuz," Ray calmly said. "That was some evil-ass shit that happened to your shorty. Man, I hope they catch that psycho fuck and burn his ass up!"

With his eyes closed, Jovan exhaled deeply and said, "You took the words right out of my mouth." There was a touch of gloom floating in his words.

Feeling left out, Monica made her presence known by nuzzling closer to Jovan and placing a gentle kiss on his neck while her hand crept slowly up his thigh. She paused and then tugged at his navy denim belt loop.

"You look frustrated, baby," Monica whispered hotly in his ear. "Why don't we go somewhere private so I can put your mind and body at ease? Let me work my magic on you."

Jovan could feel her burning gaze arousing him. "That sounds pretty good right about now," he said with a raised eyebrow. "You wanna work your sexual healing on Big Daddy, huh, girl?"

Ray noticed one of his honeys had walked into the VIP. He pulled his athletic frame off the sofa and moved to greet her. "I'll be right back, playboy. A body's calling me," he said with a wink before stepping off.

Meanwhile, Jovan was tapping his chin, his attention temporarily diverted when a statuesque beauty with a heart-shaped ass sashayed a few feet before him. Monica nudged him just when the beauty had looked back. She waved, and Jovan flashed her his killer smile. *Damn! That ass is to phat*, he said silently.

A Beautiful Satan

Monica folded her arms across her chest and pursed her lips. "I see you found something else you'd rather have," she said with attitude, rolling her eyes.

He cut his eyes and responded with a playful grin, "Don't even go there, boo." A mischievous smile appeared. "Ya know how we roll. Ain't nothing change, so don't fuck up a good thing," Jovan warned, a little annoyed. He eased off the sofa. "You wanna stir it up tonight?" he questioned as he tossed back the rest of his bubbly.

"You know I do," Monica replied. "Please don't play with me."

"Alright," he said, caressing her cheek. "Chill, have some Dom, and be ready for me when I get back." Jovan smiled at Monica and left her staring at his back.

The sounds of Lil Wayne's "Bedrock" coaxed the crowd out onto the dance floor.

Jovan slid up next to Ray, who was standing near the VIP entrance talking to three attractive women. The first lady Jovan didn't recognize, but he knew the other two: The pretty red-bone was Tammy, and the other was Ms. Heart-Shaped Ass!

"Baby boy, looks like you could use a little help," Jovan said coolly, draping his arm over his partner's shoulder.

Ray acted surprised and asked, "Ey, what's good, dawg?"

"Ya know, breathing easy, baby, breathing easy," Jovan grinned, his eyes glued to Ms. Heart-Shaped Ass. Then he made his move. "Oh my," he said softly, taking her hand in his. "Who is this gorgeous beauty?" She told him her name was Malaysia. The two stared at each other, eye to eye, as if they were already a hot item.

Jovan was a very charismatic and charming man, and this honey-coated beauty was being drawn in by his intoxicating magnetism. Jovan could sense the heated vibe radiating from this divine creature.

Meanwhile, back over on the VIP sofa, Monica was getting nice and toasted. She was grooving to the up-tempo music pumping throughout the club. She decided since Jovan was taking her for granted tonight that she wasn't going to let his ass disturb her groove. She popped the cork off the second bottle of Dom P.

"Jovan thinks he so damn hot," she mumbled to herself while refilling her glass for the fifth or sixth time. "Leave me over here while he flirts with them bitches." She glared across the lounge. "Pretty as I am that nigga must be crazy!" Monica conceded as she offered up a toast. "Fucking bastard!" she hissed and threw her head back to gulp the bubbly.

"Monica!" Jovan shouted abruptly, causing her to spill the drink on her gold designer gown. "D--damn!" she stammered with a shocked look.

"You ready to bounce?" he asked, snatching the bottle from the ice bucket. He tossed it back when he realized it was half empty. "What the fuck?!" he exclaimed with dismay while eyeing Monica. "Damn, baby girl," Jovan said easily, holding the bottle up to the light. "You've been over here having yourself a good ole time, I see, 'cause you just punished the Dom." He tossed his head back and turned up the bottle.

"I hope you know you're not driving," Jovan stated bluntly, placing the bottle on the glass tabletop. "The Hotel Topaz ain't that far anyway," he added casually. "You can catch a cab back to your ride in the morning, alright?"

Monica regarded him with a look of skepticism. "Why can't you bring me back?"

"Because I'll be home. I'm not staying out all night," he said pointedly.

"Awww!" she whined and began twisting and turning in her seat as if she was on the verge of having a hissy fit.

"'Aww,' shit," Jovan interrupted. "Finish that drink," he clapped loudly. "It's time to bounce," he commanded.

A Beautiful Satan

The next morning Jovan awoke in his own bed to the sounds of birds chirping outside of his window. He got up and made his way into the bathroom still half asleep. He relieved himself, then stumbled to the sink to wash his hands. Suddenly Jovan's head cocked to the side with a questioning look when he noticed his cell phone on the marble counter between the double sinks. He remembered leaving his phone on his nightstand. "What the hell?"

Chapter 7

Ding! The elevated stopped on the 13th floor. Natasha stepped out but saw an empty floor. She pulled her long blonde ponytail over her left shoulder, allowing the hair to snake down to her 36-DD bosom, and adjusted her red-framed Louis Vuitton shades.

She looked provocative in the flaming-red catsuit, which accentuated her thick hour-glass figure as she strutted down the hall clutching a red and gold LV bag at her side.

"Coming! A feminine voice announced from inside. The door opened and the aroma of potpourri and sunlight spilled out into the hall. "Natasha? Girl, why you here so early? I'm still getting ready."

Natasha gave the attractive brunette a frosty stare. "Ariel. What, would you like for me to leave and come back when you're ready? I didn't realize the traffic would be so light this time of day. My bad," she said, gripping her hips in a sassy, playful manner.

"No, girl, you don't have to do that, "Ariel protested quickly, swinging the door wide. "Come in and make yourself comfortable. I'll be ready in no time."

A Beautiful Satan

While Ariel was in the bedroom getting herself together, Natasha roamed around her living room. She was checking out the white girl's modest décor.

The white bitch is attractive, Natasha said to herself as she made her way around the room examining the photo gallery of Ariel's life, all meticulously arranged in chronological order throughout the apartment.

"This girl's a damn picture freak," she mumbled under her breath. Suddenly Natasha's body stiffened as if she had been hit with a few thousand volts of electricity. Rage flashed in her eyes as a digital frame flashed to life. Natasha's arm extended and her fingers brushed the surface of the digital frame. Digital images of Jovan and Ariel were flashing across the digital picture frame. They were a collection of her most recent and prized photos.

The images were so vivid. There was a photo of the two happily leaning against the hood of Jovan's Mercedes. Another image showed the couple in a swanky nightclub, both of them dressed. The next image depicted Jovan sandwiched between Ariel and some Asian-looking chick. Both women were groping his groin!

Ariel walked into the living room, startling her. "Natasha," she said, "see, that didn't take long at all." She noticed Natasha was paying close attention to her new digital picture frame. "You like those digital frames too, girl?" Ariel asked casually as she sat her black Coach bag on the dining table, fishing through its contents. "That one there is the priciest. It was $250, but it's worth it. I just adore it," she expressed with a warm smile while spreading clear gloss across her pink lips. "It was a gift from my fiancé. That's probably why I adore it so." Ariel glowed as thoughts of him filled her mind.

Natasha's vision blurred as the tears coursed down her face. "Your what?? You bitch!" she hissed, scowling. Natasha's head seemed to twist completely around, like a scene right out of the "Exorcist." Her palms began to sweat and her heart was beating rapidly as she looked into Ariel's eyes.

An eerie feeling struck Ariel in the pit of her stomach when they made eye contact. "Okay ..." said Ariel slowly, "is something wrong?"

"Is he your fiancé?" Natasha inquired with a nasty tone as she snatched the digital frame off the shelf.

Ariel could see the pain behind her eyes. She hesitated. "Uh, yes, that's my man," she weakly answered. "What's the problem, Natasha? You know him? We've only been dating for about a year."

"What?" Natasha blurted out. "You've been dating for a year?" She could feel her blood pressure rise.

Ariel could feel the pain and hurt in her voice. "Why? What's wrong, Natasha? What, has my fiancé done something to you?" she asked in a compassionate tone. Natasha laughed. Her laugh was dark. Cynical. Loud. Ariel looked at her as if she were crazy. "Am I missing something here?" She was trying to be very selective with her words, but Natasha cut her off.

Suddenly, without warning, Natasha backhanded Ariel across the bridge of her nose with the digital picture frame. The blow dislocated her nose, letting off a sickly crack.

Ariel staggered backwards, grabbing at her twisted, bloodied nose. "Why the hell you do that?" she asked in a whiney tone.

Natasha's demeanor was toxic; it was as if a dark, unholy spirit arose in her. "Bitch!" she growled insidiously. Her piercing gaze was fierce. "Don't nobody fuck Angel's man and live!" A demonic haze suddenly billowed in her eyes.

Ariel was shaken.

Thirteen floors below, bystanders and pedestrians heard the sound of breaking glass followed instantly by the chilling scream of a terrified woman. Then Ariel's body hurled through the air and did a flying twisting pirouette

A Beautiful Satan

before her body crashed head first through the roof of a Metro transit bus. Blood and bones exploded from her body, which was mangled and mutilated beyond recognition.

An hour later the vicinity surrounding the apartment building was teaming with a crowd of uniformed officers, detectives and media crews. The scene conjured up visions of a major catastrophe with an intense investigation that was unfolding on the premises. There were so many suits crowded within the yellow crime scene perimeter you would've thought that the President had just been assassinated.

The Dynamic Duo, Louis and Clark, slithered through the mix of uniformed and undercover agents. "Looks like our victim did a swan dive from way up there somewhere, huh, guys? The detective with the spit-shined head said while sipping on his cup of latte.

"I'll say," said a gruff-sounding sergeant resembling Fred Flintstone. "She tore a hole right through the roof of this here Metro bus. Poor little thing. My gosh, she made a terrible mess in there."

Inching his way over to his partner, the arrogant detective Louis, placed a hand on Clark's shoulder. "I got word the deceased here may have been thrown from the 13th floor. She was heard screaming all the way to her death," he said.

The detectives eyed one another knowingly, as if reading one another's thoughts. Without another word they walked towards the building entrance.

Upstairs on the 13th floor, inside of Ariel's apartment, the detectives found their worthy confidant and forensic scientist, Tony. He was meticulously canvassing the crime scene, collecting any and all pertinent evidence that would be put to use in solving this case.

"Tony, my man," Louis greeted his scientist friend, sounding carefree, "What it look like from up here, suicide or homicide? You make the call."

Tony was in the process of dusting for prints when the duo ducked into the apartment under the crime tape. He was focusing diligently on one particular area of a wooden shelf when he noticed the two characters scoping the crime scene.

"This is definitely a homicide, gentlemen, no bones about it," Tony remarked, his tone reflecting the gravity of the situation.

"Nice-looking young lady," Clark commented as he examined the victim's photo collection. "She's got quite a substantial photo array here. Think she's a model? 'Cause she damn sure pretty enough to be one."

"I agree; she's very photogenic," added Tony.

Over at the window, Louis was surveying the broken window frame. He let out a low whistle and said, "Damn, that was some really foul shit they did to our little lady." He glanced over his shoulder. "Any good prints there, Tony? You've been working that same spot for a minute now."

"No prints, but we do have here a missing picture frame." Tony studied the area closely, then added with forensic savvy, "And from the particle dimensions I've been able to incur, I'd go so far as to say that the missing frame is one of those contemporary digital models. Uh, the, uh, more pricier model, I believe."

The Dynamic Duo moved in to get a closer look at what the forensics agent had uncovered.

"A high-end digital frame you say," uttered Clark, peering over Tony's shoulder. "Well, I guess that's a good enough a start as any. You wouldn't by any chance have a make and model on that, uh, runaway frame, would ya?" Louis shook his head and gave his partner a quick elbow to the ribs.

Tony smirked. "If you think you can do any better, detective, be my guest. But if I were you, I'd do my damnedest to track down that, uh, runaway frame. Because whatever is on it, someone felt it was important enough to kill for."

Chapter 8

The mesmerizing sounds of Marcus Johnson resonated off the aged brick walls and wooden rafters as the curly haired Sax Master serenaded a crowd of jazz enthusiasts relaxing by candlelight after finishing their meals.

Jovan and Angel were enjoying the live performance inside of the legendary Blues Alley in Georgetown.

An aura of love engulfed the Risings as they held hands lovingly in the center of the table. Angel loved when her man showed open affection. It was times like this that made her silly putty in his hands.

Jovan gazed across the table at his wife. *Wow!* he thought. She was perfectly Angelic in her floral Jan Taminia creation. He couldn't help but smile at Angel's beauty as she blushed like a young schoolgirl under his admiring eyes.

Moments like this Angel cherished and held dear to her heart. She realized that it was these special loving moments of joy that kept her going, kept her love growing strong, kept her pushing on no matter how hard times got. It was these endearing moments in their relationship she was able to draw strength from when times got hard. *My love for this man is what keeps me sane*, Angel told herself.

Outside, it was a balmy night in Washington. The Risings strolled the sidewalks of Georgetown hand in hand.

"I had a wonderful time tonight. Thank you."

"Well, it was my pleasure, baby," Jovan said warmly.

"Why can't every night be like tonight? Doesn't this feel good—being out on the town together, enjoying what we have together as husband and wife? This is living. This is how a loving couple enjoys life together."

Jovan nodded and said, "You right, baby, and I love being out like this with you. I love going places with you, sharing myself, my time and my life with you. Angel, I married you. You're my wife, baby. Don't you know there is no higher pedestal that a man can place a woman on? When a man makes his woman his wife, that is the ultimate crowning, baby. And you are my crown jewel." Jovan stopped and gazed deeply into Angel's eyes. "I love you, girl. Don't you know that? You're a part of me," he said, heartfelt.

Emotions were running high. Jovan watched as Angel's soft, assenting eyes turned misty. He pulled her close to his body and crushed Angel's lips to his own during a heated embrace.

Crowds of passersby moved past the couple as they embraced, expressing their passions under the stars in the middle of Georgetown. They were in their own world and no one else mattered.

It was after midnight when the Risings returned home. They were still caught up in the moment; they teased and touched one another all the way home, like they couldn't get enough. Things were heated. During the drive, Jovan had to pull the car over a couple of times before continuing.

They burst through the doors of their bedroom in a heated frenzy, brimming with lust, tugging on one another's clothes.

A Beautiful Satan

Jovan grabbed the stereo remote, and the sound of the Isley Brothers leapt from the speakers to the ceiling and walls in a crescendo of intoxication and desire.

Across the room, Angel turned on the fireplace; the fluttering flames glowed softly, creating a sensually arousing ambiance that ignited the room.

She floated to the middle of the floor, her hips swaying in rhythm to the slow, tantalizing groove. Angel closed her eyes and smiled when she felt the tender touch of her husband's hands on her skin.

Jovan eased up behind his wife and glided his fingers slowly down Angel's neck, along her delicate shoulders. He then gently caressed her arms. He felt her body shudder when he gripped her firmly around her waist.

Tenderly, he kissed the nape of her neck, enjoying the feel of her smooth, silky skin against his lips as their bodies grinded salaciously to the love behind the melody.

Angel's silk dress fell around her ankles. Jovan expressed his appreciation for her loveliness with a warm, vibrant smile and placed a trail of moist, warm kisses straight down the crook of her back and then painted her voluptuous derriere from left to right with sensuous passion marks.

He lay Angel down in front of the fireplace, placing several pillows under her, exposing her pudenda, leaving her vulnerable and anxious. With care, Jovan kissed her pink, sensitive flesh. Small sounds escaped her as he gripped her tightly. Jovan sucked the juices from inside her and caressed her moist tender parts with his tongue. She squirmed. She shook. She came. Angel was caught up in the rapture.

Jovan climbed to his feet, gloating with a devilish grin. He shed his ivory Gucci button-up. "That was good, wasn't it, baby?" he inquired, his voice deep and moving.

Angel hadn't gathered her senses yet. She was in a semi-comatose state, her hot juices still bubbling between her legs.

"Yea, I know baby," he said, enjoying the provocative sight of her squirming around in ecstasy. Jovan stood over his wife undoing his pants. "I hope you ready for this," he expressed with a fiendish look.

Chapter 9

Inside an elegant restaurant in downtown D.C., Angel was having lunch with her close friend Jo-Jo and their overly vivacious and giddy girlfriend Tina.

Laughter emanated from their table, thanks in large part to Tina. Tina was short and looked half Asian. She was as known for her loud, ditzy laug, as she was her tight Chinese bob hairstyles and big butt. Her ass was so round and plump you could sit a glass of water on it while she stood.

"Angel, girl, you are too much!" Tina exclaimed, still giggling uncontrollably. "That nigga made you blank out?"

"Girlfriend," Angel said, smiling from ear to ear as she smacked the table and took a sip of wine, "I was seeing exploding stars and shit—and my eyes were open!"

The trio erupted in a chorus of giddy laughter.

"Damn! That's some good fuckin' there, girl," Jo-Jo conceded with a look of astonished envy. "Make me wanna fire my little youngin'," she added with a critical stare while slicing a portion of lobster tail and drenching it in hot, melted butter.

Tina interjected loudly, "That shit makes me wanna call Steve and tell his ass to clock out early today so he can come home and wax this ass real good! Shit!"

"I thought you cut youngin' off, Jo-Jo?" Angel inquired politely with an intuitive stare as she sank her teeth into a colossal shrimp.

She sighed. "I did for a minute, but I'm like you girl— I'm weak for the dick. Shit, I was missing that nigga hitting it!" Jo-Jo paused and looked up from the table. Her eyes met Angel's. "I think I gotta problem."

Tina almost choked. "What? What's up, bitch! You burnin'?" They both turned to Tina and eyed her harshly. "What? I say something wrong?"

Jo-Jo decided not to answer her; she needed some medical insight from Angel. "For real, I think I may need some kind of help."

"What makes you say that?"

"Girl, I had told myself that I wasn't fucking with youngin' no more. Day one, I was okay. Day two, I wanted some dick. I know that was a want. But by day three …" Jo-Jo stopped short, her head shaking with a look of defeat. She looked at Angel, her eyes then traveled quickly to Tina and back to Angel's. Jo-Jo smiled self-consciously and said, "I couldn't control the flow between my legs. My pussy was soaking wet! I took a cold shower and bath, but that shit ain't work! Girl, the dick made me weak. I gave in when youngin' called again. I told him to bring that dick to me!" There was an intense, animalistic look in her eye when she spoke.

"Go 'head, ho," Tina cut in. "You know damn well you called up youngin' and went running to his ass."

A flash of anger crossed Jo-Jo's face, but she quickly covered it.

Angel waved Tina off. "I understand," she said softly. "I don't think there's any cause for help. You were just going through it, that's all. We all have our moments of weakness when we allow that special man to get inside of our heads and hearts. When that happens, it's only natural that our body will eventually follow."

"That's the bottom line," Tina added with her boisterous mouth. "You falling for that young, untamed piece of tender-oni." She laughed while pouring another glass. "Mmm, mmm, mmm. Fucking with y'all horny bitches, y'all got me thinking about raping me a nigga. Damn!"

"Go 'head, bitch," Jo-Jo retorted. "You've been wanting to do that freaky shit for years." Tina's hand shot up in protest.

"No, girl, get it right. I told you that I wanted two niggas to act like they were raping my ass. That's what I said."

Angel asked in a shocked voice, "Why the hell you want two niggas to rape you?"

"Yeah, ho, you on some real freaked-out shit. What you doing, poppin' E's again?"

"Bitch, y'all know I rolls from time to time. Ain't nothing wrong with a few stacks every now and then. Shit, y'all should try it sometime. Get together with your man and explore some new territory." She giggled and speared a large scallop with her fork. "Don't knock it, girls, 'til you've tried it," she said as she stuffed her mouth and then winked slyly.

"Look, Tina," Jo-Jo said defensively, "I know just what kinda shit you up to, and that shit not happening over here, so you and Stevie can get your Ecstasy clientele elsewhere, girlfriend."

"Steve selling ecstasy?" Angel asked, faking surprise. "I thought that little rough-around-the-edges nigga was working now." She knew Steve was working. She also knew that he was diligently working his way up the ranks of the illegal Ecstasy trade. But at the moment, she was enjoying the fact that she was being a thorn in Tina's ass.

"What the hell you just say?" Tina asked sourly, casting a bitter look Angel's way. "'Cause my baby do work, for your information. You got shit twisted. My baby working his shit on both ends of the fence. You better check yourself. Shit, what that nigga Jovan doing? Besides running them streets, running from club to club and running his dick up in every piece of ass that looks his way! So don't even go there." Tina smiled coldly and folded her arms aggressively.

Angel's eyes flared dangerously. "I saw you looking his way," she said venomously. "So what's going on? You got something you wanna get off your chest?" She pushed back from the table.

Jo-Jo was taken aback by Angel's response. She could sense that she was on the verge of attack.

"C'mon now, girl, what are you doing??" Jo-Jo said quickly, resting her hand on Angel's shoulder. She felt it unyielding, a sure sign of her anger. She attempted to defuse the situation before sparks started really flying. "Angel, get real. We girls. Why you gonna go there?" Jo-Jo said. "We don't do that, we don't cross the line. We don't fuck around with our friends' men. You know that."

Tina snickered. "Don't tell her nothing, 'cause I'm down for mine. She can get crazy if she wants, 'cause I can get crazy right along with her ass. Angel don't scare me. Fuck that shit! I can fight too. I put the fucking 'whoop' in whoop ass!"

Jo-Jo shot Angel a critical look, as if to say, "Yea, right."

Angel looked at Tina in disgust. "Little bitch don't know what to say out her mouth sometimes!"

"Ain't that some shit," Tina laughed, "You can kiss my ass."

"Girl, you feeling okay?" Jo-Jo asked, looking at Tina as if she were losing her mind. "I'm trying to kill this rift and you trying to keep it going."

"That's alright, Jo-Jo, leave her ass alone," Angel said, half smiling. "We know her short ass is all bark and no bite. I don't even know how I allowed myself to get so bent out of shape."

A Beautiful Satan

"I know that's right," Jo-Jo agreed with a sense of relief, "'cause I think she had one too many Mai-Tai's."

"Speaking of which, I gotta go tee-tee," Angel said as she stood up. She cuffed her Prada bag under her arm and rushed off.

Angel was standing at the counter in front of a wide-frame mirror applying a fresh coat of Mac lipstick when two loud-mouth ladies came stumbling through the doorway. It was obvious from their slurred speech and silly giggling that they both were totally wasted. *This early?* Angel frowned, indignation flared in her expression. "Drunk bitches," she mumbled under her breath and rolled her eyes.

The ringtone for Drake's song "Fancy" featuring T.I. and Swizz Beatz blared from one of the rowdy broad's purses. "Oooh, Gail!" the scarlet-clad Beyoncé wannabe gushed excitedly, as if she were about to have an orgasm. "This is my boo now. Oh, shit! Quick, how do I look? How do I look?"

"Answer the damn phone, Monica. That nigga can't see you," smirked her redhead girlfriend.

"Hello," Monica breathed into the cell phone.

"What's good with you, baby?" Jovan asked.

"Jovan, is that you?" she said, barely able to control the excitement brimming inside of her.

Angel froze in motion as a petrified look exploded across her face. She gripped the lipstick so tightly the whites of her knuckles appeared.

"Don't play with me, shorty. Play with them little boys. When I call, you get on your grown-woman shit, alright?"

"Excuse me," she said, nudging her girlfriend. "My bad, I won't let it happen again."

"Where you at?" he asked.

"I'm downtown at McCormick & Schmick's having lunch with my girl, Gail. You remember her? The fly-ass cracker freak that swear she's blacker than Lauryn Hill."

"Look, I'll be in town within the hour, so finish your lunch and get rid of the freaky white girl. Text me when you ready."

She covered the phone and let out a joyful yelp. "Gail! My baby wanna hook up!" She leaned against the counter trying to gather her composure. Monica felt the woman with the tight-ass Prada bag staring at her in the mirror. She rolled her eyes with a nasty leer. "Text you when I'm ready for what, boo?" she asked, turning to Gail.

"You got jokes, huh? Well, when you get your shit together."

Monica cut him off, "No, no, no! I'll be ready. I'm ready now. Let me drop this freak off at home and then we can hook up."

Suddenly Angel brushed past the two women. Her intentions were blatant and rude. "Freak bitches," she spat over her shoulder without looking back.

Monica and Gail stared after her in disbelief.

"Damn, what was that all about?" questioned Gail.

"I don't know, but that bitch got serious issues."

"Probably not getting enough dick at home."

"Hey, girl," Monica laughed, giving Gail a high-five. "A no-dick diet is a sure way to turn any sane bitch into a scary-ass she-devil!" Both women bent over and started laughing hysterically.

Angel walked up to the table and slammed down a fifty dollar bill next to Jo-Jo. "Here, put this towards the check," she said, her eyes looking wild. "I gotta run; an emergency just came up. I'll call you later." Before anyone could get a word out, she disappeared in a huff.

ⓦⓦⓦⓦ

The incident in the ladies' room left Angel rattled beyond comprehension. Could this really be her Jovan this bitch was speaking to and arranging to meet? Her mind was racing in every direction, and her emotions were on a roller-coaster ride.

Angel had her sights locked on a burnt-orange 350Z and the two bitches riding in it two cars ahead of her Benz.

Please, Lord, don't let that be my man that bitch going to meet. Please, she said to herself through tear-flooded eyes. Angel mashed on the gas, and the Mercedes zipped in and out of traffic. She was driving recklessly, but she didn't give a fuck.

Angel felt ruthless at this moment; she couldn't understand why such a dark yearning was suddenly pumping through her veins. For some odd reason she felt madness pervading her soul.

The Nissan turned right off North Capital and onto Hawaii Avenue. The car proceeded down a steep hill, and at the bottom Angel watched the sport coupe stop in front of a beige brick house. Gail hopped out. The orange automobile sped off before she was halfway up the steps.

Angel typed the address into her cell phone as she coasted by slowly in her in Benz. She stepped hard on the gas; she had to catch up to the real target: Monica.

She didn't have to go far. The orange Nissan was making a pit stop at the neighborhood 7-Eleven. Angel parked three cars away.

Angel had a clear view of the counter and register. She watched as Monica chit-chatted with the Abdullah-looking cashier. The way she was carrying on, it was obvious that she was one of the store regulars.

A violent jolt rocked Angel as she witnessed the cashier take a box of Magnums from the shelf, place the prophylactics into a small paper bag and hand the bag over to Monica. Her vision flashed blood red.

The 350Z made a right at the light, drove halfway up the hill and bust another right turn into a quiet garden-style apartment complex called The Heights.

Angel pulled up to the building Monica had just entered and watched through the glass entrance as the scarlet-clad bitch paused for a second before disappearing into the first apartment on the right.

Night fell over the area. It was calm outside of the complex. On Monica's balcony, the sliding glass door was partially open. Inside, the smooth vocals of Alicia Keys floated throughout her modishly furnished spread.

"You don't know my name!" Monica's loud voice drifted from the bathroom. She was enjoying a nice, hot bubble bath, still reeling from the hurting her lover Jovan had put on her ass earlier. She felt herself falling too hard for this man; she was in a total free fall over this married man! And she felt too helpless to do anything about it.

Jovan was different from all of the other men who had passed through her short life of 24 years. He was so smooth, charming and confident. He made Monica beam inside. And the nigga dressed his ass off! When you walked into a room on his arm you felt like a movie star—all eyes were on you. Then to top it off, the nigga got the bomb dick game! He had that bomb shit that made a bitch all crazy over his ass!

"That nigga know what he doing," she said out loud while toweling off. "And I can't do a damn thing about it." Monica shook her head. "Damn ... I'm in love with a married man," she concluded, coming to grips with her feelings.

Monica wrapped her towel around her and smiled when she heard the intro to her favorite tune, "A Woman's Worth." The doorbell rang, and when she swung the door open, a blonde-haired, blue-eyed female wearing a black warm-up suit burst in, startling her.

Monica grabbed at her chest. "Bitch! What the hell you doing in my house?" Her surprise quickly turned to rage until the flash of steel dangling at the intruder's side caught her attention. When the women made eye contact, Monica 's persona shrunk when she observed the wicked fury burning dark in her eyes.

Natasha's jaw tightened as she wielded the blade in the air. It was as long as her arm. Monica froze as a cold chill ran down her neck. The blade came down in a swooping arc, plunging deeply into her chest. "Dirty bitch!" Natasha yelled.

Sheer terror erupted across Monica 's face as the violence unfolded. She stumbled backward in a futile attempt to escape her attacker and tumbled back into the tub screaming.

Natasha was impulsive, volatile and lethal as she converged on her mortally wounded ho. "You like fucking married men, Monica?" she laughed brutally. "I know, bitch! Trifling ass!" Natasha hissed, twirling her fingers around her blonde ponytail. She reached down and snatched Monica viciously by her hair. "Bitch, you'll never fuck another married nigga!" Natasha dunked the terrified woman's head into the water, pushing her face to the bottom of the tub with uncanny strength. She then snatched her head back up and put the blade to the side of her temple. She hissed, "You slut!"

Monica was coughing and crying and trying to catch her breath all at the same time. "Please ... please ... let me go ... I'll never ... do anything like that again. Please!" she begged as she struggled to get out the tub. She opened her mouth to scream, but Natasha plunged the blade deep into her mouth and out the back of her head. Monica's legs flailed about as the life drained from her body.

Afterwards, Natasha sat in the bathroom on the edge of the tub and cracked a wicked smile as she watched the blood mix into the bath water. In the background, the soft voice of Alicia Keys continued to sing as death permeated the air.

Chapter 10

Jovan sat in his den, sipping cognac and watching the latest videos on the plasma. Shit was extremely hectic as of late, and he needed some alone time. He had been busy overseeing his rental properties, placing ads on the Web, in newspapers and in auto trader magazines. He was trying to sell the three cars he had copped from the dealer auction last week as well as keep tabs on his partner, Ray. They had recently pooled their finances and negotiated a good-ass deal for two keys of pure Colombian snow. Ray had a crew of dealers moving the shit over in S.E. on Orleans Place. So far, so good.

The humming sound of the garage door alerted Jovan to his wife's arrival. He glanced down at his Omega timepiece. It was just before midnight. *Where the fuck is she coming from at this time of night?*

Okay, it was around eight o'clock when I left Monica's, he remembered. When he got home and turned on the plasma, his favorite sports commentary had just gotten underway at 9 p.m. on the dot. He had been home for three hours. *Damn, how time flies.*

A Beautiful Satan

Angel waltzed into the room wearing her lavender nurse scrubs. "Hey," she smiled. "How was your day?"

Jovan looked at her with a questioning stare. "You went to work? I thought you said you were off today?"

She waved him off. "No, silly," Angel said crossing the room. She leaned over him and planted a wet kiss on his lips. "Your baby had to go to work," she told him in a husky voice. "Not everybody is gifted with those entrepreneurial abilities like you. Most of us have to work for our money. What, you forgot?" Angel pushed herself up from the chair. "Let me go change out of these scrubs," she said walking toward the stairs. She looked back. "Are you coming up soon to keep me company? Or are you spending half the night down here keeping yourself company?"

"I'll be up in a little while." There was an inquisitive look in Jovan's eye as he watched Angel disappear. For some strange reason that brief exchange between them troubled his inner spirit. He couldn't put his finger on what it was, but something just didn't fit.

For one thing, Angel smelled too glamorous to have just come from work at the hospital. She never puts on perfume after work and always complained about feeling gritty and dirty after her shift at the hospital. She couldn't wait to get home and take a bubble bath. *I could've sworn Angel told me she was off today.* That bothered him.

Another thing that concerned Jovan was when Angel said "most of us have to work for our money." *She doesn't have to work for jack-shit ever again in life if she doesn't want to. Her fucking ex-husband left her a few million. Even though she said it was only a million.* What Angel didn't know was Jovan had recently found some forms about offshore banking. *What was that all about? Something isn't right. Another man? Nah.* Jovan quickly dismissed that notion. *Angel ain't that crazy. She know I'll put a slug in her head and the bamma's ass.*

So what the fuck is it then? Something happened, I'm 100% sure.

The sudden sound of his cell phone startled Jovan out of his reverie. A voice squawked over the speaker, "What's good, cuz? You in the city tonight or what?" It was Ray's rude ass.

He snatched the cell from the glass end table. "Nah, nigga, I ain't down the way tonight," he said curtly. "What I tell you 'bout busting through like that, huh? You gotta alert me dawg, straight up. You don't know what I might be into or who I'm with, capice?

Ray didn't hesitate. "My bad, playboy. These bitches got a nigga all twisted up and shit. It won't happen again."

"What's good? Where you at anyway, nigga?

Ray laughed, glancing from side to side at the two Asian hotties cuffed under his arms. "Playboy," he began, feeling extra, "I'm down here at Ibiza chillin' like a villain with a mob of pretty bun-buns! I was hoping you could swing through this joint and take some of these buns off of my hands. Me and you could have ourselves one helluva orgy! I'm talking a smorgasbord of delightful asses!"

Jovan exhaled deeply. "Nah, not tonight, I'm a take a rain check, man. Sounds good, but I've been smashing all day long, ya dig? So I'm in for the night, Champ."

"I feel ya on that, but damn, cuz." Ray was silently hoping Jovan would change his mind as his eyes swept around the VIP lounge. Beautiful ladies stretched as far as the eye could see. It was a beautiful thang! One of the Asian girls started playing with Ray's earlobe, causing him to quiver. "You don't know what you missing; I'm telling ya, I got 'em in flavas up in the VIP joint! I got mocha chocolate, honey, French vanilla, hot latte and butter pecan twirl buns, playboy. I got whatever flava your taste buds desire. It's on my menu." Jovan's attention was temporarily diverted when he heard a sudden movement to his left. Wifey was snooping about.

A Beautiful Satan

"Hey, check this, right—I'm getting ready to go chill with the wife, so we'll get things straight tomorrow, a'ight? I'm out."

"Who was that?" Angel inquired, stepping from the shadows. "Sound like somebody was selling ice cream or something like that. Is that what I heard?"

He watched Angel sashay across the carpet, her cream silk nightie swaying enticingly as she moved. With a thoughtful gleam in his eye, Jovan started to stroke his chin as he looked up at her from his seat. He laughed mockingly. "Now, precious, what you talking about, girl? He cupped her ass and released his killer dimpled smile. "That wasn't nobody but crazy-ass Ray fucking with a nigga. His crazy ass lonely and looking for company, that's all."

Angel seemed uneasy with the blustery interplay between her husband and Ray. She cast a questionable look his way. "That pimp nigga lonely? Looking for company?" she said, twisting her lips.

"C'mon now, baby, everybody knows that pimps need love too," he joked,
trying to lighten the mood.

"That's not what I heard," she smirked, suspicious. Jovan folded his arms across his chest. "Is that a fact? Well, why don't you enlighten me on what it is that you know concerning this matter?" he asked, sounding interested.

Angel thought for a second, then decided to steer the subject matter into more stimulating territory. As she leaned down, her hand grazed his manhood and it stiffened. She spoke in hushed tones. "Well, what I heard about pimps is them niggas all on the down-low. A bunch of undercover fags is what they are." Angel peered deeply into his piercing gray eyes.

Jovan keyed in on his wife's provocative intentions, and he was more than happy to evade her lingering question and oblige her naughty interest. "Is that a fact, my love?" he whispered in her ear. His deep Barry White voice made Angel's heart flutter.

His wife had an overwhelming sexual thirst for which Jovan eagerly set out to quench. He tickled her kitty while she tickled his fancy. Angel adored that tickling sensation. It drove her buck wild. And Jovan aimed to please.

Chapter 11

It had been quite a violent night in the District. There was a triple homicide over on Savannah Terrace in S.E., a fatal stabbing in the entertainment district of Adams Morgan in N.W. and the grisly discovery of a slain woman in her bathtub over at The Heights apartment complex in N.E.

"Damn," Detective Clark said. "That's some cold-blooded shit somebody did to the poor girl. Why would they cut out her fucking tongue?"

Detective Louis sighed loudly. "Yeah, that was fucking foul," he said. "I mean the girl was taking a fucking bath for Christ sake! What the fuck is the world coming to?" He stormed out of the bathroom in frustration. It was evident the bloody crime scene was getting under his skin.

"C'mon now, Rich." Clark stepped into the living room to support his partner. "You gotta keep it together, partner," he urged, placing an arm over his shoulder. "You've been doing this too long to let this shit right here get to you like that. Channel that negative energy like you've been trained to do so we can put this evidence in perspective and find the scumbag who did this shit and get his foul ass off the street."

Louis took a deep breath and then exhaled. "Yeah, you're right, Will. I know the drill, and I know what I gotta do." Louis looked across the room. "Hey, Chavez," he called the young Puerto Rican rookie who had the task of interviewing all the building's occupants. "What you got so far, kiddo?"

The young rookie started flipping through his notepad. He shook his head. "Nothing so far, detective. One thing we found to be very odd, though. We don't believe anything was taken. It don't figure, right?" The rookie paused, staring at the detectives. "Is this really a burglary?" Chavez asked, tossing the question in the air for the seasoned vets to ponder.

"Shit doesn't make sense," Clark agreed. "Why such a vicious slaying on such a helpless woman? This wasn't a random act." Louis turned to his partner.

"No shit, Sherlock," he said sarcastically. "This was a senseless act of violence," he stated firmly.

"You hit the nail on the head with that," said the geeky-looking Tony Woo as he entered the room. Referring to his notes, he added, "We have an extremely volatile predator here, gentlemen." Tony eyed both men. His look was stoic. "This person or persons are stalking their victims."

"Victims?" Louis interrupted. "There's only one body here!"

"What are you getting at, Tony?" Clark asked sternly, clasping his hands behind his back. "Lay it all out on the table for us. What's the deal?"

The little scientist was tapping his glasses. "The writing's on the wall, gentlemen," he said point blank. "Our predator has graduated to status of serial killer."

Louis frowned. "Serial killer?" he enunciated as if the word put a bitter taste in his mouth. "Where the freaking hell did you come up with that label all of a sudden?" Louis looked very uncomfortable.

"This crime scene, gentlemen, is connected to our 13th-floor diver in Cleveland Park and our eyeless victim over by

A Beautiful Satan

UDC. Three slayings committed by the same perpetrator earns them the title of serial killer."

"Where's the connection, Tony?" Clark demanded.

"Well, for starters," Tony began, focusing on his pointed finger, "all three women were extremely attractive." He paused, eyeing both men for effect. They were still waiting for the connection to be revealed. Tony continued, "Secondly, the cleaning agent used at all three crime scenes was consistent." Both detectives' eyes widened, startled. A small smile creased Tony's lips when he noticed their reaction. That was the silver bullet they had been searching for. That gave them an angle and focal point from which to build their investigation.

"The cleaning agent used to sterilize each crime scene had a rich alcohol-based chemical component and isn't sold to the general public, which means only a licensed buyer within the medical field has access to this agent. So, like I was saying in the beginning of this investigation, our predator is well versed in the field of forensic or medical science." The scientist tore a page from his notebook and handed it over to the Dynamic Duo. "This is the key to catching our killer."

Clark took hold of the paper, and both detectives studied its contents.

"Yeah, it's about time this scumbag slips up, wouldn't you agree there, Tony?"
Clark inquired casually.

"Gentlemen," Tony Woo began as he stared over the top of his wire frames and regarded them both with a no-nonsense expression, "this guy didn't leave any forensics on the first three victims. He's not gonna get sloppier, he's gonna get better."

It was a glorious October day. The sun's low-slung amber rays shone down on Jovan as he exited the Gucci boutique on Wisconsin Avenue in upper N.W. Shopping bags weighed down both his arms.

Jovan checked his Rolex and noticed it was still early. He had stacks of cash and the rest of the day to do whatever he pleased—at least until Ray finished dealing with them cats over in S.E. He figured he'd slide through the campus of Howard University, see what was jumping and probably bag one or two shorties at his favorite pussy haven: the premier women's high-rise at Howard called The Towers. He climbed into his Benz and began his journey across town.

"Yeah, this the move," Jovan concluded. "Soon as my whip rolls up outside, them hot youngins gonna be geekin' to get up in my ride and go party like a rock star. That shit never fails to amaze me."

The shimmering black Mercedes coupe seemed to glide along 7th Street as Usher's "Like a Freak" thundered from the interior. Jovan was slouched behind the wheel looking smooth as silk, peering through his new gold-framed Gucci shades. He was feeling it—the music, the mood, the whole scene—as he scrutinized the world from inside his posh confines.

His cell phone vibrated. "Yeah!" he snapped as he snatched up his cell. A soft, silky voice caressed his ear. "Hello, may I speak with Jovan?" He pulled the phone from his ear and looked at the screen displaying "Unknown." He huffed, "I hate that shit."

"Um, hello."

"May I ask who's calling?" He was ready to hang up.

"Yes. Tell him this is Malaysia calling, please."

"Malaysia," Jovan repeated, and then his demeanor softened instantly. "Is this the gorgeous wildflower of a beauty?" he asked smoothly, envisioning the sparkle her eyes made when he used that same line as his intro the night they were acquainted. "The same Malaysia I met a few weeks ago at Ibiza?"

"Yes, this is she." She sounded so sweet.

A Beautiful Satan

"Well, what's going on with you? What you do, lose my number? And now it's found all of a sudden, huh? What's the deal, baby girl?"

"Don't be mad, please. There's a logical reason why you haven't heard from me since the night we met."

"Go 'head, I'm listening."

"Well, I've been through a lot," she began. Her silky voice sounded a bit stressed now. "There was a tragedy in my family that called for me to return home. My father passed, and since I'm the oldest child, numerous responsibilities were required of me."

"Baby, I'm so very sorry to hear that," he said, expressing his heartfelt condolence. "Are you okay? You need anything? Just let me know."

"Aw, that's so sweet of you. Thank you very much, but I'm okay, Jovan. Thank you."

"So where's your home located? I know you could've at least left me a message or e-mail or something."

"My home is in Thailand," Malaysia replied, matter-of-factly. "When I got the call early the next morning, I did a rush job getting my personals together. I messed around and grabbed my old BlackBerry. Your information was on the new one I had just purchased. Believe me, Jovan, I wasn't right when I realized the mix-up. I've been thinking about you the entire time I've been away, and I couldn't wait to get back here and hopefully get to see you again. Very soon." She paused for a second, then said, "I want you to know that I'm usually not this forward. But, um, I was um ... I was really digging you, and I would like to see you." Malaysia was straight and to the point.

Jovan was surprised by her openness, but he was loving it. He sensed that this Thai beauty was uniquely refreshing and a definite keeper. "Damn, girl," he responded easily while holding his composure in check. "I appreciate your openness 'cause you've been on my mind constantly also. Getting acquainted with you, that's all I want to do." He licked his lips hungrily as visions of him smashing that pretty Thai ass materialized in his mind. They agreed to meet in the near future.

The black Benz thundered through the intersection at 7th and Florida, where 7th turns into Georgia Avenue. A second later, the sleek coupe roared past Howard U Hospital. The dorm where Danielle lived was on the left. Jovan stepped out of the Mercedes looking as sharp as ever in his black Gucci ensemble. All eyes were on him as he glided over to the entrance of The Towers, where two familiar shorties were standing. The first one's name was Melissa; she was a hot-mocha shorty with a nasty bow-legged stance and a set of lips so juicy they were meant for only one thing. The second girl's name was Candy; she was a high-yella shorty, slim in the waist, pretty in the face, with a nice round onion on her back.

"How are you ladies doing today?" Jovan greeted them both warmly. At the same time, he inventoried a slew of hot, young prospects loitering along the walkway.

"Just fine," Candy answered as her eyes crawled up his frame. Slowly, she undressed him in her mind. "How you doing with your fine-ass self? Damn!" Her girl Melissa looked star struck. She just stood there gazing and smiling at him like he was her knight in shining armor.

"Where's my baby, Danielle? She upstairs chillin'?" He was talking to Candy's hot ass. He already knew from the look she was giving him that she was in game mode. Hell, they both were.

Candy's lips smacked. "Danielle's at work," she said saucily. "She won't be back 'til late tonight sometime. Why, what you trying do?"

He rubbed his hands together, contemplating his next move. "Well, if Danielle was here," he said slyly, "you know I'd be getting it in."

She pursed her lips and said slowly, "Oooh, I know all about you and that." Candy fixed Jovan with a heated stare.

A Beautiful Satan

"Since your boo not around to take care of that for you, let me ride with you. See how I handle that thing." Candy's eyes locked on his crotch.

"Oh yeah?" he replied in a low drawl, matching her look. Jovan dipped his Gucci frames and eyed Candy's body with purpose. "Mmm, you ready to go for a ride, huh? You sure 'bout that?"

She bit her bottom lip and shot him a steamy leer. "I've been ready for that ride since the first day I laid eyes on you."

Jovan stepped aside. "Mmm," he breathed. "Oh, I can't wait to see your work." He motioned for her to lead the way. "After you."

"Hey," her girl Melisa said suddenly, "I'm game and ready to ride too."

His head whipped around. "Do you even know where we're going?" he said.

"It's whatever," she said.

"What?" he smirked.

"Yeesss," she whispered eagerly. "Like I said, it's whatever."

"Ladies first!" Jovan said as they led the way to his coupe.

Chapter 12

Angel was rattled from her sleep. She felt someone was watching her, and the feeling was unnerving. Then she spotted the piercing blue eyes that appeared from the shadows. Her outstretched arm moved along the wall searching for a light switch. She felt it, and flicked it on.

The haughty-looking eyes disappeared as soon as the blinding white light flooded the bathroom, reflecting off the polished white tiles in stark fashion. The sound of running water echoed through the air. The intense illumination caused Angel to wince as she sought out the source of the water. She could see white shower curtains drawn around a bathtub, and she moved in to investigate by pulling back the curtain. Angel recoiled in horror at what she uncovered. A gruesome bloodied corpse was floating belly-up in the crimson-tainted water with a large blade protruding from a woman's mouth.

Right then and there, a startling revelation occurred to Angel. She knew the dead woman. Her name was Monica. But how do I know her? she wondered. The question disturbed her deeply.

A Beautiful Satan

Suddenly the sound of something scratching on the door drew her attention. "Who's there?" she called out. The scratching continued, only louder this time. Angel approached the door cautiously and reached for the knob. Suddenly the door abruptly burst open, revealing a thick cloud of darkness hovering in the doorway like a black ghost.

The haughty blue eyes were back. They seemed to glow in the darkness; their penetrating gaze gripped Angel with fear. Her heartbeat resonated in her ears. She stood paralyzed, unable to move, unable to breath. She could feel a menacing presence radiating from the eyes, drifting into the room. Angel's eyes watered as her body tensed with anticipation. A loud whimper escaped her lips. The eyes and the darkness exploded upon her and then swallowed her whole.

When Angel's eyes popped open, she jumped upright in bed. "Oh my God!" she gasped, clutching at her chest. "It was just a dream!" she said, relieved. Angel looked over at her sleeping husband. "J," she whispered, needing to feel the comfort of his arms around her. "J, wake up, please."

She pulled back the comforter. A bloodied, eyeless corpse rolled over to greet her. The hideous corpse of Tara snarled, "Ho!"

As Angel sprang into a sitting position, she could feel her heart racing. "Lord, what's happening to me?" Angel said, out of breath. Her eyes swept the bedroom, making sure that the room and everything in it was safe. She reached out for Jovan, and her heart sunk when she realized that the covers were undisturbed. "Fucking bastard," she said vehemently as she crumbled into the empty space. Teary eyed, Angel curled up into the fetal position and cried silently in the dark.

Chapter 13

Jovan hit a "J" as he walked across the room butt naked and stared out the balcony window. Candy and Melissa lay across the bed naked watching videos.

He was sporting a cocky, triumphant expression when he peeked back over his shoulder. He cracked a smile as he pictured the both of them taking turns singing at the top of their lungs every time they switched positions after they talked that shit and then couldn't take the dick. All that goddamn screaming and hollering and trying to get away. "I'm surprised ain't nobody call the damn police," he chuckled under his breath.

Candy noticed him checking them out. "I see you. What you grinning about?" she inquired. "Your girl Dannie wasn't lying—you the bomb, hands down!"

Melissa's soft, chocolaty frame rolled over. "Mmm," she moaned, glowing with delight and massaging her hard, puckered nipples with one hand and in between her legs with the other. "Girl, you ain't never lied," she said. Melissa agreed that shit was the truth. "Please don't forget to give me your digits. You can call me up anytime."

Jovan got hard watching Melissa play with herself. And watching his penis blow up like a huge parade float set Melissa's ass on fire.

"What the hell," Melissa whispered to herself in astonishment. The triple stack E-pills she popped earlier smacked her head all of a sudden. Her pussy was craving to have that dick stuffed inside of her. The room started to spin, and she felt hot all over. Melissa closed her eyes and felt her inner body erupt in ecstasy. Her back arched as her pussy exploded like a volcano. Her hands caressed her vagina.

Melissa looked momentarily star struck when she opened her eyes and found her girl Candy licking and sucking on her pussy. Melissa's mind said stop, but her body was loving every second of it. Then she watched Jovan crawl across the bed, his long, thick shaft hanging low as he moved into position next to her head. He grabbed a pillow and propped her head up nicely.

She surprised the hell out of Jovan when she suddenly latched onto his joint with both hands and forced the swollen head of his penis into her mouth like she was eating an apple whole.

"Oh yeah, baby," Jovan moaned with a smile as he watched her work her mouthpiece all over his rod. *She might can't take no dick,* he thought, *but she can slob a knob viciously.*

The steel-gray Crown Victoria was snaking its way along Connecticut Avenue at the height of the evening rush.

Detective Will Clark waved anxiously to the driver in the burgundy Jeep Commander. "Will you get the hell outta my way," he demanded, stomping on the gas pedal when he spotted a break in traffic. The Crown Vic darted into an exposed gap, which opened up due to a waiting Metro transit bus that was loading passengers at the entrance to the National Zoo. "Fucking asshole!" he muttered as he cut in front of the jeep.

"Next time just hit the siren on their ass," Detective Louis offered. "It saves a lot of aggravation," he explained while studying the contents of a thick manila folder.

Clark sighed. "Yeah, I know the drill, Rich," he said flatly, and shot him a hard look. "So what else does forensic say besides the mystery DNA?"

Louis, uncertain, began sucking his teeth and tapping his pen on the dash. Then he finally spoke up, "Fucking scumbag really must know his shit."

"What brings you to that conclusion?"

"It says in here this fucker is vacuuming the crime scene as part of his ritual after each murder."

Clark groaned. "A genuine Mr. Merry Maids we're dealing with here, sounds like to me," he gritted sardonically. "What's it say? Is he toting a vacuum around to each crime scene or some shit like that?"

"Well," Louis said, reading deeper into the report, "from what they've gathered thus far, looks like our sicko used the first victim's own vacuum to sterilize the scene." He paused and looked over at his partner.

"What, they find the victim's vacuum missing a bag?"

He nodded with a gleam in his eye. "Will," he began slowly, "we're dealing with a very cool, calm character here. Remember, he plucked the eyes from our victim's skull. That was one of the bloodiest crime scenes I've ever come across," Louis confessed.

Clark detected an uneasy note in his partner's voice. He cut his eyes in Louis' direction. "Don't go getting all weirded out on me there, Rich. I need your head on straight and your in-depth expertise in order for us to crack this case."

Louis regarded him with an intense look. "Don't worry, Will," he said stoutly, "I'm with you on this no matter how long it takes."

A Beautiful Satan

Clark nodded and drove past the Uptown movie theater on his left. He abruptly hit the brake as the upcoming traffic signal turned red. He huffed in frustration, then turned to Louis. "Anything in there about why his pattern changed up all of a sudden?"

I believe that's our job, Will," he said, frowning when he flipped the page and found the photo of the eyeless corpse. His jaw tightened as he shuffled through the collage of grisly photographs. He could feel a migraine coming on. Detective Louis slammed the folder shut and dropped it at his feet. He let his head lean back and rest on the headrest and began massaging his temple.

"You alright, partner?" Clark asked when he heard the folder hit the floor.

"I'm cool," he said. "It's these damn migraines again, that's all." He attempted to play down his condition, but Clark wasn't fooled.

"If you need to stop past the CVS, just say the word before we get up to the college."

"I'm good," he reiterated. "Let's just get up to UDC so we can interview those witnesses again."

Clark studied his partner for a second before focusing on the mounting traffic up ahead. It was apparent to him that the vulgarity of this case was really weighing on his conscious. What troubled Clark was why. Louis is a seasoned detective; he's dealt with violent cases of this magnitude in the past, so what's the deal with this case here?

As Detective Clark maneuvered the cruiser along the gauntlet of rolling traffic, his mind did its own maneuvering. He couldn't stop thinking about the instability of his partner. He had a funny feeling, and it bothered him immensely.

Chapter 14

After dropping the two hotties back at Howard, Jovan remembered that the party was at Ray's tonight as he headed out the city towards the Potomac suburbs.

The crowds outside of the palatial Potomac estate were growing by the minute. Jovan took notice of the swelling crowd as he stared up the long, winding driveway toward the entrance. None of the attending partygoers would have anything to worry themselves over. Potomac, Maryland, was an affluent suburb of Washington, D.C.; it was often referred to as the Beverly Hills of the Washington region. Celebrities, sport stars and high-ranking political figures gravitated towards and called Potomac their home.

Jovan was in deep thought as he scanned the grounds of the estate. *Ray's party is jumping off. I guess my man knew what he was talking about when he said he wanted to rent out the Potomac Mansion and throw a fly Playa's Ball. All I need now,* he told himself, *is for Malaysia to show her face in the place. With that ass on my dick, my day will be complete.*

Inside, the party was hot. D.C.'s premier disc jockey, D.J. Mini, was on the ones and twos, blazin' the airwaves with

A Beautiful Satan

R. Kelly's "I'm a Flirt." Jovan moved through the main room and the ultra-hip crowd of partiers. He was searching for Ray when he inadvertently bumped into one of Ray's protégés, a young slickster by the name of Finesse.

"Nigga, where's the love!" exclaimed the flamboyant young pimp, grinning broadly and extending his open arms.

"Whaz up, baby," Jovan replied. Both men greeted each other with a strong hug.

"Where's Ray?!!" Jovan asked.

"He chilling by the pool," Finesse replied while checking out the ladies in the background—a small clique of groupies all geekin' out over Jovan.

Ray was lounging on the lower level in the pool house. When Jovan and Finesse entered the room, a fog of marijuana smoke assaulted their nostrils. He spotted Ray right away. He was chilling over at the poolside.

Ray greeted Jovan with a lazy smile. Two young and pretty Asian honeys, clad in skimpy two-piece snakeskin bikinis, were keeping him company. "Playboy!" he said, extending his free hand. "Smooth, fly-ass nigga!" He reached into a platinum box and produced a quarter-pound Ziploc bag stuffed with the prettiest green hydro. The groupies' eyes all lit up. "Here, puff on this crucial."

Ray held up a thick smoking blunt. "Now that you here, we can get this party started."

Jovan took three hard pulls and gagged. "Whoa!"

"How ya like that there?" Ray flashed his victory smile.

With watery eyes, Jovan held up a finger as he attempted to catch his breath by stifling his cough. "Yeah, this that shit right here. Goddamn!" He passed the blunt to Finesse.

Jovan and Ray moved off to the side away from the women. There was some important business that demanded their prompt attention.

"Playboy," Ray began, as he made a neat bow with the black satin belt around his plumb-purple smoking jacket. He made himself comfortable on a poolside lounge chair. "Here, take a seat," Ray offered, patting the empty spot beside him. "I got some bad and good news to lay on you."

"Bad news like what?" questioned Jovan with a skeptical frown. The mention of bad news caused his temperature to rise. He shed his leather before taking a seat next to his partner. "You know I ain't the one to handle bad news lightly, dawg," he warned, folding his arms across his chest aggressively. They were face-to-face now.

Ray sucked his teeth for a second, pondering his partner's words. "Don't worry," he said with a wink, then pulled a healthy looking stack of fifties from the pocket of his smoking jacket. "Here," he tossed the money to Jovan. "That's you, playboy."

He eyed the money in his hand for a moment. "What's this supposed to be?" he asked, thumbing through the bills. "That's a part of your profits from Orleans Place today," Ray answered easily.

"This ain't shit," Jovan retorted dryly. "Where's the rest of my cake? You know not to fuck with my loot." Jovan paused and aimed a cold stare at Ray. "Don't fuck with my family, and don't fuck with my funds," he explained sternly. "That's the rule of thumb I live by."

Ray's hand flew up in a submissive gesture. "Whoa, whoa ... hold up, playa. I know how ya operate," he said smoothly. "That right there is nothing but the early a.m. profits. That's your fun money. The serious paper rolls in during the p.m. That right there is the good news. The bad news is my peoples took a hit today, but don't sweat it," Ray said, wearing a false smile. "That's on me. I'll absorb the loss from this bullshit that went down."

Jovan remained silent. *Five G's* he voiced silently when he reached the end of the stack.

A Beautiful Satan

"I was trying to make that move on them Barry Farms bammas, and shit got all fucked up. But like I said, that's on me. I'll take the loss 'cause you never said that you wanted in on the move."

Jovan's brow shot up when it dawned on him what Ray was referring to. They had a conversation a few days ago about opening shop in the Barry Farms housing project, one of the most violent projects in the city. "What? What you do?" he asked suddenly. "You went ahead and put a half a brick over that joint anyway?" He was more than a little annoyed.

"Nah, I ain't do the half a bird," Ray replied quietly, shaking his head. "I put a quarter key over there instead, and some bammas hit up my squad."

"They got the whole quarter joint up off of 'em?" Jovan inquired with a raised eyebrow.

"Yeah, they got 'em," he said. "But don't worry, I'm putting a hit squad together as we speak. Them bammas fucked with the wrong peoples!" His voice turned coarse, "Don't even worry, I got this," Ray assured, pounding on his chest with a distant glare in his eyes.

The men were suddenly distracted. A boisterous group of women spilled into the pool house talking loudly and acting raunchily. It was obvious the women had too much to drink; a few of them were stumbling as they moved toward a corner sofa.

One of the ladies, an attractive Italian with long brown trusses, froze in her tracks when she caught sight of the two men staring at them from the poolside. She stormed across the room like she had a bone to pick with somebody.

Looking puzzled, Jovan asked, "Who the fuck is this bitch? One of your hos?"

Ray shook his head, "I don't know shorty," he replied without hesitation. "But she would make a hot addition to my stable," he admitted slyly.

She stomped over to Jovan with a mean look on her face. "What kind of bitch-ass nigga are you?" she snapped, rolling her head and grabbing her hips.

He stared up at her, trying not to laugh. He found the situation to be amusing. "Um, excuse me, miss," he said politely, "but, uh, I think you might have me confused with some other brother. I don't know you," he said softly, licking his lips and eyeing her physique with a lustful look. "But, uh, if this is your way of introducing yourself to a man like myself ..." Jovan stopped short, stroking his chin arrogantly. "This act right here," he waved his forefinger in a scolding manner, "this is not the right angle to get next to a man like me."

"What?" she rolled her eyes, looking hostile. "You got shit twisted, don't you? Do you know who I am? I'm Ariel's best friend, Tiffany! No, let me correct that. She was my best friend."

A quizzical look flashed across Jovan's face. "So you coming at me with that wacked-out bullshit because you and my girl Ariel beefin'?"

Tiffany looked at Jovan like he was crazy. "Beefin'? We don't have no beef," she protested defiantly with her head just a rolling. Tiffany propped her hands on her hip and scowled, "My girl passed away! And you got the audacity not to make it to her funeral. Who the hell do you think you are? You're a monster! That's what you are."

Jovan was processing her words. He responded in an almost breathless voice, "What? Ariel is dead? What the fuck happened?"

Both men were blindsided by the story Tiffany laid on them. Someone had murdered the pretty, outgoing and kindhearted French native. Jovan was more affected by the shocking revelation than he was letting on.

The French beauty was Jovan's secret love. They had been carrying on a secret life together under the radar. Not even their friends knew. Jovan was even contemplating how he could go about pulling off a secret wedding in France to the lovely Ariel. Now some crazy muthafucka had taken her away. *First Tara ... now Ariel?* Thoughts of the two murdered women caused a dull ache to implode inside his heart. How had two of his love interests suddenly become murder victims? Anxiety swelled in the pit of his stomach as the reality of the situation settled on his conscious.

After listening to Tiffany's startling revelation, Ray sensed that his partner needed a little time to get himself together. He rejoined his female companions while Jovan silently gathered his senses.

All of a sudden, as if the air was sucked out of the room, the noise from the crowd dropped a few octaves.

Although Jovan could hear Ray's voice calling in the distance, he felt like he was emerging through a dense fog. When his vision cleared, Ray was motioning for him to look. When Jovan noticed Malaysia moving through the crowd, he felt like Lazarus rising from the dead.

Malaysia's presence energized him, bringing him suddenly to his feet. Jovan strolled across the floor, winking at the cutie eyeing him, never breaking his stride.

As Jovan closed the distance between them, his eyes roamed over her hot, curvy frame with excitement. He loved how the tight-fitting dress clung to her curves, beautifully accentuating that hot body of hers. Her nipples were protruding through the sheer pink Dior. *They are perfect*, he thought, his piercing gray eyes absorbing every delightful inch of her with joyful glee.

"Hello, gorgeous," Jovan softly spoke, leaning into her ear. He took her by the hand and looked deeply into her eyes. "Seeing you tonight was definitely worth the wait," he said, licking his lips while admiring her. "Mmmm, mmm, mmm, Malaysia," he whispered smoothly. "Baby, you are breathtaking."

"Thank you, Jovan," Malaysia blushed. *This fine brother has me beyond horny*, she silently confessed. Jovan's salacious stare was intense. She could feel the heat radiating along her body. *It was amazing*, she thought. This man reached into her and touched her womanhood with just his look.

"God!" Malaysia exhaled, as their eyes connected.

His impish smile made her heart do somersaults. Watching him move across the floor like a male lion coming to stake his claim put butterflies in her stomach and made her pussy wet. His persona radiated confidence, passion and finesse in a way she had never experienced before. Point blank, Jovan set her soul afire. His touch sent goose bumps racing up and down her arm. *Wow,* she thought. *This is how it feels—love at first sight.*

"Pretty lady," he said, his low, sexy voice massaging her ear. "How would you like it if we rolled up out of here and found us a more intimate setting? You know, someplace where we can explore one another's mind, body and soul. Our insatiable desires would make for a hot topic also, wouldn't you agree?" A devious grin crawled across his lips.

Malaysia turned to him, and her emerald eyes smiled with radiance so warm he couldn't help but smile. "Mmm, that sounds very interesting," she softly murmured in his ear. "Do you have somewhere special in mind?"

He thought for a moment, stroking his chin. "Sure thing, pretty lady," he smiled, offering his arm. "Shall we?" She happily grabbed hold of him.

Jovan gave his partner a look as he escorted his Thai beauty toward the exit. "Call me later," he mouthed with a wink before the alluring couple disappeared into the stairwell.

ꙮꙮꙮꙮ

Before the stroke of midnight, Jovan and Malaysia were cruising the trendy restaurant district in Bethesda, Maryland. Not long after their arrival in Bethesda, the black SL-550 pulled to a stop outside of the posh Paramour Restaurant and Bar, an exclusive gathering den that catered to an affluent clientele of swingers. For those in the know, "paramour" was French for "illicit lover."

Paramour's theme was an intoxicatingly romantic setting with flaming torches adorning walls painted with exotic murals. Private dining booths with cozy iridescent tables were aglow in candlelight as soft Polynesian melodies filled the background, creating an atmosphere charged with erotic sensuality.

Jovan and Malaysia walked into the restaurant hand in hand right after the valet attendant relieved Jovan of his car keys. A tall, tanned Australian wearing a sharply tailored black tux greeted the couple warmly, and Jovan returned the greeting. "Hello, Ty," he said as he shook hands with the majordomo.

"Mr. Rising, sir," he said, his voice thick with that "down under" accent, "we are so pleased to have you grace us with your presence on this lovely evening." Ty paused momentarily and then stepped behind the rosewood podium. In less than two seconds, Ty stood before them holding a shiny platinum-engraved goblet above his head. "Selena will be at your beck and call this evening," the majordomo advised, passing Jovan the goblet. "Ah, here she is now," Ty smiled graciously.

When the attractive Latina maitre d' appeared, she was all smiles as she hurried over to greet them. "Hola, Mr. Jovan!" she said, beaming. "Right this way, Senor." She led the way, escorting them to their private dining area, which was a nice secluded booth.

Flames from a stone fireplace licked the air directly across from them, establishing a nice, romantic touch to an already arousing atmosphere.

"Come here often?" Malaysia asked with a pleased look as she absorbed the sexy scene and its unique décor. She eased into the booth thinking, *This brother definitely has plenty of class.*

"Oh, I come here every now and then," Jovan said speaking casually. "Ya know, when the mood moves me, or should I say, when that *special* someone moves me." He slid close to her. Jovan inhaled and filled his nostrils with Malaysia's sweet smelling fragrance. "Ahh," he sighed, ingesting the intoxicating aroma into his system.

"As you can see, this is not your ordinary restaurant," Jovan explained with a wave of his hand.

Malaysia nodded in agreement. "Members only. I gathered that much."

He smiled at her response. "Oh, really? You been to a joint like this before? Is that what you telling me?" He watched as she shook her head. "So I'm your first," Jovan continued, drawing his lips close to her ear. "That's nice to know because I reserve this place for very special occasions."

"Is that so," she replied smiling. "Well, to what do I owe this special honor?" Jovan's cologne and his sexy-ass voice had Malaysia's ass all hot and bothered. She had to get a grip on herself. *Damn! I hope he doesn't notice,* she thought.

Jovan stroked her long, pretty hair, admiring the soft texture as he followed the flowing strands down to the small of her back. "Malaysia, your beauty alone makes you special," he whispered in her ear as he pushed her hair back. "Your look, your scent," he inhaled deeply. "Your presence … everything about you girl is special," he said smoothly.

This brother is too suave, Malaysia thought. His voice, his words, his demeanor were all so hypnotic. She had to snap out of it. "Mmm," she moaned, planting her hand firmly on his thigh. "You're charming," she confessed with a smile. "I know you've got an army of women in line waiting for you. Where's the wife? I know you got one 'cause you're too dreamy to be floating around unattached."

He was concentrating on Malaysia's neckline, tracing it lightly with his index finger when she dropped the wife bomb on him. Without hesitation, Jovan answered calmly,

A Beautiful Satan

"My wife should be at home." He never broke stride with his finger.

"What?" Malaysia blurted, looking stunned. She turned and grabbed his left wrist. She stared at the blinged-out wedding band as disbelief spread across her face. "You have a wife at home, and you're out on the town wining and dining another woman? Oh, baby, you have issues," she expressed sarcastically. "I don't know about this." She shook her head dejectedly. "I can't be having that type of drama in my life."

His hand went up. "Hey, pump your brakes, baby girl," Jovan began, initiating his tactful rebuttal. "Now listen to me." He caressed her face with both hands and turned her toward him. They were face-to-face and eye to eye. "Am I married? Yes. Do I have a wife at home? Yes. But it's not what you think. My marriage is a marriage of convenience with major financial implications involved," he explained. His tone was firm but calm. "Now, I really don't like talking about my situation. But you can rest assured and believe me when I say this façade will be coming to a head very soon. When it does, I'll be looking to start my life anew with a brand-new slate. Hopefully, with someone who's as intriguing and beautiful and as lovely as yourself. I know what I need to complete me, and all that I hold in my hands right here is all that I will need."

Malaysia's head was spinning now. Her feelings had just run the entire spectrum of her emotional scale. She had just experienced love, shock, disbelief, contempt and compassion, and now her heart was beating in rhythm to Jovan's voice. Malaysia was eating out of the palm of his hand. She thought to herself, *If this man is feeding me bull, this shit sure tastes good.*

Jovan watched as Malaysia went through a profound transformation right before his very eyes. He knew he had her, hook, line and sinker. Malaysia's mind, body and soul were trailing close behind.

Damn, I'm good, Jovan said to himself, stroking his own ego. *Sometimes, I even surprise myself. I think I might be falling in love with me too.* Tickled laughter filled his insides.

"So, baby," Jovan said, his gray eyes piercing her soul, "are you feeling me? 'Cause I'm feeling you. Just let me know if we taking this ride in the same car or not, okay?"

Malaysia didn't answer him; she just sat gazing in his eyes.

Chapter 15

The windswept pines moved against the coming storm as lightning flashes ignited the dark clouds rolling across the sky.

Jovan hurried up the walkway, bracing himself against the blustery wind as thick raindrops pelted him in the face. His pace quickened as he neared the low-rise apartment building. He reached for the door, which swung open abruptly, startling him.

He stepped into the empty lobby with the wind nipping at his back. He paused as the door slammed shut and a dead silence swept through the lobby.

Jovan stood in front of apartment #101 and rang the doorbell. Monica appeared in the doorway looking hot as she danced around, showing off the powder-blue silk nightie he had recently surprised her with.

Monica stopped dancing and propped her hands on her shapely hips. "What the hell are you doing?" she yelled.

The sound of the swirling wind sounded behind him. Someone else must've entered the building, he thought. All of a sudden, a rushing wind blew across the left side of Jovan's *face. His eyes slammed shut out of reflex, and something wet sprayed him in the face. Monica playing games, Jovan thought.*

"What the fuck?" he cursed as he wiped his eyes. "Kind of games you playing, girl?" When Jovan finished wiping his eyes clear, the sight of his blood-soaked hands rattled him. As he looked up slowly, what Jovan saw rocked his entire foundation. The scene was ghastly. A butcher knife was embedded in the middle of Monica's forehead with blood gushing from the wound. The crimson gore cascaded down her face and spilled onto her nightie.

"No!" Jovan shrieked, rushing to aid her. He couldn't reach her, though, for there was a glass wall blocking his path. He pressed his palms flat against the glass and gave it a mighty shove. "No!" he yelled as he watched Monica fall to her knees. He desperately wanted to save her, but it was too late.

Behind Jovan, the sound of swirling wind drew his attention. He quickly spun around on his heels and was surprised to see that dark shadows had engulfed the lobby; a thick cloud of black smoke was crawling across the gray tiled floor. He jumped when the eerie sound of demonic laughter erupted from the darkness. Jovan's body stiffened, and the hairs on the back of his neck turned prickly.

Inside of the billowing darkness Jovan could hear the sound of blades slashing through the air. His eyes were of no use to him as the threatening sound drew closer and closer with each swing. His breathing grew louder as his pulse elevated. Jovan's eyes shifted from side to side, fear and trepidation swirling around him.

Suddenly the flash of a blade caught his eye as it sliced through the darkness, down the front of his body. Jovan's eyes went wide when he saw his erect penis standing at attention. The menacing blade swooped down on his protruding organ like a guillotine in the act of a beheading. The blade sliced through his membrane with the ease of a steak knife chopping

A Beautiful Satan

through a stick of butter. He stared in utter shock as he witnessed his penis separate from his body and tumble to his feet.

"No! No! Nooo!" Jovan screamed incoherently while kicking and squirming and grabbing at his groin.

Angel tugged on the covers and called, "J! Wake up, wake up, Da. You're having a bad dream, baby."

Jovan's eyes blinked wide open and then darted wildly around his bedroom. He realized that he was holding his jewels in the palm of his hand. Jovan squeezed them a little too hard. "Ooh fuck!" he cursed himself, doubling over in pain. All of his parts were still intact. Thank God that was just a dream.

"Are you okay," Angel asked, looking concerned. "You need anything?"

"Oh, fuck," he said, still moaning and rocking in pain. "Leave me alone," he growled.

Angel pushed the covers aside, threw her legs over the side of the bed. "I'm hungry," she said as she stood. "You want a Spanish omelet and some bacon? That's what I gotta taste for."

He nodded, looking groggy. "Yeah, baby, that sounds good," he muttered, rolling toward her. "Why don't you put on some fresh coffee while you're at it?"

She glanced over her shoulder as she walked around the bed on her way to the bathroom. "You ain't gotta tell me that. I know how my man likes his coffee in the morning. Let me handle this. Just relax."

After Jovan watched his wife disappear into the bathroom, he rolled over and stared up at the ceiling. Thoughts of the disturbing dream slowly trickled across his mind. The horrible images were so vivid they made him cringe. *What kind of crazy-ass dream was that?* Jovan wondered silently. He shuddered when the entire vision played out in his mind. Then a disquieting thought popped into his head: Tara. When he had the dream about her, she wound up a victim of a gruesome slaying.

"Oh my God," Jovan said with a strained, fearful look in his eye. "Please, not Monica too." The thought caused a deep, queasy feeling to push into his gut. Jovan didn't want to admit to himself, but his gut instinct was telling that Monica was no more. Jovan wished the dreaded feeling away. He hoped and prayed that what he felt was nothing more than his gut instinct running amok.

Jovan took his time before he finally decided to crawl out of bed, get himself together and journey down the stairs to have breakfast with his wife.

From the top of the stairs, Jovan could hear two female voices coming from the kitchen. "Who in the hell?" he said as he descended the stairs.

When Jovan walked into the kitchen, he was taken aback by what he found. Angel was standing alone in the kitchen, hovering over the range in the midst of preparing her prized Spanish omelet dish.

"Weren't you just talking to someone?" he inquired. "I know I'm not crazy."

A warm smile flashed across Angel's face. "What you talking about, boy?" she uttered, waving him off. "You hearing things. Ain't nobody down here but me."

He moved over to the granite island and perched himself atop a bar stool. "Were you just talking on the phone? I'm not trippin'; I know what I heard, and what I heard were two women talking to one another."

Angel reached across the counter and caressed his cheek. "Maybe you heard somebody outside or something because I haven't used the phone today. I've been down here preparing this delicious meal for my husband all by my lonesome, waiting for him to join me. Now, since you're here, would it be too much to ask you to get a couple of mugs down from the cabinet and pour us some coffee, please?" She finished with a wink and a kiss.

A Beautiful Satan

Jovan's shoulders sagged in defeat, but his mind was on point. He shook his head with uncertainty written all over his face as he hopped from the stool. *What kind of games is Angel playing with me?* he thought as he pulled their favorite matching red his-and-hers mugs out of the overhead cabinet.

"So what's on your agenda for today?" Angel asked while preparing his plate. Her flirty, conniving look didn't jibe right with her husband. Jovan eased back onto the stool.

"Nothing in particular. Why?" he retorted.

"Well, you know your girl Alicia Keys in town tonight," Angel said with a knowing smile. She knew that would get his attention, if he didn't already know.

"Oh yeah?" he replied with a raised brow as he stuffed a hefty piece of omelet in his mouth. "I ain't know that. Where she gonna be at?"

"Well," she said softly, picking through her omelet, "I'll tell you where she's performing if you promise to take me to see her."

Jovan chuckled, "What? All I gotta do is make a call and find out where she gonna be at. C'mon now, get real."

"That may be," she grinned cunningly, twirling her fork. "But that don't mean
you'll be able to get tickets. Catch my drift?" she chuckled.

"Oh, you got tickets already, huh?" Jovan was amused. He knew Angel's game, and he didn't mind. It was time he wined and dined his wife. Lately, he realized that he had been spending more and more time away from the house. Fucking with Ray's hot ass took up more time than he had anticipated.

"Sure, precious," he said quickly. "You want to go and see Alicia Keys tonight with your Daddy? Well, you better look extra sexy tonight." He blew her a kiss.

A triumphant smile appeared instantly on Angel's lips. She dropped her fork, whirled around and snatched the cordless off its base. "What's going on now?" Jovan asked.

"Nothing, baby. I need to get my nails touched up," she said while dialing, then returning to her plate.

"So where is she performing at tonight?"

She put her hand over the receiver.

"Hogate's on the waterfront."

"Yes, Angel Rising here. Is my girl Nia available today?"

"She is."

"What's her next availability?"

"She's booked."

"Well, I'm one of her preferred clients."

"Mrs. Rising?"

"Yes, that's me."

"Oh, she has an opening in the next hour."

"Yes, that'll be perfect, honey."

"I'll see you then. Thank you."

Angel hung up the phone, scuffed down two bite-size pieces of her omelet and grabbed her coffee mug as she headed towards the stairs. "I have to go get ready," she said. "Whatever you do, make sure you're here by eight so that we can be there on time." Angel disappeared up the stairs.

Jovan polished off the rest of his breakfast before pushing away from the granite isle. He stood and stretched, then moved in front of the bay windows. He enjoyed the view of the tree-lined backyard. The scene was tranquil. The brilliant autumn sun's warm rays cascaded down through the birch foliage. Jovan smiled as he watched two squirrels dash from one tree to the next, chasing one another in a game of tag.

You little guys don't know how lucky you are, he said to himself. *All you have to worry about is finding nuts and busting nuts. My world is much more complicated.* Suddenly the repulsive images of his disturbing dream began to invade his thoughts. Jovan realized these images were going to haunt him the whole day though.

It was like Monica was calling out to him. The shit felt weird. The nightmare had sparked a strange yearning inside of him. *That's it,* Jovan decided, *I've got to find out if she's okay.*

A Beautiful Satan

That's the only way I'm going to get over this. With his mind made up, Jovan did an about-face, and headed for the stairs.

ⓌⓌⓌⓌ

A polished black Mercedes truck rolled into the empty parking slot in front of Monica's apartment building.

There were three young dudes loitering by the wooden fence outside of the building, trying to look hard.

Jovan flipped open the armrest and pulled out a healthy-looking .40 caliber. He looked sinister as he stuffed the gat in his hip and then hopped out. He shot the youngins a hard look before moving up the walkway. It was obvious them niggas ain't want no trouble.

When Jovan stepped into the lobby, the creepy nightmare flooded into his mind. He walked quickly to Monica's door and rang the doorbell.

"Where in the hell is she?" he mumbled under his breath. "She's not answering the damn phone, "she's not answering her fucking cell. Now she's not answering the door!" Frustration was starting to get the better of him.

The sound of a door opening echoed behind him. Jovan spun around and found a little old lady peering through the crack with a cautious eye.

"Don't nobody live there no more," she said in a small voice. "They took her body away days ago."

Jovan blinked twice. "What?" he gasped, his heartbeat pounding in his chest. "They took her body away? Who took her body away?" He knew the answer before the words tumbled out of his mouth.

"Them detectives and them policemen," the old lady said cracking the door a little wider. "Should've seen 'em; they was like something off of the 'CSI' show."

Five minutes hadn't gone by before the black ML 500 was double-parked at the bottom of Hawaii Avenue, in front of Monica's girlfriend's house.

Jovan was surprised to see the usually perky and saucy redhead looking so demure and placid. It was as though all of the life had been sucked from her and all that was left was a pale, freckled-faced shell of a woman. It took Gail a few seconds to recognize who Jovan was. When she realized who he was, she burst through the screen door and fell into his arms and began to sob openly.

"Oh, Jovan," she cried. "Have they found out anything? They find out who killed my girl?" Gail's voice broke off to a frail whimper.

It was obvious she had been devastated by the death of her friend, so much so she was not the same person he remembered. Jovan wasn't prepared for this, another of his love interests murdered. And they had just gotten back together after at least a monthlong hiatus. This situation was too daunting for him to digest right now. The murders, this woman, whom he barely knew, falling apart on him. How had this travesty come upon his life out of the blue like this?

What have I done? Why is this happening to me? Jovan asked himself, feeling torn and confused.

Chapter 16

It was Saturday night, and Jovan kept his promise to his wife. The Risings were arm in arm, as they walked into the ritzy Hogate's restaurant and lounge. The view along the S.W. waterfront was picturesque.

Jovan and Angel drew admiring stares as they entered. They looked perfect together, the couple who had the best of everything. Jovan was dashing in his olive-green Giorgio Armani suit, while his lovely wife bedazzled the eyes in her magenta Chado Ralph Rucci pantsuit. They complemented one another superbly.

Angel loved music and dancing, and she loved it that much more when Jovan was added to the equation. As the couple journeyed through the crowded club, Angel felt like the belle of the ball hanging on her husband's arm.

She was bubbling with excitement, watching as a number of familiar faces greeted Jovan and paid homage to her husband like he was a superstar. Angel was riding high, absorbing every aspect of the evening: the ritzy club, the sexy, showy crowd, the live music and the intoxicating atmosphere.

She was caught up in the moment and loving every minute of it.

When the couple took their place at their reserved table, Angle threw her arms around Jovan's neck and planted a nice, juicy kiss on his lips, expressing her excitement and appreciation.

"Thank you," she said happily. "I'm having so much fun!" She snuggled close to his ear. "Look at those tramps over there," Angel whispered. "We look so good they can't keep their eyes off of us. They hating for real."

Jovan smirked, "You don't know that. Why can't they be admiring our style, huh?"

Angel smacked her lips. "What, you know them bitches?" she whispered with an attitude. "That's why you taking up for 'em?"

Jovan frowned. "Get real," he shot back quickly. "I don't know none of them broads. I'm here with you," he said, easing his arm around her. "You all that matters to me. Don't you know?" He peered deeply into his wife's soft amber eyes. "You're my world, precious," he said, his tone low and deliberate. "And you're everything that's good in it."

Angel started feeling all warm and fuzzy inside. *Damn, this nigga knows how to get to me*, she confessed to herself. She exhaled deeply, "Awww, that's so sweet." Angel kissed him tenderly on his neck, then relaxed her body against his.

A pair of young ladies made their way through the crowd, giggling. As they walked past the couple's table, both of them smiled and eyed Jovan, waving as they walked by.

"The nerve of those little hussies," Angel spat with a look of disgust. "They don't have no damn respect. Damn, if they act like that while I'm with you, I know how hot in the ass they act when I'm not around. Them trifling sluts don't have no respect for themselves, let alone having respect for someone else!" That little insignificant gesture had really ruffled Angel's feathers.

A Beautiful Satan

Jovan waved them off. "Fuck them bitches," he grumbled sharply. "C'mon, baby, don't let them get under your skin like that," he urged, trying to lighten the mood. "Me and you doing this thang tonight. This our night; we're in our own little circle, our own lil' sphere. So don't let nobody disturb our groove, okay? He was cool and collected when he spoke. That was the only way to get through to his wife when she got like this.

Angel pursed her lips. "Well, since you put it like that," she muttered in a submissive tone, "I suppose you have a point."

He watched her closely. "What was that? I didn't hear you." He scowled slightly.

Angel knew what he was getting at. She knew that look. "Okay, you're right," she slowly relented. "I'm not going to let any outsiders disturb our groove, okay? Does that suffice?" An instant smile appeared on her hubby's face.

"Well," she said, now standing, "I'm going to the little girls' room. Would you be so kind as to have me a drink and something to munch on when I return?"

"Baby, girl, that's being prepared as we speak," he said. He blew her a kiss. "So you just hurry your sexy ass on back here, and don't make me come looking for you. 'Cause if I do, I'm a put it in you for real."

She moaned playfully, "Oooh, I don't know, I just might like that." Jovan smacked her on her ass before sending her off.

While Angel was busy in the restroom, a couple of familiar faces noticed Jovan and decided now was the perfect time to make their presence known to him. It was pretty clear they were hoping for a lot more once they showed themselves.

Jovan felt good. He was glad that he decided to take his wife up on her offer tonight. Crazy-ass Ray had tried to talk him out of going with his wife. Something about a hotel party at the Washington Plaza. He figured it wouldn't be nothing but a bunch of gold-diggers on the prowl at the hotel.

He'd rather party with his wife tonight than deal with them money-grubbing bitches. *Now if Malaysia would've called, things would have been different.*

"How are you doing tonight, J?" a gentle whisper caressed his ear from behind. Whoever this was, he felt they were infringing upon his space.

He glanced over his shoulder and caught sight of the pretty little freak, Candy, and her bow-legged sidekick with the vicious head-game, Melissa. She was standing beside her, smiling and waving as Candy hovered over him. *What the fuck do these dumb-ass bitches call themselves doing?* he wondered.

Jovan made no attempt to conceal the mounting indignation in his expression. "What do y'all want?" he inquired with obvious distaste in his voice.

Candy's smile faded. "We just wanted to say—"

He cut her off with a wave of his hand. "'Just wanted to say' my ass!" he snapped. "I'm with my wife, bitch! I dare you to act like you don't know. Don't fucking play with me! Play with your pussy, bitch!" He was seething now. These freaks had crossed the line, and they knew it.

Both of their eyes grew wide. Jovan looked like he was ready to knock their heads off. Melissa shook her head in disbelief when she witnessed her friend's demeanor crumble on the spot.

"I told you this was a bad idea," Melissa said, grabbing Candy by the arm. But her girl was being defiant.

Candy's head whirled around, and her lips curled into a sneer. "Get off me!" she barked, ripping her arm from Melissa's grip. "Who this nigga think he is? King fucking Tut or something?"

"Look, girl," Melissa fired back, "Don't take your hurt out on me. I ain't the one," she warned, rolling her head and her eyes.

Candy took a couple of deep breaths, summoning the courage to contest this man's blatant disregard for her and her feelings. She whipped her head around and was startled to find Jovan bearing down on her with a look that was cold and icy. She literally shrunk under his gaze.

"Why you still standing here?" His voice was sharp. "I told you I'm with my wife. You gotta fucking comprehension problem or something?"

"What's going on?" The sound of Angel's voice cracked the tension in the air, replacing it with apprehension. "Who are these girls?" she asked with growing disdain as she eyed each woman from head to toe. *Young hussies*, she thought to herself.

"Nobody," he replied slowly, sucking his teeth and holding Candy with a steely stare. "These a couple of Ray's girls," he added as an afterthought. "They were just leaving."

Ray's girls? Melissa didn't like the sound of that one bit. Her eyes narrowed as they bounced from Jovan's wife to Jovan to Candy. How was she going to handle this situation with this man dissing the both of them? But the tables had turned. Now that Wifey was here, the trump card was now in their possession.

As cocky as Jovan as acting, you would've thought that he was still in the driver's seat.

Candy played along. "Tell Ray I said to call me," she responded meekly, "as soon as possible, please."

Angel kept a watchful eye on both women. Her womanly instincts had kicked in, and warning bells were sounding off. She walked around to her seat, placed her expensive Ralph Rucci bag on the table and waited for the unwanted company to depart.

Just as Candy was moving away and Jovan was about to exhale a deep sigh of relief, the shit got nipped in the bud. Melissa made a callously bold move, which was very ill advised on her part.

She walked up to Jovan, who was staring wide eyed with his heart thumping in his ears. "I don't give a damn about no Ray," Melissa expressed, her tone pompous, her look seedy. She rested her manicured hand on his chest. Jovan chuckled nervously; his eyes shifted from Melissa to Angel and then back to Melissa. "So I advise you to give me a call," she demanded bluntly.

Angel's usually warm eyes had chilled into chips of ice. If looks could kill, Melissa would've dropped dead right there and then. *If this bitch don't get her fucking nasty-ass paws off my man,* she thought. Her insides were boiling.

Melissa's nails dug into Jovan's chest. She went on to say, "Then maybe we can iron all of this Ray nonsense out, okay?" She shot Angel a look of disgust before walking away.

Angel was about to pounce until Jovan intervened. He grabbed her by the wrist and locked his grip. "C'mon, baby, let's have a seat," he offered, pulling her chair out. "Them bitches not worth it," Jovan said calmly. "They're nobodies just trying to start some bullshit."

Jovan attempted to soothe the situation, but the damage was already done. He was talking, but Angel had tuned him out. She didn't hear a word of what he was saying. Her eyes were locked on the departing hussies. Her mind churned violently as her subconscious devised a plan with devilish intent.

Unaware of his wife's subtle transformation, Jovan never realized that Angel had left the building. In her place, a wicked presence now resided.

As the night progressed, Jovan was getting an eerie, uncomfortable vibe from his wife. Apparently, she was still disturbed about the exchange with them dumb-ass bitches. If he didn't know better, he'd swear on a stack of Bibles that the woman accompanying him was not his wife.

Besides the minor disturbance with the college girls, the remainder of the evening went relatively smooth. They enjoyed themselves dancing and drinking and had a nice time together.

A Beautiful Satan

"Baby, you wanna wait here while I go to coat check and get our coats?" Jovan asked as he stood up. "I can see the coat check line is pretty long."

"Okay," Natasha replied, while inspecting her manicured nails.

Jovan's brow frowned as he watched her. She was still acting all weird and shit. *What the fuck is going on? Aw man, I hope her ass not fucking with any of those experimental drugs from the hospital.* He was becoming concerned. "I'll be right back," he muttered, moving off into the crowd.

Her eyes trailed Jovan until he was swallowed up by the crowd. A devious grin crawled across Natasha's lips, and she giggled to herself. As her eyes swept over the crowd, she began to hum a tune to herself. She stood up and tucked her purse under her arm before moving away from the table. Moments later she slipped into the ladies' room.

The party was just starting to wind down. Half of the patrons were making preparations to leave, while the other half were still getting their groove on. Robin Thicke's hit tune "Sex Therapy" still had the party rocking out on the dance floor.

Natasha materialized from the ladies' room. Instead of her usual ponytail, tonight she wore her hair out; her long blonde tresses flowed below her shoulders. She donned a pair of dark Donna Karan shades for cover. Her piercing eyes swept over the sea of bodies, searching out Angel's transgressors.

Like a deadly snake on the prowl, Natasha slithered through the crowd, her forked tongue seeking out the unsuspecting prey.

Somewhere on the patio, in the midst of all the party action, Natasha's search was suddenly rewarded when she stumbled upon the two women.

Natasha watched the sluts from across the room. An intense feel of loathing bubbled inside of her as she witnessed

Candy's and Melissa's promiscuous behavior. She began to gradually drift through the crowd toward her intended targets.

As she closed the distance, Natasha could sense the rage pumping through her veins with her heart and pulse rate quickening. She could feel her chest heave as her breathing deepened.

"Alright, ladies and gentlemen," DJ Flex boomed over the microphone, "thank you all for coming tonight. I want you to be safe and have a safe trip home. Until next time See ya!" His voice trailed off, and the unique singing voice of Ayo filtered into the air: "Down on my knees ... I'm begging you ... please, don't leave me!"

The thick mass of patrons began to make a slow surge toward the large, winding staircase and the exit below.

Somehow Natasha was able to maintain her cool. She was right up on the backs of her intended prey. She bit down hard on her lower lip in excited anticipation as she fumbled inside of her bag. She moved along with the flow of the crowd. Her hands shook with an uncanny rage as she reached out to touch them. Something silver flashed in her hand.

The blade disappeared swiftly in the back of Melissa's neck, over and over, as Natasha delivered a succession of quick, fatal thrusts.

A terror-stricken look exploded across Melissa's face. She froze and grabbed the back of her neck. Crimson goo poured from her mortal wound, and Melissa's manicured hands were covered in blood. She stared at her hands, totally horrified by what she saw.

Suddenly a horrified scream cracked the air when the woman beside Melissa caught sight of the bloody mess. She pushed into the crowd, struggling to get away from the grisly scene.

Melissa dropped to her knees, panting for air in obvious agony. Candy grabbed her friend and screamed in shock. A second later, a sharp, excruciating pain tore through her stomach. Candy's face contorted in pain as she doubled

A Beautiful Satan

over clutching her exposed intestines. Blood covered her hands. She realized she had been stabbed. Candy wavered for a moment before collapsing onto the floor in a fetal position.

A frenzy of panic swept through the crowd like a fierce wildfire. Women screamed in horror at the sight of the bloodied pair, and people moved hastily to put as much distance as possible between themselves and the carnage.

Outside, Water Street quickly became a sight of mass confusion and mayhem as the nervous, frightful crowd flooded the streets and sidewalk.

Jovan found himself caught up in the fray as the raucous stampede swept him away. Before he realized what was going on, he found himself standing outside in the midst of the melee.

Nervous chatter filled the air as red, white and blue police cruisers descended on the scene.

Jovan pushed through the crowd. "Angel! Angel!" he shouted, frustration etched deep in his face as he struggled against the dense surge of bodies.

Suddenly a bullhorn blasted in the night. "Please, ladies and gentlemen," said a police officer, his voice booming with authority. "We need you all to please vacate these premises. This is a crime scene, and I need your cooperation in this matter. Anyone who may have witnessed this attack or any strange behavior, please step over to the entrance of the club. Everyone else, we need you to please vacate this property now!"

As the crowd began to disperse, Jovan pressed on with his search. He crisscrossed Water Street for an entire block, calling out his wife's name as he maneuvered from side to side.

In the middle of the street, Jovan stood frustrated and perturbed. *Where in the hell is Angel*, he thought with mounting concern as the crowds dissipated and still she was nowhere to be found. "Angel! Angel!" he yelled at the top of his lungs. *Where is she? Could she be inside Hogate's?* The thought struck a chord in Jovan, and he cringed.

A stark feeling began to bubble inside of him when he realized the startling fact that Angel could possibly be one of the injured victims.

Jovan took a deep breath, slung his black Armani leather over his shoulder, whirled on his heels and marched back down Water Street toward the sea of flashing lights.

ⓌⓌⓌⓌ

It was a quarter past six in the morning when Jovan walked through the garage with his head slung low. He flipped through his key ring and fumbled at the door. "Fuck!" he cursed in a state of ire.

Once he located the house key, he unlocked the door. Angrily, Jovan slammed his shoulder against the door. He stumbled into the house grumbling under his breath.

"What are you over there mumbling about?" Angel said from the family room as she sat upright on the sofa adjusting her floral bathrobe.

The sound of Angel's voice startled him. He froze, staring across the room in clear astonishment. Jovan closed and opened his eyes, refocusing them. When he realized his mind wasn't playing tricks on him, a broad smile crept across his lips, and a massive weight seemed to lift from his shoulders.

Jovan felt a rush of excitement, all traces of his irritable mood gone. He was full of energy now as he strode into the family room.

"Baby! Where did you go? How did you get home?" he asked, amazed. Jovan plopped down on the sofa beside her in relief. "I looked everywhere for you. I talked to the police. I was even trying to get back inside Hogate's to make sure nothing had happened to you. Where did you go?"

Angel merely stared at Jovan and smiled. "I can't remember," she said softly.

A Beautiful Satan

Jovan's smile faded. "You can't remember?" he uttered, looking troubled. "What do you mean, you can't remember? If that was the case, how in the hell did you get home?"

"I got home in a cab," she said matter-of-factly. "I thought you put me in the cab." Angel cast an eerie look his way and whispered, "Oh my gosh, if you didn't put me in a cab, who did?" The question hung in the air.

Chapter 17

"This one here," the incredibly stunning homicide technician said as she examined Melissa's body. "Her carotid artery has been severed." The lovely Malaysia looked no-nonsense, clad in a crisp white medical smock that was buttoned up to her neck. She pushed her clear-framed specks onto the bridge of her nose, and her piercing emerald eyes swept the small coterie of homicide detectives who seemed to be paying a little too much attention to her and not enough to the crime scene at hand.

"Excuse me, gentlemen," the Thai beauty spoke up suddenly. "Are all the parties involved in this matter on the same page here?" Malaysia's edgy demeanor caused an uncomfortable silent ripple effect. With that said, she tied her hair back into a ponytail and knelt beside the second bloodied corpse—Candy.

"Our victim here," Malaysia began with indifference as she carefully studied the wound pattern, "was stabbed in the stomach, then slashed completely around to her spine." She hesitated, shaking her head in disgust. "I believe our perp's intention," she added as an afterthought, "was to eviscerate this woman on the spot."

"So in layman's terms," Clark's deep, baritone voice interrupted as the Dynamic Duo appeared on the scene, acknowledging the rank and file with a slight nod, "what you're trying to say is that the killer was attempting to disembowel our victim here?" Clark regarded the tech with a wary eye.

Malaysia turned to the arrogant pair and shot each a steely look. She had been warned about the pompous twosome. She watched the men slip out of their dark trench coats, then step around to the second victim without so much as a look her way.

"What do we have here?" questioned Louis as he squatted over Melissa's corpse. Clark took a knee opposite his partner, and with an awkward grunt replied, "That's a pretty nasty neck wound." He eyed his partner with an unassuming look and mumbled, "Severed windpipe, looks like to me."

Malaysia cut in unexpectedly, "Why don't you try severed carotid while you're at it?" she said, snickering under her breath.

The technician's condescending tone didn't go over well with the prized pair. Clark's brow creased. "You don't say," he glanced over his shoulder and smirked. Louis appeared unfazed by her comment. "I think we may need Woo's expertise for this one here," he suggested looking concerned.

Malaysia's head whipped around. "What?" her voice cracked as she glared at the duo with obvious apprehension. "This is my crime scene!" she stated loudly, springing to her feet. "I dare you to infringe on my authority."

"Whoa, there miss—uh, what's your name?" Louis said, standing.

She peered at the Canadian suspiciously. "Tomay," she remarked with bitterness, "Malaysia Tomay."

"Well, Ms. Tomay," Detective Louis said smiling, "we've been hearing some very commendable comments about you," he replied, side-stepping Melissa's corpse. Louis noticed the uneasy look his partner was casting his way. Louis decided that it was in their best interest to have a smooth working relationship with the newly acquired homicide tech. Besides, Ms. Tomay was gorgeous; he was hoping to get a date with her in the very *near* future.

"Don't get it wrong, Ms. Tomay," Louis expressed cordially, staring into her eyes. "My partner and I are in no way attempting to step on your toes. What I was referring to when I mentioned Mr. Woo was the fact that Detective Clark and myself are involved in an extremely tactical investigation of an extremely violent serial killer." He paused, eyeing the group of suits milling in the background. Louis added with a wave of his hand, "These two here," he said referring to the two corpses. He paused. "There's a very strong probability that these slayings are connected to our investigation."

Detective Clark interjected smartly, "These would make number four and number five on our growing list of murder victims."

Malaysia looked stunned, clutching at her chest, "A serial killer! Why wasn't I or anyone on my team advised of this situation?" Her tone and demeanor grew testy.

"Protocol didn't warrant any departmental advisory on this particular and very sensitive matter," Clark stated. He stood beside his partner with his hands clasped behind his back. "Does anyone have a problem with departmental protocol?" His voice was heavy with contempt.

Louis lowered his head, waiting for an answer.

Malaysia's shoulders sagged in defeat as she released a deep sigh of frustration. She shot the overbearing detective a cold and distant look before turning on her heels.

Clark patted his partner on the back. "You alright?" he asked, gloating triumphantly. "Hey, Gomer Pyle!" he called to

A Beautiful Satan

a young, dorky-looking detective he liked to clown. "Where's the, uh, witness list there, buddy?"

The detective shook his head vigorously and answered, "My name is Peter Jackson, sir, and there is no witness list."

Clark fell out with laughter. "You hear this shit, Rich? We have a fucking club filled with hundreds of people! Two young women get chopped up like minced meat, and we don't have a fucking eyewitness to the attack? Who's the commanding officer tonight?" Beads of perspiration broke out on Clark's nose, which was a telltale sign of his growing wrath.

"Lieutenant Broody is the shift commander. He's in the back talking with the manager," Peter advised him while scribbling on his notepad.

Clark glared. "Let me go have a few words with Broody," he snapped and then stepped off in a huff. "You coming, Rich?" he shouted over his shoulder.

Rich Louis was a very subdued man. Cautiously optimistic is how he described himself.

Malaysia clamped her jaw tight and kept a watchful eye on the dynamic pair.

"Well, gentlemen," Louis said casually, "Let me get with the lieutenant and get the lowdown on this murder investigation." He turned to face Malaysia. "Ms. Tomay, I would like to get together with you later and exchange notes."

Louis held up his hand in anticipation of her answer. She ignored him, her expression tight and grim. "I don't see any need in us doing that," she said, frosty.

She slid her specks onto her forehead and stared him in the eyes. "My report will be filed. You and your partner can follow the proper protocol to extract the desired information you seek." Malaysia could see through him, and she recognized the lust in his eyes the moment he approached her. On-the-job flings and relationships were taboo in her book.

Malaysia dismissed the detective with a blatant gesture that needed no words. She returned to the meticulous process of examining the deceased without a second look. Then out of nowhere, for reasons she couldn't explain, thoughts of Jovan popped into her head.

Chapter 18

It was 11:30 p.m. and the dark streets of the Barry Farms housing project were in full swing. Two area drug crews were operating on the block tonight. Luckily, the coke business was brisk, so static was low, though moral and testosterone was running high amongst both crews.

A black Dodge Charger crept slowly through the housing project. Three young gunners from Ray's crew were stalking the Barry Farms territory in search of a big square-headed dude who went by the name Top Cat. He was the O.G. who ran shit over in the Farms.

The young gunner pushing the whip was called Dank, a high-yellow cat with dirty brown dreads and a big-ass cross with dripping blood tattooed on the left side of his grill. He was a crazy ass youngin' with a thirst for violence. "Soon as you see that bamma, let me know 'cause I'm a blast on these bammas," he said to his brother Psycho.

Psycho rode shotgun, glaring out the window, itching for something to jump off. This youngin' wasn't to be fucked with at all. He was an exact replica of his older brother, except he was a little lighter in the ass and rocked a bald head.

Psycho was the type of youngin' who didn't give a fuck about life. "America's Most Dangerous Nigga" was tattooed on his back, and "Death Wish" was tatted across his chest in bold red letters.

Psycho looked at his brother and sneered, "Yeah, I can't wait to clap these bitches," he said in a raspy voice as he fingered the .40 caliber Desert in his lap. "Show these bammas how true killers get down."

"These bammas in for the surprise of their life!" boasted their homeboy Mike, who was bouncing around in the rear seat. His hazel eyes jumped with anticipation as his big, burly frame rocked from side to side nervously.

The Charger slowed in the shadows, then pulled behind a U-Haul rental truck and parked. Dank and Psycho slipped from the car unnoticed, then melted into the shadows. Mike climbed behind the wheel, all giddy over being the getaway driver.

Under the straining glow of the towering street lamp, four crew members were huddled together, sitting on concrete steps, toking on a thick blunt of Purple Haze and guzzling 40s of Steel. Laughter and small talk could be heard drifting from the group.

Suddenly one of the men sprang to his feet. "You left all my shit down Dale's house?" he blurted excitedly. "Ah, fuck! I need dat. Shit, I gotta go get dat. I'll be back in ten minutes, so y'all niggas be ready." He hopped behind the wheel of a steel-gray Crown Victoria. The voice of Lil Wayne blared from the interior as the car peeled out.

Fifty yards down the street, the Crown Vic rolled past a champagne-gold 745 BMW. The car was parked on the corner and looked out of place. Behind the Beemer's tinted windows, Ray sat perched at the wheel, clocking everything that moved on the corner where the crew was huddled. Jovan was sitting in the passenger seat.

A Beautiful Satan

"Man, I wish these niggas would hurry up and take care of these cats," Ray said with a hint of anxiety in his voice.

"Dawg," Jovan began, exhaling a cloud of smoke from his nostrils, feeling good, "are you sure this shit is going down tonight?" he said, coughing. "Why the hell you got me out here for this shit anyway? We suppose to be up in Layla or the Park checking out some ass, not checking out no clowns down on the rip."

Ray waved him off. "C'mon, playboy, give me a break," he complained. "The club ain't but five minutes away. I just wanna make sure my boys handle this money." He jumped suddenly. "I see my youngins now. Look."

Psycho emerged from the shadows brandishing twin .40-caliber Deserts. The trio sitting on the steps froze in place.

"Nigga, where your man Top Cat?" Psycho growled, waving the burners from one bamma's head to the next. "Bitch-ass nigga! Where that nigga at?"

The trio glared at the gun-toting assailant like he was insane. The bamma wearing the black Redskins cap cocked to the side looked antsy. He was about to make a move.

Dank rushed in out of the blue and smacked the bamma across the nose with the butt of his P-94 before the clown knew what hit him. His cap went sailing to the pavement followed by a fresh blood spill.

"Muthafucka!" Dank snarled, hovering over him, "What the fuck's wrong with you, huh? My man asked you a question!"

The other two bammas stared dumbfounded. "Who you talking about, cuz?" the dude in the black skully stammered nervously. "We not rolling with slim."

That was the wrong answer. Psycho glared with bloodlust in his eyes.

"Since you bitches got jokes, then you bitches gettin' rocked to sleep," he explained coldly. Then without warning, in the same emotionless demeanor, Psycho placed the barrel of his .40 caliber on the top of the dude's head Dank had just smacked. He uttered, "Starting with this bitch ..." Psycho pumped two slugs into the top of the clown's head without batting an eye.

The muffled blasts caught everyone off guard. The two crew members' hearts jumped into their throats as they gaped in shock at the sight of their homeboy's brains splattering on the sidewalk. His body crumbled to the ground in an unnatural, twisted heap of flesh and bones.

Up the block, inside the 745, the abrupt sound of gunfire startled Jovan; he jumped and forgot all about the smoking blunt in his hand as it went tumbling to his feet. "What the fuck!" he gasped in disbelief. "He shot the nigga?"

With a cynical smirk playing around his mouth, Ray inhaled and said, "Yeah, that shit was sweet, and we got front-row seats too. Can't get no better than this, baby."

"What?" Jovan muttered, looking thunderstruck. *Ray must've lost his goddamn mind*, he said to himself. *Now I'm a witness to murder!*

There was a slight pause, and then Jovan's whole foundation shook when he saw a sudden burst of gunfire erupt on the corner. A succession of popping sounds echoed through the air.

"Ray!" Jovan shouted with a strained look of exasperation splashed across his face. He grabbed his arm. "Nigga, what's your damn problem? Your peoples just killed the whole fucking corner! And you got me out here watching this shit like it's legal. Nigga, if you don't get me the fuck outta here!"

A few yards behind the BMW, the gray Crown Vic eased into position, creeping through the shadows with dark headlamps. The driver parked at the curb and crawled out into the night.

Ray revved the engine. He looked in the rearview mirror and the whites of his eyes went wide. Behind the whip he caught a glimpse of the O.G., Top Cat; the bamma was fumbling beneath his jacket. Something shiny and chrome appeared in his hand. Ray put his foot on the pedal and floored it. A split second later gunfire exploded behind them, and the rear window shattered once ... twice ... three ... four ... five times before the entire window caved in from the gunfire.

The gold Beemer bent the corner so hard its tires screamed. Ray snatched the wheel back, caught the straightaway, and the sedan thundered out of the projects onto the main road. Seconds later, the 745 was racing up Suitland Parkway, heading out of D.C.

⑭⑭⑭⑭

Jovan hopped out of the BMW, seething. He slammed the door so hard, it was a miracle that nothing was damaged. Jovan fell against the door, struggling to control his growing rage.

The entire trip, from the time they hit the Parkway, until the moment they arrived at Ray's house, Jovan hadn't spoken one word.

Ray moseyed around the car, giggling and holding his stomach. He planted himself in the spot beside his man. "C'mon, J, I know you ain't gonna hold this shit against me, dawg," he said, tossing his hands in the air in submission. "C'mon now, playboy, we better than that," Ray said, his lips contorting just before a loud cackle slipped out. He was tickled pink by the crazy look on Jovan's face.

Jovan glared at Ray, his expression acrid. "Nigga, what you take me for, a joke?" he snapped, then lost control.

Ray was simultaneously stunned and dazed when he caught the full blast of a stiff right hook across his chin. Ray's knees buckled. He wobbled as he attempted to gather his bearings. Jovan followed up with a hard left to the temple and a vicious right body shot.

By the time Ray realized what had happened, he was on his hands and knees gasping for air. Jovan hovered over him, chastising him sharply for putting his livelihood at stake.

Suddenly a stream of halogen lights spilled across the ivory driveway, distracting Jovan. He stared down the black car as it charged down the pavement and skidded to a halt with just two feet to spare.

Jovan mugged the trio with an intense look as they hurried over to aid their fallen boss.

"Main man, what's going on?" Psycho voiced, matching Jovan's tough look. He and Dank hoisted Ray to his feet and leaned him against the hood of the Dodge.

"Chill," Ray grumbled, snatching his arm from the gunner's grasp. "This between J and me." There was a heavy scowl hanging from Ray's grill as he adjusted his dark denim jacket and straightened his jeans. "I got this," he muttered more so to himself.

Ray's devious look didn't go unnoticed. "Yeah, I hope you got it," Jovan fired back coldly as his eyes turned an icy gray. Aggressive animosity pulsated from his form as he strolled to his Mercedes Benz.

Jovan's unyielding nature served as an obvious warning sign to Ray and the crew as they watched with a look of sheer prudence.

Hopping into his coupe, he whipped the ride around and went roaring up the ivory pavement, disappearing into the night.

Chapter 19

"Hey," Angel said in a feisty tone, "I thought you weren't going to be out half the night. So what happened?"

Jovan sighed. "I'm sorry, precious. I'll make it up to you, I promise. I just got caught up and lost track of time. That's all."

"You'll make it up!" she stated sourly. "That's your favorite line. Can't you think of anything else to say when you fuck up? I'm getting sick of that shit!" Angel snapped harshly. She flipped the cell phone shut and stared at the device like she was expecting the phone to reveal something magical. When nothing happened, Angel slammed it on the hard oak desk with such force the outer shell shattered. She palmed the phone in her hand, glaring at the damaged frame, anger billowing in her eyes. Without thinking, Angel hurled the cell phone across the room and watched as it smacked loudly against the door and broke into pieces. "Fuck him!" she spat, madness leaping from her eyes.

The office phone beeped. "Mrs. Rising," the secretary's voice sounded over the intercom. "Is everything okay? I heard something hit the door. Do you need anything?"

Angel's finger moved to the intercom. "No, Diana. I'll call if I need anything," she said, short. Angel swiveled in her chair and stared across the lush green campus of the NIH facility. This serene panoramic view from the 12th floor usually helped soothe Angel's inner being. But not today. She wasn't feeling it. In reality, Angel wasn't feeling herself. Lately, for some strange reason, she felt this dark, icky sensation crawling around inside of her. Angel thought it might have something to do with these new experimental pain killers she had been secretly popping. She cut back on the pain killers, but the sensation persisted. She found herself grasping at straws, trying to figure out this nagging, eerie void that seemed to be growing stronger each day.

Moments later, Angel emerged from her office, pulling the black leather strap to her Gucci purse over her shoulder. She secured the office door and then stepped over to the secretary's desk.

Diana, the office secretary, was a petite brunette with thin, emaciated lips and an extra-long nose that seemed to jump out at you.

She turned and smiled. "I take it you're leaving for the day, Mrs. Rising?" The office phone rang. "One moment, please," she said softly, placing the caller on hold.

Angel eyed Diana as she slipped her black leather coat over her burgundy nursing scrubs. She replied, "Ah, yes, Diana, I'm leaving, so screen all of my calls. Any emergencies please forward to my cell. I'll see you tomorrow," she said, and walked off without giving her a second look.

Ding! The elevator sounded. Angel's pace quickened when she heard the elevator door slide open. She rounded the corner just as the door was closing. At the last second, when she thought it was too late, the elevator door stopped abruptly, and opened.

"Wow, a beautiful Angel," the promiscuous Dr. Saint greeted in a slow drawl, "You're a sight for sore eyes at the end as well as the beginning of any day." His eyes slid up and down her frame, attempting to undress her. "That Mr. Rising don't know how lucky he is, does he?" the flirty doctor muttered slyly.

The flirtatious Dr. Saint was considered the facility's playboy. He was a fairly handsome white man with salt-and-pepper hair, a stocky build and captivating blue eyes. He was the type of man who didn't take kindly to the answer no.

Angel glanced over her shoulder and smirked. "Thank you for the compliment, doctor," she acknowledged with her back turned to him, "but some things are better left unsaid."

The doctor couldn't resist the challenge. He eased up close behind her. Angel's sweet fragrance excited him. "Some things are better left unsaid," Dr. Saint whispered in her ear, startling her. "But this, my dear, isn't one of them." His hands caressed Angel's waist. He went on, "You see, we have an untapped carnal bond that is itching to be explored." His breath was hot and heavy on her neck.

His touch caused Angel's blood to boil. "Did Angel give you permission to touch her?" Her voice was dripping with acid.

He had a serious problem. Instead of heeding the warning signs and backing off, Angel's testy response aroused him even more.

"Ooh, yeah," he groaned excitably, as if she was really stroking his manhood. "That I like, that I like."

Natasha whirled around. Their eyes locked, and Dr. Saint's heart dropped to his knees. A frigid chill swept through him like a powerful blast of arctic air. The whites of her eyes were gone. In their place, simmering crimson pools framed him with ferocious intent. Dr. Saint couldn't believe his eyes. Who was this woman standing before him?

"Good Lord," he muttered brokenly and stumbled back against the elevator wall. Natasha pounced on him like a lioness protecting her cubs. The doctor screamed like a bitch when she sank her teeth into his hard, buffed chest. Her eyes smiled wickedly at the sight of the doctor's horrified expression and the growing blood stain on his clean white cotton seersucker Polo.

"You've been warned," she snarled. "Don't fuck with me!"

Dr. Saint's pride had been mortally wounded, but at least his life was still intact. He stood trembling, unable to move as he watched the crazy nurse turn and exit the elevator like nothing happened. He waited for the elevator door to close, and then he sank to the floor, heaving a sigh of relief. "What a crazy fucking cunt!" he said. The urgency of it all wasn't lost on him. The doctor knew he had just stared death in the face and lived.

Chapter 20

Demonic laughter echoed in the darkness. The sound made the hairs on the back of Jovan's neck stand at attention.

"What the fuck is this??!" Jovan cursed when he realized his hands were bound. He tried to lift his head and choked. There was a bar across his neck a half-inch above him.

Jovan felt something hot hit his chest. "Ow! What the fuck??!" Laughter erupted above him, and something hot landed on his stomach. "Ow! Shit! What the fuck is going on?"

"Where have you been?" He heard Angel's soft voice talking to him in the dark. "Angel, where are you?" Jovan asked quietly, straining to see. "I need you, precious. Please ... come help me. Ow!" Something hot fell across his nipple. A loud eruption of cynical laughter followed, resonating in the darkness and echoing from every direction.

"Are you a king?" a raspy-sounding voice hissed. "Who's king are you? Ha, ha, ha!" The taunt sent goose bumps racing down his arm.

A succession of heated drops marked a hot trail descending along Jovan's abdomen. "What the fuck is this shit? What in the hell are you doing?" he yelled, sounding distressed. "Who the hell is that in here with you, huh?"

"I love you ... please stop hurting me," he heard his wife say in the distance. He screamed, "Angel! Where are you? Come help me, please!"

The eerie-sounding laughter bellowed across the darkness. "She can't save you!" the strange, raspy voice mocked. "You don't wanna be saved!"

Suddenly Jovan's vision cleared. He could see a flickering flame that floated in the darkness. Jovan watched with wide eyes as the liquid flame cascaded through the dark and collided with his exposed manhood.

"Fuck you!!!" he shrieked in pain, squirming to break free. A cacophony of wickedness bellowed in the background. "Fuck you!!!" he screamed vehemently.

His eyes fluttered and then opened slowly. It took him a few seconds before he could focus. The digital alarm clock over on the nightstand came into view; the time was 9:37 a.m. He had just awakened from yet another nightmare.

Jovan peered across the room and popped upright when he realized he was lying nude on his bedroom floor. He stared around the empty room. The only thing out of place that caught his eye was the white folding chair positioned by the fireplace. *What's that doing up here?* Jovan wondered. *That chair belongs down in the basement.*

When Jovan took a look at himself, he was surprised to see splashes of dried white candle wax splattered all over his body. Suddenly a floodgate of memories went reeling through his mind.

The dark vision struck him with panic, and Jovan grabbed his dick with both hands. It was coated with dry wax.

"Ain't this a bitch," he mumbled. "I thought I was dreaming." Jovan's expression turned serious. "Where the fuck is Angel?" he grumbled, jumping to his feet. "Angel!

A Beautiful Satan

Angel! You got some helluva explaining to do," he yelled, storming out of the bedroom, peeling wax from his frame.

Downstairs was empty. He peeked inside the garage. Angel's Benz was gone. Jovan did an about-face and headed for the kitchen. There was a note on the granite isle: "Gone to the hospital, had an emergency meeting to attend. Could you please pick up my coat from Bebe that I ordered last week, please? See you later...Love Your Angel."

"Ain't this some shit," he huffed. "Yeah, I'll scoop the coat for you, but I got a bone to pick with your ass," he told himself, crumbling the note before heading back upstairs to get ready for the day's agenda.

ⓌⓌⓌⓌ

Jovan strolled into the crowded Bebe clothing boutique.

"Hello, how may I help you today?" asked a warm, friendly voice.

The voice caught Jovan's attention right away, and he stopped suddenly in his tracks to investigate the source. He couldn't help but smile when he saw her.

Her name was Manika. She was a five-foot-nine bronze beauty with beautiful, hypnotic gray eyes and a flawless physique.

Their eyes seemed to touch, and instantly sparks ignited between them. When Manika smiled, Jovan swore the sun was shining. Her smile was that radiant.

"Mmm, mmm, mmm ... you just took my breath away, gorgeous," Jovan said, giving her a heavy dose of his smile. Manika blushed with an innocence so radiant Jovan was completely captivated by her spirit.

They both found themselves vibing off of one another as they proceeded to walk and talk, moving to the rear of the store.

"What time do you get off work today?" Jovan inquired. "I was thinking if my schedule works out right, we could probably hook up a little later on. Would that interest you in any way?"

Manika's eyes twinkled. "I would love that," she replied softly, "Do you have anything special in mind for us to do?"

He chuckled lightly. "Do I? Mmm, mmm, mmm."

Manika took a deep breath and muttered, "I'm going to get your coat." She rushed off through the doorway that led to the rear storage room.

A few moments later, Manika reappeared with a full-length chocolate shearling coat draped over her arm. When Manika saw him, her heart suddenly went pitter-patter for this man she barely knew. Manika was at a loss for how her emotions were flipping totally out of whack for this man.

"Thank you, gorgeous," Jovan said politely, "This is for me, right?" he asked, grabbing the coat. He slung it over his shoulder and with a sweep of his hand, he said smoothly, "After you, my lovely princess."

His deep voice sounded so good in her ear. Manika thought how sexy Jovan would sound whispering in her ear while he was working that body. She gazed at him with a steamy look of lust in her eye.

"I'm really looking forward to seeing you, Jovan, so please don't disappoint me." She stopped short and peered deep into his eyes. "And I promise you," she whispered, drawing close to his ear, "with all my heart, I will not disappoint you."

Jovan liked the sound of that immensely. Thoughts of Manika's naked flesh colliding with his were an absolute turn on. As he checked the information she had typed in his phone, he could feel his excitement brewing inside of him.

Chapter 21

The Homicide Division was located on the fourth floor of the police headquarters in downtown D.C. Inside the large, cluttered office over by the window, Detective Clark was kicked back in his chair with his hands folded behind his head contemplating their next move when a loud crack sounded off suddenly, startling him from his reverie.

He jumped. "Okay, buddy, I get your drift," he said gritting his teeth, looking wide eyed and disoriented. "By that stupid-ass smirk on your face, I take it you got some good news to lay on me." He got up and lumbered over to the coffee station and poured himself a hot cup of java.

Clark crossed the dull tiled floor and perched his wide behind on the corner of his partner's desk. "Well, you gonna lay the news on me or what?" he asked, slurping loudly from his coffee mug.

Detective Louis was busy tapping out a beat on his chin with the tip of his Bic pen. He eyed his partner and said glibly, "I did some re-interviewing of the Monica case on my own, buddy." He got to his feet and started for the coffee station. "I took a detour past The Heights and stumbled across a few of the neighborhood thugs." Louis hesitated as he poured a cup of coffee. He turned with his cup in hand. "Guess what I found out." He allowed his statement to linger while he focused on his hot beverage.

His burly partner waited with growing anticipation. Apparently pleased with himself, Louis went on to say, "Our victim had a special male friend in her life ... and this friend owns a black Mercedes Benz convertible."

Clark's brow shot up in surprise. "You don't say," he muttered. "A black convertible, huh?" he repeated with a growing look of speculation. "Our jumper over in Cleveland Park—we've got witness accounts saying she was involved with a mystery man who drove a black convertible."

A broad smile slid across Louis' lips. "You just answered the million-dollar question," he replied, looking jovial. "This might be the vital connection we've been looking for, buddy."

He grinned warily. Could this be the link they had been searching so diligently for, trying to put a name and face to a violent serial killer on the loose in the nation's capital? He hoped that it was.

Louis watched the contemplative expression on his partner's face. "What's on your mind, Will? We gotta keep our heads together on this. You know that, right?"

He shook his head, and he tried to wave it off as nothing. "No, no ... my mind's in overdrive right now," Clark said with a dubious look. "I think my imagination is stretching itself a bit, that's all."

"Well, go ahead and put it on the table, buddy," Louis said quickly, "We're leaving no stone unturned in this case, remember?"

"It's nothing really, Rich," Clark said, taking a sip of coffee. He sat his cup down before saying, "Just a touch of wishful thinking on my part, so bear with me on this. Our first victim over by the college, she had gone out to run a few errands earlier that morning and returned home early evening, at which time our killer strikes. But her car hadn't been moved since the day before."

Louis wondered where his partner was going with this. He shrugged, "Okay, so she didn't drive that day. She could've walked; she was known to be an avid walker. Or maybe she decided to take the Metro that day. We have no witness to her mode of transportation on the day she checked out."

Clark put his hand up in defense. "Okay, just humor me for a second here, Rich." His voice dropped a few octaves, and he continued in hushed tones. "How much credence would you say our case would have if we could place a black vehicle at the scene of our first murder?" Clark's eyes made a cautious sweep of their area as soon as he stopped talking.

A quizzical look rolled across Louis' tanned complexion. "Just what type of tree are you barking up here, Will?" he asked, sounding doubtful.

A cryptic smile crawled across Clark's lips, and he replied, "You know what the book says, partner: If you can't place the suspect on the crime scene, place the crime scene on the suspect."

Louis frowned, "Yeah, I know exactly what the good book says, but we don't have a suspect or any name of a potential suspect to place anywhere."

Clark threw his head back and laughed. "Oh, that's simple. Whoever we tie to that black Mercedes to, that's our sick psycho fuck right there." He continued to laugh, sounding just like a wounded hyena.

Louis watched his partner's polished bald head bounce around. He felt a touch of anxiety swell in his gut and the start of a migraine tapping on his temples. Louis wasn't really feeling what Clark was trying to sell. This wasn't the type of case where you could make a suspect. There was a violent, sadistic serial killer walking the streets of D.C. So whoever they nabbed as a suspect would have to be the real perpetrator.

Chapter 22

Natasha was home alone, sitting in the garage behind the wheel of Jovan's prized convertible.

She was busy admiring herself in the visor mirror, combing her soft blonde tresses, when the ringtone to the song "Love" by Musiq Soulchild began to permeate the vehicle's cockpit.

Natasha froze in motion when she heard the tune. Her facial expression went from happy-go-lucky to a contorted Tasmanian she-devil in the blink of an eye.

She wrestled the cell phone from the pocket of Angel's ruby satin robe. "Why the fuck did Angel program this lovey-dovey shit for his dirty-dick cheating ass??!" Natasha spat bitterly, before answering the call. "Hello? What do you want?" she snorted, greeting Jovan with an obvious attitude.

"What?" Jovan shot back gruffly. "Is that any way to answer my call? What, you bump your damn head or something?"

Natasha glared at the phone and thought, *This nigga crazy*. She grumbled sourly, "No, I ain't bump my damn head! Did you bump your damn head?"

A Beautiful Satan

"Hold the fuck up," Jovan said sternly, "Last night you was playing sick-ass games, burning me with fucking candle wax while I was half out of it! And now you cracking slick over the phone?" He paused when he heard her giggle over the line. "Oh, you find this shit funny, huh?" His wife's giggle grew into raucous laughter. "What the fuck?" Jovan mumbled, staring at his phone in disbelief. *Angel gots to be high off of something*, he told himself, then said coldly, "You must not want this fucking Bebe coat I picked up for your ass."

Natasha smiled to herself. "Baby, why you gotta bring the coat into this?" she asked calmly with a measure of control in her voice. "The coat has nothing to do with what went on with us last night. Now that's your wife's coat and your wife deserves to have the coat she has been waiting so patiently to have."

After some hesitation Jovan conceded. "Well, I suppose you got a point there, but that still doesn't dismiss that bullshit you pulled on me last night!"

"Look, nigga," Natasha fired back with heat, "you better get your dirty-dick ass in line before something really fucked up goes down! Last night I was just playing with you and your dick. Keep it up and I'mma cut it off." She broke out in laughter.

Jovan didn't like the sound of that at all. *What the hell had gotten into Angel,* he thought. This didn't sound like his wife at all.

"Man, what the fuck are you saying, huh?" he barked angrily. "What the fuck is the matter with your ass? Are you on some of that experimental shit from the hospital?" When she didn't respond, Jovan asked, "Angel, what are you doing?"

"Let me tell you something, Mr. Rising." Natasha's tone was adamant. "Angel isn't doing anything she's not supposed to be doing. That's your department. What Angel is doing is trying to maintain her sanity for your ass! Word to the wise, Mr. Rising: Each of us have our voices." With that said, Natasha hung up.

After the exchange with Angel, Jovan was on another planet, shaken and confused. He sat behind the wheel of his Mercedes truck wondering who in the hell had he just finished talking to on the phone? Angel was totally off her rocker. It was like he was talking to a total stranger. *Man, I'm gonna have to get my wife some help*, he reasoned.

Jovan didn't make much of it, but something sinister was definitely at play. A knock on the passenger window distracted him. Manika slid gracefully into the seat, and her lovely smile changed his mood instantly.

"I like your truck," Manika said softly while fastening her seatbelt.

Jovan grinned. "Is that all you like?" he asked.

"Well, that all depends," she said quietly, batting her eyes and licking her lips. "Because I like many things. What do you like?"

He put the vehicle in drive and chuckled. "What I like, baby girl, might just blow your mind."

She gave him a lustful look. "I like how that sound," said Manika's in a husky tone. "Because my lips … they find joy in the most unusual places."

The words she spoke were like a symphony to Jovan's ears. The silky black SUV leapt from the curb and quickly merged into the flow of traffic.

ⓌⓌⓌⓌ

Back in the garage, Natasha was just finishing up under the stern. She doubled-checked to make sure that nothing was left out of place. She was pleased with her work and after making one last inspection of the driver's area, closed the car door.

Angel's gonna be so happy with me, Natasha said to herself as she walked around the car. She started to hum her favorite tune as she headed back into the house.

A Beautiful Satan

ⓌⓌⓌⓌ

Jovan and his new bronze showpiece walked through D.C.'s Chinatown area. Next door to the Verizon Center, business was brisk inside of Clyde's. The cute couple strolled through the doors and were greeted by a polite Asian maître d'. They were escorted to their dining booth by the window, which boasted a view of 7th Street and DC's lively nightlife.

"So," Jovan said, breaking the silence, "you ever been here before?"

Manika smiled warmly and said, "No, I've never been here, but I have been to Clyde's before—the one in Columbia, across from the mall. I think it's called Clyde's on the Lake?"

"Yeah, that's it," he confirmed. "That's my favorite Clyde's restaurant."

"So why did you bring me downtown to this one?"

"So that we could make a night of it," Jovan told her bluntly. "'Cause from here we've got access to nice clubs and fly hotels. You get my drift?" He gave her a knowing wink.

"Yeah, I know you got the whole night planned out. You strike me as a man that
has everything together."

"Oh, I do, do I?" Jovan muttered with a devious gleam in his eyes. "So what else have you figured out about me? Enlighten me a bit."

Manika stared at him for a moment and with a lighthearted smirk said sarcastically, "I can tell you're conceited as hell."

His hand went up to stop her. "It's not conceit, baby," Jovan corrected, "its called confidence. And, yes, I'm one confident nigga."

The waitress interrupted, "How are you wonderful people doing tonight? Are you ready to place your order, or do you need a little more time to decide?"

Without hesitation, Jovan replied, "We need some time to decide on the entrées, but while we're deciding you can bring us two mojitos. That'll be all, thank you," Jovan said to the waitress.

"Okay, sweetness," Jovan said smoothly, staring across the table into her eyes. "Back to you and I ... what's going on in that head of yours? I saw that smile, and from the looks of it, something good must be rolling around up there." He reached out and caressed her hand. "I'm not psychic, but I want you to know that I'm feeling you," he said seriously. "And from the vibe I'm getting, I can tell you feeling me too. So whatever your thoughts are, I want you to know that you can share them with me."

"You are too much," she giggled. "There's no doubt in my mind that you know everything you're doing and just how to do and say it. And, yes," Manika whispered, like she was letting him in on a secret, "I'm feeling you."

"Well, is that good or bad?" Jovan asked, already knowing her answer.

Manika drew closer to the table. "That's good, boo," she said softly. "It's almost as good as a fucking orgasm!" Manika said, then excused herself from the table. Jovan leaned back in his seat, admiring her booty as she sashayed off to the ladies' room.

ⓦⓦⓦⓦ

While Manika freshened up in the ladies room, an uninvited guest decided to pay Jovan a visit.

He was thoroughly surprised when Angel's hot-in-the-ass girlfriend Tina rolled up on him out of nowhere. Jovan could feel a cold chill run down his spine when the bitch stood over him, staring. He smiled uneasily, his eyes focused on the menu in his hand.

"Is there something I can help you with, miss?" he inquired, tightening his jaw. Jovan never took his eyes off the menu.

A chuckle erupted from Tina's mouth. "Help me?" she uttered smartly, placing a hand on her chest. "You got it twisted, don't you, Mr. Lover Man?" she remarked with her hands trailing slowly down the platinum silk body dress that was clinging tightly to her curves. Tina's hands came to rest on her hips. At the same time, a cunning grin was playing around her silver-coated lips. She rocked back on her heels in a provocative stance.

"The question should be," she said leaning into his ear, "how can I help you." There was no mistaking the pretentious aura billowing from her short, curvy frame.

Jovan caught a hint of something else in Tina's mood. He turned to face her, almost expecting her not to move. She didn't budge. They were staring eye to eye, so close their noses were about to touch.

Tina licked her lips enticingly. "I know you wouldn't want your precious
Angel to find out anything about your little rendezvous down here at Clyde's, now would you?"

While Tina was gloating in the moment, Jovan was making a mental assessment of his unfortunate dilemma.

"Alright, Tina," he snapped. "What is it that you want, huh?"

Tina gazed deep into Jovan's eyes, lust leaping. She put her lips to his ear, and in a sensuous tone said, "Don't play with me. You know damn well what I want."

A cold chill swept across Jovan's neck when Tina's wet tongue slipped into his ear. He was stunned.

"What the wifey don't know won't hurt her," she stated casually. "Hey, who's gonna tell her? I'm sure as hell not." Tina stood up and wriggled her hips a little as she adjusted her dress. "I'm gonna let you get back to your date. Don't let that bitch damage the goods before I get a chance to sample it," Tina said. She blew him a kiss before she walked off.

When Manika returned to the table, she found Jovan with a stony look plastered on his face. She looked around and then eased into her seat.

"Is everything okay, Jovan?" Manika asked with obvious concern. "Did something happen while I was away?"

He shrugged. "Nah," Jovan replied coolly as he gathered his composure. "Everything good." He hesitated, then added, "A thought did occur to me, though. Maybe we could go somewhere with a more intimate atmosphere. Would you like that?"

Manika knew he was hiding something, but who was she to question him? She was happy to be in his company and dying to get more intimately acquainted with a man of his caliber.

"Sure," Manika agreed, smiling. She was up for whatever Jovan had in mind. "Where are we going?"

Jovan rose from his seat and plucked a crisp fifty from his wallet before downing his drink. He threw his head back and drained the mojito.

Jovan stepped from the booth. "After you, lovely," he said smoothly, motioning for her to lead the way. He glanced to the rear of the restaurant. Jovan was very perceptive and knew without a doubt that Tina was somewhere in the crowd watching him.

ⓦⓦⓦⓦ

Outside, Jovan hopped behind the wheel, pulled the frames off his face, and then, without saying a word, leaned across the seat and locked lips with Manika.

Suddenly Manika pushed him away, breathing heavily. She stammered between breaths, "Could we have our food delivered instead?"

Jovan smiled at her. "Sweetness, you must've read my mind," he said a second before Manika's hand gripped the back of his head.

Expressing her aggressive desire, Manika smashed her lips onto his. "Oh yeah," he said breathlessly as she sank her teeth into his lower lip. "It's on, baby!"

Chapter 23

The sun was peeking over the horizon by the time Jovan made it home. He parked his black Benz truck in the driveway, climbed out and stretched before heading up the walkway with his suit jacket slung over his shoulder.

When Jovan stepped over the threshold into his domain, he was greeted by an unsettling darkness with an eerie silence that seemed to echo throughout the house.

His eyes panned across the darkened expanse of the first floor. For some strange reason, Jovan felt somebody was watching him as he peered through the dark.

Jovan proceeded to cross the living room. When he realized there was no natural light streaming through the window, Jovan paused in the middle of the room. The dark burgundy drapes had been drawn shut. *That's odd*, he thought. They always left them open. They had both agreed natural light gave their home a warm, inviting feeling. *What the hell is going on,* he wondered.

At the bottom of the stairs, Jovan flipped the light switch on but nothing happened. "What the fuck?" he mumbled, continuing through the dark. He made his way into the kitchen and was startled when he found the wooden shutters on the bay windows pulled shut.

A wave of apprehension hit Jovan when he tried the light switch in the kitchen and found it didn't work either. The first floor was pitch black.

"Angel!" Jovan yelled. What's up with the lights and windows? He figured the problem with the lights was more than likely a blown fuse. *But why are the windows all covered up?* he wondered as he moved toward the basement door.

Jovan pushed the door wide open. "Okay," he sighed, feeling a touch of relief when he saw that the lights were on in the basement. "At least there's light down there," he said as he flicked on the light switch for the basement landing. Nothing happened. "Fuck!" he cursed.

Something shuffled in the dark. Jovan heard something move off to his right, and in the same instance he detected movement out the corner of his eye. His body stiffened when he turned to look, and a blonde streak leaped from the shadows a split second before a blow to the back of his head sent him tumbling down the basement steps.

He crashed hard into the wall on the first landing. At the top of the stairs, a dark silhouette of someone wielding a bat stood in the doorway. Just before Jovan slipped into unconsciousness, he remembered seeing those piercing blue eyes with a crazy, cynical look glaring down at him.

Jovan came to several hours later. Wincing in pain, he got up slowly. His phone was sounding off in the darkness, a familiar ringtone blaring loudly. He fumbled around in the dark until he spotted a tiny beacon of light on his phone a few feet away on the floor.

Squinting at the lightened screen, Jovan spoke groggily. "Whaz up, precious?" He had a terrible headache for some reason.

A Beautiful Satan

"I know you're not just waking up?" Malaysia shot back almost immediately. Suddenly Jovan felt fuzzy. *Where the hell am I?* Dazed, Jovan used the cell's light to look at his timepiece. It was past noon. He then used the light from his cell to illuminate the area around him. *What am I doing down in the basement?* he wondered.

"I took a little nap," he said, sounding confused. "Are you okay with that?" Suddenly a vision of blue eyes flashed in his head. Jovan was stunned for a second. The eyes were sinister. They looked so real, like they were right upon him.

"Why are you asking me if I'm okay with you being asleep on the eve of you escorting me to the annual jazz symphony at the Kennedy Center?"

Standing now, Jovan cringed. *Damn, I feel like shit.* He moved toward the bathroom. "Oh, precious, I'm sorry," he said awkwardly. "I've been so busy, the symphony totally slipped my mind. Don't worry, I'll make it up to you. I promise."

"Excuse me?" Malaysia pressed, lowering her voice to an urgent whisper. "But you promised already that we were going to this event. And I've had my heart set on this." It was obvious from her tone Malaysia wasn't taking no for an answer.

Jovan groaned in disbelief. "Oh, alright," he said, doing his best to remain polite. "Since you put it like that, I can't disappoint you. I couldn't do that if I tried." He heard what sounded like lips smacking over the line.

"Is that so?" she replied, her tone softer now. "I just love the way that sounds. Let me see what else you're willing to do to make sure that your precious isn't disappointed." She snickered, then added, "I'll be ready at seven. By then, I'll have something special in mind for you to make me happy. See you soon."

What was that all about? Jovan wondered, turning on the bathroom light. He gazed tiredly into the mirror over the sink. A look of shock registered on his face.

"What the fuck is this shit?!" he blurted sharply. The man staring back at him was covered from head to toe in black soot.

He stormed out of the basement. "Angel! Angel!" he yelled angrily. Why in the hell did you put all this black shit all over me? Have you lost your goddamn mind?!" Jovan flung open the garage door. Angel's car was gone. He realized his wife did her dastardly deed and rolled out like nothing happened. Jovan was totally incensed now. He spun around and began punching madly at his cell phone.

Angel's voice mail picked up on the first ring. Jovan was heated. "I don't know what kind of fucking games you playing ..." he began, his voice sounded like a deadly tempest on the verge of unleashing its fury, "but when I see your ass, I gotta serious bone to pick with you. You fucking with the wrong muthafucka!"

Jovan looked like a black shadow. His head began throbbing like it was about to burst. He grabbed at it and cringed in pain. There was a big-ass lump on the back of his head. A cold chill swept through him as the vision of those psychotic-looking eyes crept through his mind.

Suddenly feeling nauseous, Jovan held himself together and headed upstairs to get ready for his date with Malaysia. "Fuck Angel! She can suck my dick!"

That evening ...

It was a clear, cool autumn evening in D.C. By the time Jovan and Malaysia arrived outside of the Kennedy Center, the stars were beginning to twinkle across the darkening skyline.

The black Mercedes coupe rolled to a halt at the front entrance, where
a group of eager valet attendants loitered along the red carpeted walkway.

A Beautiful Satan

Jovan looked impeccable when he stepped out of his ride wearing a crisp black Christian Dior tuxedo. He strolled around to the passenger side and opened the door for Malaysia, who was radiant in her strapless black silk Vera Wang evening gown.

"Shall we, my precious," Jovan said, extending his hand. He helped the gorgeous Thai model from the car. Together they looked incredible.

Arm in arm, the glamorous couple proceeded down the scarlet walkway. In their wake, whispers of awe emanated from a cluster of spectators, as if their presence had just been graced by royalty.

The jazz ensemble performed fabulously. In Malaysia's mind, tonight's event was memorable, something she would cherish for a very long time. Malaysia was thrilled that she was able to share this moment with the man she felt complemented her. This man made her feel alive inside, something she hadn't felt in a long time.

In the little time they had gotten to know one another, Malaysia found Jovan to be an intriguing individual with a powerfully seductive nature. Malaysia told herself to take it slow, reminding herself the man was still married. But she couldn't help herself. When it came to looking at the bigger picture, she felt the fact that Jovan's marriage would soon be dissolved justified her actions. Those thoughts made her heart flutter and gave her that good kind of queasy feeling in her gut. Malaysia's heart was vulnerable around Jovan. She couldn't control herself or her feelings. She realized that she was head over heels in love with this man.

Later that evening ...

The shimmering black coupe rolled along Rock Creek Parkway, careening smoothly down the dark, narrow, winding road with Jovan at the wheel. He commanded the sporty whip with ease as they listened to the soft, smooth vocals of Sade's

"No Ordinary Love." The music's soothing melody permeated the cockpit of the Mercedes.

Jovan beamed with joy as he watched his Thai beauty having a good time, gyrating to the rhythm of the music. He could feel himself growing attached to this lovely creature. Malaysia was a different breed of woman, a total deviation from the normal predatory stock of women traveling through his life. Malaysia was unique, a breath of fresh air. He liked how she made him feel. He liked her smell, her touch, her individuality. Malaysia was what he referred to as wifey material, without a doubt. "I see you fucks with my girl Sade real heavy, huh?" Jovan inquired with a broad grin.

"Sade... oooh yes, that's my girl," Malaysia answered. "I love everything about her. All her music is the bomb!"

Jovan sucked his teeth. "I tell you what," he said smoothly, "The next time she's on tour, I got you. Me and you. Is that a date?"

She nodded enthusiastically. "Is that a date? I want to hear you make that a promise."

He shrugged his shoulders. "I guess I could do that," he told her easily, "but why you need me to promise you?"

"Because," she said still grooving, "I know your character, and you have a hard time breaking a promise."

Jovan smirked lightly. "Oh yeah, you think you know me, huh?"

"I know you well enough to know that I'm right about what I just said." She smiled and blew him a kiss.

The RPM's climbed steadily as the car roared past the rear entrance of the National Zoo. Jovan chuckled heartily. He couldn't deny it—baby girl knew her shit. "What, you profiling me or something?" he said jokingly.

Malaysia stopped and turned to him. "That's funny you would use that choice of words to describe me."

Jovan glanced at her with a wary eye. "And why would you find that to be funny?" he questioned with an intuitive stare.

A Beautiful Satan

"It's funny because that just so happens to be what I do for a living—I'm a forensic technician and criminal profiler for the Metropolitan Police Department. Like CSI. Get it?"

"What?" He looked surprised, then said with an even tone, "You mean to tell me that my baby is a law enforcement agent?" On the inside Jovan was taken aback by her law enforcement title. He gathered his composure well. Fuck it, he rationalized. Malaysia was already falling for him. Shit, he could use this to his advantage.

Malaysia smiled, and her warm glow made him melt. "You don't find that to be a problem do you, Jovan?"

He snickered, "Yeah, right. Why would I, precious? If anything, I feel safer already knowing my baby stay strapped. You are totin', right?" he asked, only half joking.

She eyed him playfully. "How you know that?" Malaysia said, smacking her lips. "'Cause we're supposed to stay armed at all times? And, yes, I've got a little something that I keep in my purse. Oh, I'm so glad you feel that way, Jovan. Because most men—when I tell them what it is that I do they, tend to shy away from me." Malaysia felt so relieved she could express herself so openly with this man.

Jovan laughed and placed his hand on her thigh. "Has the thought ever crossed your mind that those men may have been involved in some type of criminal activity?" He was cool, calm and confident, taking it all in.

Her head bobbed vigorously. "Yep, that thought had crossed my mind."

He decided this was the perfect time to change the subject. "Do you know what thought is crossing my mind right now?" There was a mildly deceptive look in Jovan's eye.

Malaysia's lips curled into a playful sneer. "Hmmph … I'm not sure that I know what it is your getting at," she played along.

Jovan was stroking his chin with a thoughtful look. "Weren't you supposed to be thinking up something for me to do, that in your words, would make you happy?"

"Yep, I forgot all about that," she said, grinning from ear to ear. "Thank you for being so kind to remind me. Now that you've got me thinking … hmmm …" Malaysia hesitated and allowed her mind to roam for a second. "Oh, I know," she spoke up suddenly. "My feet could use a nice massage right about now, if that's alright with you." She paused, studying his facial expression closely.

"Now that's funny that you used that choice of words."

"Why? Don't tell me you make your living as a masseuse?" she smirked.

"Naw, boo, just so happens that these hands of mine are so in tune to your fantastic physique, they would be so thrilled to massage your feet and any other part of your luscious anatomy that might need special attention and catering to. You feel me?"

"Oooh yes," Malaysia sighed, "I'm definitely feeling you. Matter of fact, we could just go to my house and have some drinks instead of going to that expensive restaurant and club. I'm sure we could have a much better time together with just the two of us."

Jovan replied, "Are you sure about that?" He had picked up on her steamy demeanor instantly.

Malaysia didn't say a word; she let her eyes do the talking.

"Okay, precious," he voiced gladly, "point me in the right direction."

ⓌⓌⓌⓌ

It wasn't long before Jovan's sleek roadster was parked outside of a spacious brownstone in the uptown section of NW D.C.

A Beautiful Satan

Malaysia came floating down the stairs, singing her favorite Sade tune. She had changed into a comfortable platinum silk gown that flowed down around her ankles.

Across the living room, over by the fireplace, Jovan sat on a gold chaise sipping on a glass of straight Hennessy while gazing into the fire. He had this hazy look in his eye, like the flames had cast some kind of spell over him.

Leaning into his ear, Malaysia whispered provocatively, "Love, would you mind if I relieved you of your jacket?

Jovan almost jumped out his seat. "Whoa!" You got to give a brother a warning next time, baby."

Malaysia waltzed around and flopped her softer-than-a-baby's ass backside on the sofa next to him. "Do you like?" Malaysia smiled, wiggling her French pedicured toes for Jovan to admire.

Admiring her pretty little feet, Jovan moaned, "Do I like?" he said looking pleased. "That would be an understatement, to say the least," he replied quietly.

Slowly, Jovan proceeded to massage her feet, starting with the right one. He made deep, slow, purposeful motions. His focus was intense.

"Ooooh yessss," Malaysia sighed, arching her head with a growing look of pleasure. "Jovan, were you pulling my leg when you said you weren't a masseuse?" she moaned in a sultry whisper. "Because you know exactly what you're doing, like you've had plenty of practice. Oooh!" she gleefully stated, when Jovan blew on her toes and kissed them tenderly. She shuddered with excitement.

Jovan watched her closely. "Could you imagine what it would be like, precious?" he asked softly, placing a kiss on the top of her foot.

"Imagine what?" Her voice was just above a whisper.

He could see that she was feeling him. Her joyful expressions said it all. "Could you imagine us together as one?" His tone was smooth with a serious edge.

Malaysia dropped her head, and her emerald irises were filled with lust as she cast a heated look his way. "That's all I do is think of you. I can't help myself, love. You are an amazing man, to say the least."

"Thank you for the compliment," he said, peering into her eyes. "And you are an incredible woman yourself. Like I said before, my feelings for you are mutual, and I'm feeling you in more ways than one."

Jovan studied her, while he meticulously worked his way up her soft, creamy thighs. He smiled mischievously, before telling her, "Just lay back and relax. Close your eyes and open your mind and body to me."

Malaysia did as he directed and made herself comfortable. She settled back, relaxed and closed her eyes.

His sensual hands continued to massage her long, soft legs. Jovan maneuvered closer to that buried treasure awaiting at the top of her thighs. The swollen lips protruded through her thin silky thongs.

Malaysia squirmed and moaned in heat. She liked everything Jovan was doing to her mind and body. She was completely captivated by his provocative sensuality.

His hands were exploring her, and she was responding to his every move and gesture, just the way he expected. Jovan was manipulating Malaysia's body like a pianist playing on a baby grand.

Sounds of euphoria escaped Malaysia's lips as she gyrated passionately under Jovan's lustful embrace.

Malaysia felt like a virgin being deflowered for the first time.

Chapter 24

Meanwhile, Natasha was on the hunt ...

Emerging from the shadows, Natasha moved stealthily up the deserted corridor. Dressed in black, like a panther on the prowl looking for prey.

The Bebe boutique were Manika worked had closed its doors almost an hour ago. The last two employees, Manika and her manager, a skinny brunette named Janet, were in the process of closing up the store and were about to set the alarm.

Earlier this evening Natasha paid the store a visit during normal business hours. She wanted to get a close-up of her next victim.

The trifling slut could never have imagined when she awoke this morning that today would be her last day. Manika will never see the sun rise again, Natasha thought, smiling wickedly as she lingered in the corridor peering through a heavy set of metal doors directly opposite the front entrance of the boutique. Natasha thought to herself, *The dumb bitch had the audacity to call my girl Angel's house! Dumb bitch fucked up though when her weak-ass charades hit a wall. She*

145

was fucked up when she heard a woman's voice answer the phone. Looking for Jovan, weren't you, bitch? Yeah, I know. You fumbled the ball, though, when my girl asked you why you were calling, stupid bitch! You really fucked up when you said you were calling about her Bebe shearling. Didn't' her husband pick that up a few days ago? Yea, you fucked yourself and your life up by fucking with a married man.

Both women donned their dark overcoats before they set the alarm and stepped into the deserted mall. A look of enthusiasm jumped in Natasha's eye at the sight of Manika. Slowly, she drew a machete from the inside of her black North Face. The chrome blade looked menacing in her grasp. Natasha grinned devilishly, anxious to kill.

"Bye, Alex," the women spoke in unison to the hefty Hispanic security
guard walking down the escalator. "See you tomorrow." They both waved and walked toward the delivery corridor. When Manika pushed through the door, a loud slam echoed abruptly through the corridor.

Startled, both women froze momentarily, their eyes locked in a nervous embrace as they stared down the corridor and saw that the passageway was empty. Manika and Janet heaved a big sigh of relief, giggling at one another as they proceeded down the corridor.

Outside, hidden in the shadows, Natasha watched both women exit the building. The skinny brunette walked across the parking lot and crawled into a red Honda Accord.

Natasha smirked when she saw Manika get behind the wheel of a silver Volkswagen Jetta. She shook her head. *Should've known ... you look like a Volkswagen type of bitch.*

Janet rolled out first, with the silver Jetta rolling right on its heels. From the shadows, a burgundy Mitsubishi Eclipse appeared. When she saw that the coast was clear, Natasha whipped the sporty coupe around and sped off in hot pursuit.

A Beautiful Satan

The Honda was making a right turn on red as the Eclipse rounded the bend in the parking lot. Natasha was pleased to see the Jetta alone at the traffic light. Then her look of satisfaction quickly became a scowl. When the light turned green, instead of making the left turn, Manika proceeded across Little Patuxent Parkway and turned right into an Exxon gas station.

Whatever it was that Manika purchased from the window wasn't much, Natasha surmised. She was in and out within thirty seconds. Natasha wondered what the stop was for when she walked out empty-handed.

About ten minutes down the road, the Jetta was barreling along Broken Land Parkway. Suddenly, at the intersection of Broken Land and Snowden River parkways, Manika dipped into the left turning lane and whipped the Jetta around, making an abrupt U-turn.

Natasha looked on in disbelief. At first glance she thought the bitch had peeped her and was trying to get away. She was stumped for a second, until the brake lights on the silver car went bright before her eyes. She stared into the rearview mirror and watched the car start to turn.

The Jetta slowed and merged into the right turning lane. Seconds later, Manika turned into the entrance of Lake Elkhorn Park.

A feeling of relief flooded Natasha's senses when she realized Manika's doom was just within reach. The burgundy coupe bust a quick U-turn and followed suit.

Rolling through the lot, Natasha caught a glimpse of a silhouette behind the wheel of the Jetta as she peered through the rear windshield. Her feelings of relief morphed into an insidious loathing. She stomped on the accelerator, propelling the vehicle to the far end of the lot, where she pulled into an empty slot and killed both the engine and the lights.

By day, Lake Elkhorn's lush, green scenery, rolling landscape and picturesque view of the lawn were main attractions in Columbia, Maryland. But the setting of the sun changed the park's inviting appeal dramatically. After sunset, Lake Elkhorn's luxuriant landscape turned into a vast sea of forbidden darkness. The sign at the front entrance read: Park Closed After Dark.

Inside the Jetta, sounds of Erykah Badu and plumes of marijuana smoke filled the air. Manika was grooving and getting her smoke on. Using the Dutch Master cigar she had purchased at the Exxon, she quickly gutted the tobacco and rolled a nice, fat blunt for herself, taking it straight to the head. Manika was floating when a strange woman tapped on her window.

Annoyed, she lowered the window. "Yes, can I help you with something?" The sour note in her voice was unmistakable.

"I'm sorry, girl," Natasha said kindly, pressing her hand against her chest. "I'm not trying to bust your groove, but I was wondering if you knew your back tire was flat?"

Manika's face dropped. "Flat tire?" she snapped sharply. "No, that can't be. I just got here. I mean, I just pulled in here not ten minutes ago." She was rambling as she stuffed out the jay, jumped out and marched to the rear of the car. She stared at the flat tire in disbelief. "Shit! How in the world did that happen?" Manika grumbled in disgust as she squatted to get a closer look.

Natasha scanned the perimeter and noticed three vehicles parked in the lot when she pulled in. As bad as she wanted to gut this slut on the spot, she had to hold herself back. That didn't stop the thoughts from materializing in her mind. *What if I whacked her across the windpipe real fast with my blade? That would probably do it. Or I could just push her over right now while she was kneeling and put the blade through her heart.*

Beneath the thick shell of her North Face coat, Natasha's grip tightened around the handle of the deadly blade. She cast a wicked look upon the woman kneeling beside her. Rage coursed through her veins as she slowly began to bring forth the machete.

A feminine voice sounded in the distance. "Boris, could you please hurry?" said a chubby Caucasian woman strolling up the dark asphalt path. Trailing not far behind was her running mate, Boris. He was a rakish-looking German fellow with spiked blonde hair. "I'm coming, sweetheart, just catching my breath a bit," he said, winded.

This unexpected disruption irritated Natasha profusely. She groaned in protest, relaxing her grip on the blade. Her eyes narrowed into slits, watching the odd-looking Caucasian couple as they walked by.

She shot them a nasty look before turning up her nose and refocused her mind and energy on the more intimate task waiting before her.

"Okay, girl," Natasha began with an attitude, "you see the tire's flat, so what are you gonna do about it? You need a ride somewhere?"

Manika stood, distraught. "You would do that for me?" she asked, wiping at her eyes. "I mean I'll pay you for your time. That's not a problem. I just can't understand how I caught a flat so fast. I just got this car and those tires are brand new," Manika sighed in frustration. "Oh, well … I need a ride to Laurel, Maryland. Is that too far?"

As she spoke, Manika was unaware of Natasha's incessant foot tapping. Standing there listening to the ho complain was wearing her patience thin. "Well, honey, crying over spilled milk isn't gonna solve your problem, so what are you gonna do?" Natasha was struggling hard to control her violent impulses. She wanted to slit the bitch's throat and watch her strangle on her own blood so bad she could actually feel the life draining from this ho's body. It was a weird sensation. She could almost feel her nostrils becoming deeply saturated by the robust aroma of Manika's spilled blood.

Manika hung her head in defeat. "You're right," she breathed dejectedly, on the brink of tears. "Do you think that air in a can would help out at all?"

With her arms folded across her chest, Natasha answered drily, "Honey, I don't think anything but a new tire is gonna help you out of this shit, so come on if you still want this ride." She started walking away. "I do have other things to do, ya know," she said, speaking over her shoulder.

Manika stared after her, wondering why the stranger was acting so cold all of a sudden. *I didn't ask this bitch for her help. Crazy bitch offered to help out on her own. Now she wants to act all shitty.*

"Fucking bitch," Manika muttered under her breath as she bent down to take one last look at her tire. "Shit!" she cursed, running her hand along the black rubber surface. "Is that a gash in my damn tire?" she said, straining to see in the dark.

A horn sounded abruptly, causing Manika to nearly scurry under the car. She hopped to her feet and whirled around, grimacing.

"Are you coming girl or what? I don't have all night." Natasha looked pissed.

Who this bitch think she is? Manika voiced silently. She was ready to tell her to kiss off.

"You can wait around here in this dark-ass park if you want—that's on you, honey," Natasha shrugged nonchalantly.

At the mention of the word "dark," Manika's eyes went wide, then panned out across the park's pitch-black landscape, which seemed like an endless sea of darkness stretching as far as the eye could see. The darkness rattled her. There was no way in hell she was going to wait around at this spooky-looking place.

Manika made up her mind. It was better to ride with this asshole than to wait around in a dark-ass park by herself. The thought made her shiver.

A Beautiful Satan

The car blew through a red light with no discretion. Natasha looked over at Manika, threw her head back and laughed.

Manika couldn't help but wonder, *What kind of drugs is this bitch on?* "Are you sure you're going the right way?" she asked with a cautious look. "I never knew you could get to Laurel this way."

Natasha was intense, looking like a driver with a purpose, weaving in and out of traffic. Manika's comment made her snicker. "Have you ever been to Laurel this way?" She glanced at her and smirked. "Well rest your nerves, honey. I know the way."

Natasha swerved in and around two slower-moving cars. She flipped them the finger when they flashed their high beams.

The Eclipse turned right off the main road. Manika glanced over her shoulder. She wasn't feeling too good about going this way. This looked as though they were leaving civilization behind.

The road they were on was completely devoid of light and surrounded by a blanket of perpetual darkness. Manika thought the road looked like something right out of a horror movie. It was one of those dark, deserted roads in the middle of nowhere that leads to the doorsteps of some out-of-the-way decrepit house of horrors somewhere at the end of the road.

An intense feeling of anxiety suddenly began to brew in the pit of Manika's stomach. "Boy, I'd hate to break down off this dark road." Her comment hit a wall of silence, prompting a more direct statement. "So where in Laurel does this road lead to?"

Natasha didn't answer; she was concentrating on the dark road outside.

"Excuse me, miss," Manika said more confidently, "but I know you just heard me ask you a question. So what's the problem?"

Natasha started gritting her teeth. Her insides were trembling with anticipation. She faced Manika and cracked a wicked-looking smile.

"You the fucking problem, bitch," Natasha spat coldly. She couldn't contain herself any longer.

Manika looked like someone had just tossed an ice-cold bucket of water in her face. "What?" she frowned quizzically. Panic raced through her when the woman reached inside her coat and produced a huge blade.

"You like fucking married men, bitch??!" Natasha screamed out a second before she swung the machete, aiming with murderous intent for her throat.

Sheer survival instincts kicked in. Manika surprised herself when she caught the women's arm in mid-swing. "Oh, God!" she yelped in terror as she struggled with both hands. "What in the hell, bitch??! Oh, hell no!" She couldn't believe how much trouble this crazy bitch was giving her with one arm. *Damn! This crazy-ass-bitch stronger than a man!*

Luckily for the battling pair the road was devoid of traffic. The car swerved from left to right as if it owned the road.

Natasha was fighting to keep the car on the road with one hand and struggling in a heated tug-of-war with the other. Manika fought with all her might, trying to dislodge the machete from her powerful grip.

Suddenly Natasha shrieked in agony when Manika chomped down on her exposed wrist. It was as if she was biting into a tough T-bone steak intent on separating meat from bone.

The machete went tumbling to the floor when Natasha yielded to the painful bite. She snatched her wrist from the grips of her mouth. "You dirty bitch!" she snarled.

Seething mad, Natasha balled her hand into a tight fist and slammed three vicious backhanded blows to Manika's face, smashing her nose and leaving her in a daze.

A Beautiful Satan

Natasha was frantic, fumbling around blindly on the floor for her machete while trying to steer.

"Aw, you bitch," Manika mumbled, fighting through the fog in her head. "Nah, bitch, fuck this." She sounded like a drunk attempting to get her bearings.

Deciding to give up finding the machete right now, Natasha searched for the next clearing in the road and pulled the car over.

Before stepping out, she slammed another fist into Manika's bloodied face. "Fucking ho!" she hissed and then hawk-spit on her for emphasis. She popped the trunk, hopped out and rushed to the rear.

Wincing in pain, Manika summoned all of her will and strength, hopped out and tried to escape from the clutches of this crazy woman.

From the cover of darkness, Manika watched the crazy woman rummage through the trunk. She shrieked in fear when the bitch spun around wielding a crowbar.
Her eyes grew wide with terror when the armed woman stormed towards her.

What the fuck did I do to this crazy bitch? Manika's mind was running wild as she stumbled around in the dark. When she attempted to circle back around, Manika suddenly tripped and stumbled. Aloud squeal erupted when she went tumbling into a thorny briar bush. She knew she was fucked now.

Natasha popped out of nowhere. "Fucking slut!" She spit fire when she caught her. Instead of finishing her off right then and there, she wanted to see her suffer. That's how she got her rocks off.

"Thought you were going somewhere, huh, bitch?" she voiced looking diabolical.

Manika started sobbing. "Please, lady, leave me alone. Why are you doing this to me? What have I done to you?"

Natasha placed the crowbar against her forehead. "I'll tell you what you've done." Her tone was grim. "You fucked a married man. You know a nigga named Jovan? Yeah, you fucked him."

Jovan! The name echoed in Manika's head. His face appeared in her mind. *Jovan.*

Ear-piercing screams suddenly cracked the quiet of the night. Natasha went wild with the crowbar, shattering both of Manika's knee caps and shin bones in a cruel, barbaric attack.

After mangling Manika's limbs beyond repair, she grabbed the collar of her coat and with a powerful heave, Natasha hauled her victim from the thorny thicket. She deposited the battered and broken frame just beyond the hood of the Eclipse, as if she was disposing garbage.

"Please, I'm begging you," Manika cried out in desperation, her pretty face a gory mask of blood, dirt and tears. "Please, let me go. I won't say a thing. Please, I *swear* to God Almighty …" she said, her words cut short in a spasm of uncontrollable choking sobs. "Please, please … I'm begging you …"

Natasha watched devilishly as the woman cried and begged for mercy, whimpering helplessly at her feet. Her suffering gave Natasha the inner strength she needed to prosper and flourish. It ignited her soul and bestowed a dark power upon her that gave her dominion over Angel's presence. The more suffering Natasha inflicted on her victim, the more powerful she became.

"In your next life, ho, don't fuck around with married men." Natasha's voice sounded ominous. "Those deeds bring unwanted travesty into your life." She cast a vile look upon her, standing erect, unmovable, her eyes gleaming. "Bitches like you don't deserve life!" she said, looking Manika dead in the eye. A choked sob emanated from Manika, having no effect whatsoever on Natasha. Her face showed no emotions.

The blackness inside Natasha's heart erupted. Manika trembled and put up a halfhearted defense. With one quick motion, Natasha connected crowbar to cranium, and Manika's body slammed against the ground. Pain and numbness exploded in waves throughout her body as she attempted to digest why this woman had stalked her and was now attacking her with such vicious intent. An image of Jovan popped into her head a split second before another bone-shattering blow to the head obliterated all thoughts. The sight of blood only added fuel to Natasha's fury.

"Hey, there! What the hell are you doing on my property?" A strange older guy appeared out of nowhere.

Natasha whirled on her heels. A devious smile unfurled across her lips when she saw that the nosey old man was by himself.

"Is that somebody hurt over there?" the gray-haired man questioned as the platinum blonde approached. The guy shook in his boots when he made eye contact with the woman. He could see there was no denying the evil in those blue eyes. He stumbled backward. "I think you better gone get the hell off of my property," he said as he turned to leave.

A sudden pain exploded across his back. He fell forward, struggling against the pain. Slowly, he rolled over and stared at his attacker. The woman was taking dead aim at his head as she brought the crowbar down with deadly force. The old man closed his eyes, his thoughts scattered in every direction as fear and regret crashed into his mind.

Natasha glanced down at the corpse. She almost looked amused. "My work here is almost finished."

Chapter 25

Echoes of hard heels smacking against tile resonated off the walls and ceiling as Detective Clark's brawny frame strode the entire length of the fourth-floor hallway. His rigid demeanor let you know off the break that he meant business.

Clark peered into the homicide office and eyed his partner's empty desk. A smudge of displeasure showed on his face when he realized Louis was missing in action.

As he stepped through the doorway, his eardrums were immediately inundated by the constant buzz of chatter in the air and the incessant ringing of phones scattered all around the office.

"Where's Detective Louis?" he demanded as he marched into the command center.

"I don't know, sir," said Raul, a subordinate outfitted in a suit one size too small answered, shrugging his shoulders. "He was just over at his desk using the phone, so he couldn't have gone far."

Clark hovered over the smaller man, his broad frame eclipsing the light overhead. "Well, rookie," he grumbled, "I need his presence like ten freaking minutes ago, comprende?"

A Beautiful Satan

The rookie fought off the urge to belt him one good time in his bloated gut. Instead, Raul bounded to his feet and offered to go find the missing detective, mainly to get away from the arrogant, overbearing prick.

While he was waiting, Clark decided to go fetch himself a fresh cup of coffee.

"Wait till he hears this shit here," he mumbled to himself while stirring cream and sugar into his java. He checked his watch, then walked over to Raul's desk. He checked his watch again and sighed, a sure sign of his growing impatience.

"Would this by any chance have anything to do with our current case?" The sound of Louis' voice drifted into the room from the hallway.

When Louis and Raul walked in, they found Clark holding his cup of coffee, looking preoccupied.

"I'm not surprised," Clark stated in a low voice. "We've got serious business to attend to, but my partner is nowhere to be found. What would you propose I do in a situation like that?" As he spoke, the detective's sight never left the plastic stirrer in his caffeinated drink.

The words made no sense to Louis.

"If you're in one of your moods, buddy, just let me know," Louis voiced sternly with a no-nonsense look. "I had a very rough night, and I'm not in the mood."

Clark sat his cup down and belted out a hearty chuckle. "A rough night," he reiterated, sounding jovial all of a sudden. "I don't think you know what a rough night really consists of, Richie Boy."

Louis' brow furled slightly. *He knows I got a problem with that Richie Boy shit. I warned him before.* It was apparent to him that his partner was preparing to arrive at some twisted revelation.

"Okay, Bill," he said. He rolled his eyes and exhaled. "I'm sure you're gonna enlighten me on what a rough night really consists of. C'mon, bring it on," he told his partner flatly, gesturing with his hands.

Clark's burly frame rose from the desk. He slipped his dark Isaac Hayes frames over his eyes. "What if it consisted of you getting the life beat out of you? I mean beaten to a bloody pulp! Head cracked open, legs smashed up like somebody took a fucking sledgehammer to them."

"Hold up one minute," Louis stammered, interrupting, his hand in the air. He seemed to need a moment to digest the scenario Clark was describing. "This incident, does it tie into our current case in any way?" he asked grimly.

Clark hesitated briefly, then said disgustedly, "The son of a bitch struck again. In Maryland this time. Howard County."

"*How* do you know it's our guy?"

"Because our guy collects trophy pieces," he told him coldly. "This new victim had her hand chopped off," Clark said, "and I believe someone stumbled across our guy's path while he was in the act."

Louis' brow shot up excitedly. "A witness!" he gushed happily, grabbing his partner by the shoulders, ready to give him a big hug. "Why didn't you mention that before?" The look of strain on Clark's face quickly pulled the rug out from under him. "No!" he uttered in protest. "Don't tell me ..."

"Another double, buddy. An old white man this time."

A towering six-four figure with graying sideburns and a portly, clean-shaven face appeared in the doorway. He was the commander, Jack Stewart. Big Jack to his fellow colleagues.

"You two still hanging around here?" The commander's raspy voice seemed to cut easily through all the office clatter. His presence swept across the command post, and the chatter abruptly stopped. "Isn't that double homicide out there in Howard County related to your case?"

The commander's eyes moved immediately to Clark

A Beautiful Satan

"If you two superstars were on your job, I wouldn't have the chief of the Howard County Police on the line in my office inquiring about information pertaining to your serial killer, now would I?" His eyes shifted back and forth between both men.

For an instance, the Dynamic Duo looked flustered. They gathered their composure, bid farewell to the commander and made a hasty departure from the command post.

ⓦⓦⓦⓦ

The silver cruiser tore through the streets of D.C., slowing only when a vehicle came within a few feet of striking distance.

"Don't we need permission first before we cross jurisdictional boundaries?" asked Louis with an uncomfortable look.

Clark nodded. "Usually that would be the case, but in this situation, we all good," he explained confidently. "A few people owe me a few favors out there in Maryland." He turned to Louis. "So get Tony Woo on the phone," Clark demanded. "Let him know our guy took out two more in Howard County and to meet us out there at the lab to view the bodies."

The stench of death hovered in the air. The sterile, gleaming white linoleum walls of the forensic lab held a formidable presence that was cold and grave; grieving and sadness radiated profusely.

Tony Woo looked incisive, circling both bodies like a hawk preparing to dive-bomb its prey. This was the geeky technician's domain. Inside of these walls, his short, dumpy stature wasn't an issue. Within the walls of any forensic lab, Tony Woo was revered as a giant.

Louis and Clark were lounging in the background, conversing with their Maryland counterpart—the CSI supervisor, Mr. Ben Gordon. He was a strikingly dark and charismatic man from Uganda. Upon first glance, Mr. Gordon brought to mind the NBA star Dikembe Mutombo.

"The woman was the intended target." Tony's astuteness echoed across the lab as he denoted the severity of Manika's contusions. "She also was the first to pass," he said over his shoulder, his forensic senses tingling as he examined the mutilated corpses. "The old guy, he happened to be on the scene, and our guy didn't hesitate to take him out."

"Okay, Woo, you're not telling us anything new," Clark declared bluntly.

Tony decided the detective's remark wasn't worthy of a response. "Also, I believe our guy is a sadist; all the trait marks are lining up in a very morbid pattern."

"Like in sadomasochism?" interjected Louis. "Is that what you're saying, Woo?"

Tony flipped his right forefinger into the air. "Precisely, my boy," he agreed without hesitation. "I believe our guy is performing some type of ritual, and these grisly mutilations and the collection of his victims' body parts play a vital role in carrying out these acts." He paused and pointed to Manika's mortal head wounds. "Pay careful attention to the massive gash and the wound pattern."

"How can you make that assumption, Woo?" Clark questioned. "Victim number two over in Cleveland Park wasn't missing any body parts. Our two ladies at Hogate's weren't missing any limbs either. So how does that fit into your hypothesis?" He and Louis exchanged uneasy looks.

Tony's head turned slowly to his right. He peered over the top of his wire frames and said, "Just because no body parts were missing doesn't mean something else wasn't seized from the victim's bodily possession." His tone sounded extremely bizarre.

"Your guy," Ben spoke up suddenly, his heavy East African accent unmistakable, "requires bodily effects in any form to entertain these rituals." He stopped, looked from

A Beautiful Satan

Clark to Louis and said easily, "Gentlemen, hair is a bodily effect also."

Clark's face went grim. "Hair?"

Tony Woo nodded, removing his glasses from his face. "Where did our guy pick this lady up from?" he asked.

Ben flipped a couple pages on his notepad. He read: "The deceased's automobile, a silver Volkswagen Jetta, was discovered in the parking lot of Lake Elkhorn Park on the east end, just off Broken Land Parkway. The Jetta's rear driver side tire had been slashed. That's approximately 5 miles from the crime scene."

Tony Woo had a deep contemplative look swirling in his eye. "So our guy slashed the victim's tire and appears out of the blue as her hero. Takes her for the ride of her life. Perfect gentleman."

Clark cut in, "The woman just hops into this strange man's vehicle that comes out of nowhere? At night, I mind you."

"Happens all the time. You know that, Will," added Louis matter-of-factly.

Smiling, Tony took a deep breath before expressing to the men his overview of the perpetrator and the series of murders.

"Gentlemen," he began, peeling the latex gloves off his hands. "What we have here is a complex puzzle that seems to be missing one vital piece. On one hand we can assume that a number of the victims knew our guy. Like the first victim, for instance—there was no sign of forced entry."

"That was the eyeless corpse you heard about," Clark informed Ben.

Tony continued, "With the second victim, same thing—no forced entry."

Clark turned to Ben. "That was the skydiver I was telling you about."

"Third victim—same scenario."

"He carved out her tongue," Clark said pointedly.

"Victims four and five—that's the problem." Tony folded his hands across his potbelly and gazed at a spot across the room on the wall like he was looking through it. "That's the vital piece of the puzzle that we're missing, gentlemen."

Louis threw up his hands. "But they were murdered inside of a club!"

Tony looked at him sideways. "That's precisely what I'm getting at. *How* could our guy pull off a double homicide with hundreds of people around and not a single eyewitness account? What are we dealing with here, huh?"

"That's why we got you here," Clark said, looking agitated. "So you tell us just what in the hell are we dealing with?" His snide remark seemed to reverberate in the air.

Ben placed his hand on Clark's shoulder and squeezed. "What we're dealing with, my friend, is a very crafty individual." The supervisor regarded each man with a quiet stare before going on. "This individual is capable of blending into any situation without attracting unwanted attention. He's very charismatic and likable, as we can see by his selection of very attractive women. I gather that he's extremely good with dealing with women. A ladies' man, you could say. But in reality, what we're dealing with is a chameleon, pure and simple." When Ben finished, his demeanor grew intense.

Tony Woo nodded.

Tossing up his hands in defeat, Clark commented, "That's just fucking great. Let's put this shit on the 'Ten Most Wanted List.'" We gotta fucking A.P.B. out for a fucking chameleon! We'll be the laughing stock of the whole metropolitan region." He then stormed out of the room and didn't look back.

The trio stared after him and then looked to one another with obvious concern.

Tony Woo slipped his wire frames on and straightened his gray Bill Blass blazer. He said to the men as if he was explaining a dark secret, "Remember, time is on our side." He spoke in a low monotone. "When dealing with serial killers,

A Beautiful Satan

after each murder, time restarts for us. His schemes have wavered outside of his boundary lines. His attacks have gone public, out in the open. Gentlemen, our guy is losing control. This dead old man represents our guy's first fuck up. Mark my words: He's gonna slip up again. Soon."

Chapter 26

Angel gazed skywards at the milky blue heavens. Stopping on the front porch, she took a deep breath and made sure that her ivory suede Prada suit was tight. She counted to three before placing the house key in the front door and entering.

Inside, Angel walked into the family room and found her husband sleeping peacefully. She stared down at him and her eyes brimmed with tears. All she wanted was love from this man, that's all she ever wanted. To be loved and treated with love and respect by the man she held so dear to her heart. The man she loved, honored and cherished with every fiber of her being. Angel loved this man unconditionally; there was nothing that she would not do for this man. Nothing in the world. She loved Jovan more than she loved herself, more than life itself.

Angel choked and then caught her breath when Jovan's eyes popped open suddenly. She was about to step back when Jovan's swift reflexes startled her.

His hand sprung forth like a snake attacking its prey. He locked his hand around her wrist and tightened.

A Beautiful Satan

"What you doing, baby girl?" he asked, sitting upright. "You got some more tricks up your sleeve for your man, huh? Is that it?" He watched the dumbfounded expression on her face as if she didn't know what the hell he was talking about.

She tried wriggling free. "Could you stop? You're hurting me," she complained.

"I'm gonna do more than that to your ass," he stated with a smirk. "I don't know who the fuck you think you're playing with, but you know I'm not the one, don't you?" His look was harsh as he watched her emotions sway.

Angel felt a sudden surge of concern. "What are you talking about? Please, let me go. I haven't done nothing but stay out like you've been doing. What is it? You can't take your own medicine?" She stared at him, matching his look. "You lucky your wife is not a slut like them bitches you used to dealing with or I would've fucked a nigga by now!" she said scathingly. "But I think more highly of myself, and I'm too good for that. Besides, two wrongs don't make a right. And I'm the bigger person for not stooping to your level. You keep on doing what you doing. You gonna get yours." Angel's voice sounded meek, but her eyes shone with an intensity that Jovan found to be unsettling.

His uneasiness began to fade away as he found a sudden delight in watching his wife's enticing physique. He swept his hand down her backside, resting it on her ass. He exhaled and forced a calm smile.

"I'm gonna get mine?" Jovan smiled inwardly as his sights traveled the length of Angel's body. Wifey was looking fabulous in her new suit. "Don't you think that bullshit with the ashes was enough?" he replied, palming her ass. "The candle wax," he added casually. "Well, that's something we could work into our sex play, know what I'm saying?" He winked and tapped her ass.

Angel yanked away from his grip. "What the hell are you talking about? Ashes and candle wax? You got me mixed up with your other bitches!" She glared at him like he was off his rocker.

"Hold the fuck up," he objected quickly. "I don't got you mixed up with no goddamn body!" He jumped to his feet, irate. "What the fuck's happening with you?" he demanded. "Have you lost your damn mind?"

Angel took a step back in surprise. She had no idea why he was insisting that she had done something she knew nothing about. Jovan wasn't making any sense. Then it dawned on her suddenly. The memory loss and blackouts she had been having due to those experimental Oxyline pills she smuggled from the hospital. Angel's deductive reasoning kicked into gear, and the pain pills were the only culprit that stood out. She had taken precautionary measures and lowered the dosage from eight pills a day to four, but sometimes she found herself taking more; she couldn't help herself. The thought of not taking the pain pills were a dead issue. She was addicted to this new cutting-edge pain medication.

Am I actually carrying out deeds that I can't account for while blacked out? Those are symptoms more associated with an alcoholic, she said to herself.

"No!" Angel declared. "Absolutely not! Have you lost your fucking mind?" She exploded, fear and bewilderment running rampant through her mind. "You cheating son of a bitch! Maybe you should spend more time at home with your wife instead of running the streets with those hos and the people you call your friends, who in all actuality don't give a fuck about you. Then maybe some of this shit you talking about wouldn't happen!"

When Angel finished with her severe tongue lashing, she whirled on her heels and stomped out of the room.

"What the fuck?" Jovan mumbled. He looked befuddled, like he was lost in space. His brow furrowed. "Yea, you quick to talk shit, ain't you," he yelled after her. "Like I don't spend time with your ass. You're never fucking satisfied!" He stood at the bottom of the stairs ranting. "If I gave you the world on a silver platter, what would it matter? Because your erratic, unstable ass would still be mad at me the next time I went out. So it wouldn't matter what I did." He fastened his black True Religion jeans as he walked into the kitchen. "So fuck it! I'm damned if I do and damned if I don't."

Angel was standing in the upstairs hallway listening to every word Jovan was saying. When he finished, she yelled over the banister, "Don't use that as no damn excuse! You obsessed with the streets and all the crud that's in 'em, you fucking street runner!"

He smiled mischievously before answering, "Well if you understand my obsession, then you wouldn't try to change my mind, now would you, boo?" He pulled open the refrigerator door and took out a container of V-8 juice. While he was guzzling from the container, his BlackBerry blared from the sofa in the family room.

The blazing ringtone from Jim Jones' headbanger "We Fly High" emanated through the BlackBerry's speaker.

"Hey, playboy!" Ray's voice boomed over the line. "Are you good?" I need to holler at you. I got some folks that wanna check out them whips you got for sale. You cool with that or what? My folks got major bread, playboy, and they trying to pad your pockets with it. So you make the call."

It took Jovan all of one second to make up his mind. "Where you at now? You say their paper straight? Well, you and your peeps meet me at my car spot in about an hour. See you when I see you."

Instead of going upstairs to get ready, Jovan went downstairs and freshened up before slipping out into the garage. He revved up the Mercedes roadster, hit the remote for the garage door and got ghost.

Wrapped snugly in his midnight-blue Burberry overcoat, Jovan sat perched on the hood of his coupe, gazing across the asphalt. Jovan caught sight of a white-gold 745 Beemer turning into the front entrance of the Cherry Hill Business Park.

He flipped his coat collar, shielding his exposed neck as a chilly Northeastern breeze whipped up suddenly. He started sucking his teeth, his hand gripped tightly around the handle of the chrome plated .40 caliber buried deep inside the pocket of his coat.

As the gleaming white car rolled to a halt before him, Jovan never flinched, his cold gray eyes riveted to the spot on the windshield where the dark silhouette of the driver could be seen.

Ray felt uncertain how to proceed. The quarrel over the Barry Farm shooting had never been resolved. As far as he was concerned, the incident was over and done with. But he knew J, and that nigga be on some holding-a-grudge shit.

"Hey, dawg," his man Cordell spoke up nervously. "Main man here your folks, right? I mean dude look like he ready to bust off on a nigga. Is everything cool?"

Ray did his best to offer up a fake carefree response. He nodded quickly. "Yeah, Joe, everything good. That's how my man is. He one of those niggas that look like he's mad every damn day."

Cordell cast a leery eye Jovan's way. "Yea, I know them types," he said, trying to look hard, but failing. His bright-yellow complexion clashed humorously with his strikingly vibrant red cornrows and freckles. He resembled the face of the man on *Mad Magazine* but with cornrows.

Cornell turned to Ray. "I deals with them types all the time," he replied. "So don't worry, I got this."

"C'mon," Ray said, grabbing the door handle. "Let's get this show on the road and take care of business." He was unconsciously holding his breath as he climbed out. "Hey,

A Beautiful Satan

what's good?" Ray attempted to project confidence as he rounded the car to greet Jovan.

Jovan's aura was anything but welcoming. "What's good, nigga?" He returned the gesture with a curt nod as he sat on the hood with both hands resting in his coat pockets. Jovan had this impenetrable shield of inapproachability embodying his form. "These your folks?" he asked in an impassive tone. "What up, dude? Which joint you interested in copping?"

Cordell strolled around the car with a grin on his freckled face, rubbing his palms together. "Strictly business, huh?" he said, trying to come off cool and cordial all at once, hoping to receive the approval of this intimidating brother. "You my type of peoples, dawg." He shot Ray a quick look. Then went on, "I'm interested in two of them joints, right. You still got the, uh, twin turbo Nissan and the Crown Vic?"

"Yeah, them joints around back." He motioned in the direction of the red brick office structure situated about forty yards behind them.

"Okay, okay," he expressed with growing enthusiasm. "Another thing I wanna ask you about—the ad on your website, right? You asking fifteen grand for the twin turbo and twelve for the Crown Vic. I want both of them joints, right? But I'm only working with twenty-five stacks." He looked on with an expectant glimmer in his eye. "Think we could work something out for the twenty-five, my man?"

"Twenty-five G's for them two joints you want?" He paused, stroking the hairs on his chin. "If you got the whole twenty-five on you now ... yeah, champ, we can do this."

Both cars rode around to the rear of the building and parked just beyond the double-bay doors of the Laurel Automotive Repair shop. The owner/operator of the establishment, David Mister, was an old business associate of Jovan's who allotted him the lot space to store his list of vehicles for sale.

Black and orange "for sale" signs adorned the windows of four automobiles that were arranged side by side in a row: a steel-gray Nissan twin turbo, a candy-apple red Porsche 968, a dusty-brown Crown Victoria and a burgundy Mitsubishi Eclipse.

Jovan leaned against the side of his Benz and tossed Cordell the keys to the vehicles he asked to see.

Ray eased his way over to the empty spot on the coupe next to his partner. His hand disappeared inside the lining of his forest-green North Face.

"You know I've been hitting your cell up for like a week now," Ray voiced evenly. "I guess you still fucked up with me, huh?" He stopped short. When his hand reappeared from inside his coat, he was clutching four stacks of $50 dollar bills. Each stack was secured by a rubber band. "Hope this can help smooth things over a bit," he expressed flatly, placing the $20,000 on the hood between them.

Eyeing the forested landscape just beyond the rear lot, Jovan's head turned to his left. "What's that? Dude's loot for the whips?" he asked, cavalier.

Ray shook his head. "Nah, playboy, this what I've been trying to give you all week. This twenty grand—your half of the profits for the week."

The sight of dollars took the edgy sting out of Jovan's look. "Twenty stacks for the week, huh?" He scooped the bills from the hood, straining not to smile. "Where the rest of my dough at, nigga?" His continence wavered, and the beginning of a grin was tap dancing at the edges of his mouth.

Cordell interrupted their exchange when he walked over and dropped $25,000 in bundles of $100 bills in the same spot on the hood.

Jovan looked up in surprise. "What, you good, champ? You don't wanna test drive the joints?" he asked, stuffing the drug proceeds in his Burberry coat. He then shoveled off the stack Cordell just laid down. Jovan flipped through the bills like a seasoned bank teller.

A Beautiful Satan

The *Mad Magazine* lookalike told him that he had fired up both engines and checked under the hoods. From his experience working on cars, Cordell gave both vehicles a thumbs-up.

The way things jumped off with his wife earlier, Jovan pictured a gloomy, fucked-up day. It was amazing how one phone call could turn everything around. After one phone call and a quick trip down the road, the sun was shining down on him.

That's the power of money, Jovan rationalized within himself. Before leaving, he checked to make sure the other two cars were secure. He checked the doors on the Porsche. Locked. Then he moved on to the Eclipse. Both doors were secure.

"Hey, Ray," Jovan called out while walking around the Eclipse. "When you cop the new paint job on the whip?" His face turned grim when he reached the rear of the car. He paused staring at the trunk, pondering. The trunk's hood wasn't completely closed. Jovan didn't hear a word Ray was saying; he was totally focused on the car's trunk.

He swung open the hood, and a feeling of violation overcame him as he peered inside. *Someone been fucking around in here. I didn't leave this shit like this.* He started rummaging through the trunk's contents. Nothing was missing as far as he could see. There was nothing of value in the trunk worth taking anyway, so why had someone even gone through the trouble?

Probably some pipehead, he reasoned. *Surprise, surprise, muthafucka. Nothing here.*

Jovan slammed the trunk shut, pulling on it to make sure it was shut. When he turned, he was surprised to see Ray and Cordell standing by watching him.

"Somebody broke in your joint?" asked Ray. "Nothing missing, is it?"

"Wasn't nothing in there worth taking." Jovan replied, suddenly distracted by the subtle vibrations of his BlackBerry holstered on his hip.

He quickly popped the device from the clip. "Yeah, what up?" he answered curtly.

It was Angel's girlfriend, Tina. "Are you busy?"

"Why? What do you want?" Jovan retorted, not feeling this bitch at all.

"Damn, baby," she spoke softly, "Who got you all bent out of shape? My girl giving you problems? You need me to give you a nice body massage? I know that'll get you right."

He exhaled deeply. "Nah, shorty, I don't need no damn massage," Jovan replied, clearly irritated. "What is it that you want, huh?"

"Well, since you want to carry it like that ... I was trying to be nice about the shit." Tina fired back sharply. "But since you gotta act all hard about it, why don't you bring your hard ass over here to me so we can take care of our business and be done with it."

Jovan fought back a sharp comment. "Yea, alright," he relented, figuring he'd go ahead and have some fun with the little freak bitch and bang her back out. *Little bitch do got one helluva ass on her*, he thought. "I'm on my way," he said, and hung up.

Before the men parted ways, Ray told Jovan about tonight's jump-off that was going down at the Lux Lounge.

Jovan didn't make any promises. His night depended on how the remainder of his day went. So far, so good. Until Tina called him.

ⓌⓌⓌⓌ

High up on the fifteenth floor of the Chateau, in a swanky high-rise condominium overlooking the 495 Beltway, sounds resonated from the bedroom. Then a loud eruption of squealing split the air. A deep, throaty roar of a dominate male conquering its mate followed.

Jovan felt utterly spent as he rolled on his back and gazed up at the mirrored canopy, listening to Tina's incoherent utters of ecstasy. He had her ass speaking in tongues.

Jovan folded his hands behind his head, gloating over his obvious accomplishment. He blew Tina's back out, rocked her world and made her hot hole explode with joy all in one take.

"Oh my God!" Tina blurted, still gasping for air. "Now I know why my girl be putting up with all that shit you be taking her ass through. Mmm, mmm, mmm!" She squirmed and wriggled atop the silvery satin sheets like her ass was on fire.

Jovan looked over at her. "You satisfied now? I kept my end of the bargain." He paused, waiting for an answer.

Tina scooted across the bed and pressed her soft, heated flesh against his. "That shit was good!" Tina muttered. Her expression was one of complete astonishment. She propped her head on his chest and gazed into his eyes. "You can't tell me that you don't wanna hit this phat, juicy ass again. The way you was all up in my shit ... nigga, your dick and my pussy are made for each other," she said hotly. Her eyes flashed with unfettered lust.

He couldn't believe his ears. This broad was talking like she wanted to be his main bitch. He smiled at the idea of having her pretty, hot ass on the side, smashing that ass whenever he wanted. *But she's my wife's friend, and Angel only claims a couple of them. Nah, I can't.*

"C'mon, shorty," Jovan said, smiling deviously. "That sounds all good and everything, but the truth of the matter is you one of my wife's main girlfriends. We can't kick it like that."

Tina smiled self-consciously and quickly looked away. Her look of excitement waned. "I figured you'd probably go there," she whispered huskily, tilting her head to the side. "I don't care about that," Tina said as she reached out and stroked the head of his penis like she was caressing something valuable and dear to her.

Jovan's enormous mushroom head rested on his taut stomach staring Tina in the face. It was like his organ was calling out to her. She leaned her head in closer, puckered her lips and put a wet, juicy kiss on the tip of it. A soft moan escaped her lips when the head jumped at her.

She faced Jovan. There was no concealing the mounting eagerness in her eyes. "I do believe your partner here feels a lot differently about me than you do."

Jovan smiled benevolently. "Is that a fact?" His response had a patronizing tone. "Well, let's hear what else my partner has to say." He was amused.

Determination blazed in Tina's eyes. She spoke without thinking. "Yeah, let's hear what your partner has to say."

Tina released a deep sigh of built-up excitement and stuffed the engorged head between her yearning lips. Her mouth wrestled briefly with the thick mass.

Jovan gasped in glee, watching as Tina explored his throbbing rod with lascivious intent.

He caressed the back of her head. "That's it … work those lips and tongue all over Daddy's dick," he muttered, taking a deep breath. His voice trailed off, and he groaned in pleasure as he experienced an explosive orgasm.

"I think you may want to rethink my proposition," she said with a look of gratification glowing in her eyes. "Think about it: You can have all this." Her fingers slowly traced the enticing contours of her body. She crawled up next to him as Jovan eyed her with cautious intrigue.

Tina dug her manicured nails in his chest and drew her lips to his ear. "You can have me anytime. It'll be all yours."

Chapter 27

Lux Lounge is the place to be if you're a baller in D.C. Upstairs on the club's third level, an exclusive affair was underway for the area's infamous movers and shakers. D.C.'s underworld celebrities were on full blast for tonight's over-the-top all-white party.

The top floors of the club included the Double Platinum VIP Lounge.

Jovan came into the lounge just as brothers Dank and Psycho were leaving. Ray was flossing ultra-platinum style tonight. He had reserved seating in the coveted all-inclusive VIP section. This was the ultimate VIP setting within the VIP lounge, where only a select group flaunted their power and wealth with impressive disregard.

Jovan felt strong walking into the lounge with his iced Jacob jewels dripping from his neck and wrist in a dazzling display of flash. The crowd was captivated by his irresistible flair.

Ray waved him over to where he was standing.

Kanye West's "Power" had the crowd grooving all across the lounge.

Suddenly a dime caught Jovan's eye. She was a buxom bombshell with an Angelic face and a hellified body. Her name was Beauty. When she walked, Beauty was poetry in motion; she had a murderous strut and bounce that captivated the senses. Add to the mix her café'-au-lait skin tone, pearl-gray eyes and long blonde tresses—she was fire.

It wasn't long after Jovan had his sights set on the hot, ethereal Beauty that he plotted a course of action and moved in for the kill.

In no time, Jovan was kicked back on the sofa conversing with her.

On the surface, she was a fun-loving live wire. But underneath, she was a soft, innocent young woman fresh out of college, preparing to take on the world.

Beauty was unprepared for a man of Jovan's stature. She could sense off the bat this nigga was way out of her league. He was a seasoned baller. A "pro player" was the more appropriate slang she heard used to describe the rich and flamboyant hustlers and players. These were prolific philanderers with harems of girlfriends and groupies on the side. She watched him breathlessly.

"You're a player. My girls told me," Beauty said softly as she snuggled close under him. She wouldn't have dared gotten all coupled up with a man she didn't know, but Jovan was different.

He chuckled slightly. "Oh yeah? What your girls know about me?" he inquired, eyeing her.

Beauty was scantily clad, her cleavage practically spilling out of her tight gold sequin blouse. She nodded with an innocent, childlike expression. "Uh huh. They know you from Howard. The Towers dormitory. They said that you had, like, two or three girlfriends over there."

Jovan watched her, but said nothing. He decided instead to focus on the glass of bubbly in his other hand. He savored the expensive champagne for a moment before he lowered his head. His piercing gray orbs absorbed her loveliness. Jovan could sense Beauty's intense attraction for him.

"Small world," he breathed seductively in her ear. "What else your girls tell you about me?"

Beauty slowly raised her eyes. Well," she began, "they told me about all your cars and that you are, like, one of the best-dressed niggas around. I think they want you too because they made it a point to remind me of the saying."

He was amused by her innocence. He was really digging this pretty, young thang. "Tell me more. What's this saying you and your girls came up with?"

"Well," Beauty began, peering deep into his eyes, "the saying goes: Players only love you when they're playing games." She watched him, waiting for a reply.

Jovan struggled not to laugh. "What? C'mon now, baby girl. "Love"—that's a powerful word to be using in that sense, wouldn't you say? From the way I see it, looks like to me you need to do some thinking for your own self."

An odd look came across Beauty's face. She twisted her lips and said, "Like you know what love is. You know about living the high life and being a high roller."

Jovan smiled inwardly. "Baby girl, love is a state of mind. Love is that intense feeling shared between souls who have transcended the normal boundaries and made that in-depth spiritual connection together. Love is the action one makes to show that special soul how much they care about their well-being, their feelings, their worth." He hesitated, then added as an afterthought, "Always remember, love is what love does. Need I say more?"

He watched her closely. "It's obvious that I gotta passion for flashin', baby girl. But don't get it twisted—there's more to me than meets the eye. You fuck with me, Beauty, I'll show you how deep love can be."

Jovan lowered his head. He kissed her on the neck. A deep sigh escaped her lips, and she gripped his thigh with surprising strength. When their eyes made contact, it was like the first flush of attraction, intensely intoxicating.

"I wanna see you again after tonight," Beauty whispered.

"Why? I hope you're not like the rest of the women. Just want to get with me because of my money." He was playing with her head now. He wanted to see how Beauty's mind operated. Jovan finished by saying, "I just want to make sure if I get with you again, that you really want me just for me."

Beauty was startled by his remark. "Well, I'd be lying to you if I said I wasn't impressed by all your cars and your jewelry," she voiced, feeling awkward. "But you know like I know. I feel that chemistry. You know, I feel it just the same as you. So whatever happens …"

Her words were music to his ears. Jovan fell back and let his plan come to fruition. He watched Beauty get her drink on. And sure enough, after a few shots of Patron, she was good. She was zoned out.

As Jovan lead the drop-dead gorgeous Beauty through the crowd, he watched the bammas drool like they'd never seen a prime piece of ass before.

Outside, Jovan's glazed black Mercedes shimmered under the glow of the full moon as if the surface was wet.

The passenger seat was reclined as far as it could go. Beauty's long, shapely legs reached for the ceiling as Jovan struggled with his belt, trying to release the bulging mass in his pants.

"C'mon, Jovan, don't tease me like that," Beauty whined, her speech slurred.

"Don't worry, shorty," he said, "Daddy gonna take good care of that." Jovan beamed.

He gripped his dick firmly and worked the pulsating head inside her pussy. A mischievous grin parted Jovan's lips when Beauty shrieked at the top of her lungs, "Oh yeah, "Jovan murmured, salivating over the pussy. He tossed both her legs over his shoulders and locked them in place with a strong grip. Beauty's pudendum was exposed and vulnerable. Jovan licked his lips and thrust his manhood deep inside her, pounding the pussy into submission. He beat the pussy so good, he had Beauty's ass hitting falsetto notes so high, Mariah Carey would've been envious.

An hour later, the Benz coupe rolled in front of the club just as the crowds were coming out.

Jovan kissed Beauty good night and dropped her off at the curb. He smiled to himself as he watched Beauty move gingerly across the pavement and rejoin the small gathering of sorority sisters awaiting her arrival.

The black roadster leapt from the curb and sped off up 7th Street. The traffic was extremely light at this hour, so Jovan cruised, enjoying the wide-open road. He had a clear path up ahead, green signal lights were flashing as far as the eye could see.

When his cell phone rang, Jovan put the call on speaker. "Yeah, talk to me, baby. What can I do for you on this wonderful night?"

Malaysia replied quickly, "Jovan, baby, you alright? You don't sound like yourself. Do you need something, baby?"

"I'm good, precious," he spoke in a low drawl. "I was just out partying all night, that's all. I'm on my way home now."

Abruptly, Malaysia's tone changed. "Oh, you're on your way home? So you are okay. Not me. I'm laying alone in pain, baby." Malaysia's cool continence unraveled as she spoke. "But that don't mean nothing to you. You're on your way home to your wife, and I'm alone, trying to keep it together. But slowly, I feel myself falling apart."

The sound of her voice rattled Jovan. "Hold up," he voiced stoically, "Say no more, precious. Leave the front door unlocked and change into that Victoria's Secret thing I like." His confidence was surging.

"Why? So you can stop by and say good night to me on your way home?"

"'Cause I'm getting ready to rock that ass to sleep, that's why," he replied adamantly.

Jovan parked in front of the brownstone and stashed his bling in the console beside his chrome-plated Desert Eagle.

He bounced up the front steps, taking them two or three at a time. He was already feeling the tingle of anticipation before he laid eyes on his Thai prize that was awaiting him.

Malaysia's stomach started doing cartwheels as she watched Jovan step out his car from her bedroom window. She watched him race up the steps, then she rushed to her bedside and took a seat.

Jovan walked the length of the hallway like a panther anticipating a long-overdue meal. When he reached the doorway, he smiled to himself. It was already ajar, welcoming him in. He pushed the door, and it swung open. He paused in the doorway, allowing his eyes to adjust to the dimly lit room, and then he inhaled deeply. The air inside was laced with expensive perfume; the sweet aroma sent his insides into a frenzy.

Malaysia had exquisite taste; her bedroom was impeccably furnished with rich mahogany décor.

When Jovan stepped into the room, she glanced up in a bashful manner. Her soul was elated when she saw him cross the threshold of her private sanctuary. A broad smile crept across his lips when he laid eyes on the lovely sight before him.

He was like a kid in a candy store for the very first time as he feasted his eyes on her luscious physique. He loved the way Malaysia's soft emerald eyes were studying him with lust and adoration.

A Beautiful Satan

He moved across the carpeted floor. His eyes caressed her soft flesh. Malaysia's voice caught, and Jovan heard a sudden foreboding tone, a fear of expressing her true feelings. He could see it in her eyes. She wanted to tell him something. His reaction was purely compulsive. He cupped her chin in his right hand. His cologne penetrated her nostrils. She sighed heavily and closed her eyes.

"Precious, we can't erase what is meant to be." Jovan's endearing tone made her heart flutter. "We want to make this work, don't we? If that's the case, then we can't hide what we're feeling. I'm gonna let you in on a little secret: You have to teach a person how you want to be treated. Remember that."

Jovan placed a gentle kiss on Malaysia's forehead. She felt like he breathed love into the air as she floated off the bed and into his arms. She wrapped her arms around his neck and kissed him passionately.

She gazed into his eyes, loving the feel of his strong hands on her body as he embraced her with heated desire.

"Oooh baby, it feels so good to be in your arms," Malaysia wined, her voice startlingly sultry. "I'm really feeling you, baby. I mean, I'm really feeling you. I'm wanting you constantly, and I don't know what to do. You're still married, and I really don't need these kinds of complications in my life."

He watched her feelings waver as an uneasiness crossed his face. He nodded, wanting to comfort her. "Precious ..." Jovan paused, as though uncertain how to speak the next words. "Believe me when I say everything is gonna be alright. You just gotta let nature take its course."

"Jovan," Malaysia spoke up immediately. "You don't understand. You're not hearing me. I'm in love with you, and I don't play second base to nobody." Her voice sounded suddenly precarious.

With an awkward grunt, Jovan said as diplomatically as he could, "Okay, precious, I'm feeling you, and I don't expect you to play second base. I also don't want you to drift off back to heaven on me just yet either." He had to appease her conscience while at the same time stroke her femininity.

Malaysia couldn't help but smile. "Okay, baby," she sighed. "I'm gonna trust you on this. I hope you know what you're doing. Please don't take my heart and feelings for granted." She became calm and collected.

Jovan shot her a confused look and then quickly covered it. "I got you, you sexy, hot FBI agent." He tickled her playfully.

"I'm not with the FBI, silly," she giggled, nuzzling close to him. "But for you, darling, I'll be whatever your heart desires."

Jovan swept Malaysia off her feet and into his arms. She was pleasantly surprised by the move, tossing her arm around his neck, lust leaping from her emerald eyes.

"Whoa, baby," Malaysia breathed as a hot shiver of anticipation swept through her body. "I've been waiting for this moment for a long time."

"And, precious," Jovan voiced, sounding masculine and sexy, "your wait will be worth everything you hoped for. And then some."

ⓅⓅⓅⓅ

Jovan awoke, startled. He had no idea what had awakened him or how long he had been asleep. He slung his legs over the side of the bed. Standing in the nude, Jovan walked to the window and felt eyes on him. *Someone's watching me?*

The street below was dark and deserted. He watched, listening to the total stillness and silence outside. *Something's not right. I'm not getting these feelings for nothing.* Throughout the trials and tribulations of his life, Jovan learned long ago to believe his intuition. His intuition is what kept him from catching a lengthy prison bid in the past.

A Beautiful Satan

After a couple minutes standing at the window, Jovan didn't see anything outside worth seeing. *Maybe I was having a bad dream*, he told himself and pushed away from the window.

"Where you coming from?" Malaysia asked, half asleep, as Jovan crawled on top of her. "I was over at the window," he said, covering her neck with kisses. "I think I was having a bad dream. That's what got me out the bed."

"I see you're a hot-natured man." She smiled, squirming with excitement beneath him. She could feel his throbbing penis push hot and heavy against her thigh.

"Yeah," Jovan growled in her ear. "I'm hungry all the time."

Malaysia squealed, "Sounds to me like I got just what I've been searching for all these years." She reached down and grabbed hold of his engorged penis. "Whooo!" she gushed with glee. They could hardly contain themselves. Their steamy desire was that intense.

ⓦⓦⓦⓦ

On the deserted street outside, evil lurked in the shadows. A polished white Mercedes sedan appeared from the cloak of darkness. The expensive automobile's engine hummed just above a whisper as it crept stealthily along the quiet, dark street.

Inside, Natasha was livid. She trembled with rage as she peered up at the bedroom window. Her hands were shaking uncontrollably as she held her phone and snapped a picture of the brownstone. The sedan rolled to a stop alongside Jovan's vehicle and snapped another picture. Brimming with hate, Natasha slammed the phone on the seat. She became overwhelmed with emotion and began to cry out hysterically. She shifted the car into gear and mashed her foot on the gas, her tires screeching as she peeled out.

Chapter 28

A chilly arctic air mass had settled over the entire Northeastern corridor of the country. Local meteorologist predictions indicated that the severe cold front was showing no signs of moving out of the area for at least another week.

It wasn't fit for man on this unbearably cold Sunday night in the District. The street outside Malaysia's brownstone was totally devoid of life. The only thing moving outside were the bare tree branches and shrubbery shivering under the icy-cold assault of the wind.

The bone-chilling wind whipped across the barren landscape of Malaysia's home. Attached to the brown brick façade beside Ms. Tomay's mailbox, the thermometer displayed a teeth-chattering 8 degrees.

The house was dark except for a dim glow radiating from the window of the master bedroom upstairs. The interior of Malaysia's bedroom exuded a soothing ambiance. The smooth, comforting voice of Sade emanated from the speakers of a compact Bose sound system sitting atop the dark mahogany nightstand beside her stylish mahogany sleigh bed.

A Beautiful Satan

The bedroom was dimly lit by the soft glow of two flickering scented candles, one on top of nightstands on either side of the bed. Light spilled from the master bathroom across the gold Persian rug.

A soft, gentle voice drifted from the bath's enclosure, mingling with the lyrics to Sade's "Cherish the Day."

Malaysia's burgundy silk gown caressed the statuesque physique posing in the middle of the bathroom. A feeling of satisfaction filled her senses as she admired her sinuous figure in the full-length mirror. She barely recognized the woman staring back at her. Her face was covered with a thick mud mask and pink shower cap hiding the stunningly beautiful woman beneath all the synthetic gook.

"What we women put ourselves through to stay beautiful," she said. "Sometimes I have to ask myself if all this is even worth it." She answered immediately with a resounding, "Hell, yeah! Beauty takes work, and I don't mind one bit."

An important day loomed on the horizon for her tomorrow. She would be making her broadcasting debut on the local area newscast. There was no one more excited or proud of this defining moment in her life than she was. *Damn, how I wish my dad could've been here to see my major accomplishment.*

Downstairs in the kitchen, she was greedily rummaging through the shelves of the double-door refrigerator, searching for something sweet to much on. Anything sweet.

Her search yielded no goodies. She pushed the refrigerator's doors shut. When she whirled around, she saw the lazy Susan across the kitchen, right next to the smoked-glass dishwasher. The sight of the cabinet jarred her memory. *The goody cabinet! Yessss!*

The mud-faced beauty was crouched over spinning the shelves, fumbling through its contents. Suddenly she heard what sounded like muffled voices.

Startled, she jumped, striking her head hard against the silverware drawer that was poking out just above her.

"Ouch! Shit!" she cursed loudly, holding her head with her hand as she stood. She hesitated for a moment and listened. Her eyes blinked wide with fright when she heard the voices whispering again. They seemed to be coming from the basement.

That can't be, she thought as she moved across the black tiled floor toward the basement door. She pressed her ear to the door, and her mud-covered face frowned when she heard nothing but silence.

She unlocked the bolt, turned the knob and pulled the door open slowly. The door creaked as it opened. The unnerving sound caused her to cringe, and a sudden rash of goose bumps broke out all along her arms and legs.

As she peered down the basement stairs, a strong aura of stillness and silence radiated from the dark depths below. The stairs seem to disappear into a ominous black space. The dark view gave her the creeps.

"Hello? Anybody down there?" She felt stupid calling out from the top of the stairs. She began to reason with herself, *If there really were intruders down there, like they really were gonna just come out of hiding to greet me.* Well, if someone was in the basement, she would need some protection. She hurried over to the knife rack and drew out a sizeable blade, something befitting the likes of Jason from the horror movie "Friday the 13th."

She flipped on the light switch and groaned in anguish. The dim light below was hardly enough; it struggled to hold its own against the darkness.

Gripping the blade firmly, she descended the stairs cautiously. She was on heightened alert for any movement or sound.

When she reached the basement landing, a frosty breeze swept across her skin, causing her to shiver uncontrollably.

A Beautiful Satan

"Oh no," she gasped, rubbing her arms in an attempt to warm them. "There's a window open down here." Her eyes made a quick security scan of the area and noticed the big moving boxes and crates that were stacked in different areas around the basement, reaching halfway to the ceiling.

"All these unpacked boxes. No wonder it's so dark down here," she told herself as she watched her warm breath turn to fog right before her eyes.

She proceeded to move carefully across the concrete floor, brandishing the blade before her like it held some mystical power.

Halfway across the floor, she heard something shuffle to her left. She froze in place. The towering wall of cardboard blocked her view.

She wrapped both hands tightly around the handle of the knife. "Who's there?" she yelled. "I'm armed, so you better get out of here. I'm not going to tell you again." Slowly, she moved toward the stairs while keeping her eyes, ears and the large shimmering blade trained on the wall of cardboard boxes to her left.

Then it happened. The lights went out. She was surrounded by total darkness. Her mind and body went numb. Her fear of the dark suddenly imploded on her. She wanted to turn and run, but her mind and body had collapsed. She was paralyzed with fear, unable to speak or move. She heard movement again. This time the sound was more pronounced, and she could tell it came from close by, on the opposite side of the cardboard wall.

"Oh my God," she mouthed silently, holding her breath. She could hear the person breathing behind the wall.

Without warning, the wall came crashing down on top of her. The Thai woman went into a panic-stricken fit and screamed. Cursing in horror, she began kicking, pushing, and tossing boxes aside with surprising strength and agility as her adrenaline spiked off the charts.

The last two boxes went tumbling to the side, and she scrambled to get her footing. Just as she was getting her bearings, a blinding ray of light struck her in the face. She stood dumbfounded, looking like a deer caught in headlights.

"Fucking freak!" a crazed-sounding woman spat angrily from behind a bright flashlight.

The eyes behind the mud mask squinted, straining hard to see who this foolish woman was that had burglarized the property. She must be some desperate drug addict looking for a score.

"Freak?" the Thai woman muttered, her confidence rising now that she knew the person she was confronting was of lesser status. With her hands propped defiantly on her hips, she went on to say, "What in the hell do you think—" She was abruptly cut off mid-sentence.

She felt a jarring pain explode down the center of her head and stumbled backward, her back smacking violently against the wall. Red and white stars exploded across her eyes. She was dazed and confused, and her only thought was: *This crazy bitch attacked me!*

The sound of sliding boxes sent waves of fear down her spine. She knew she had to get out of there. With the room spinning out of control, she grabbed hold of the wooden banister and hoisted herself up the stairs.

"Where you running to, slut? Can't nobody save your ass!" Natasha shouted after her.

She hesitated and looked back. Her heart dropped with a thud when she caught a glimpse of the eyes from hell. She turned and bolted to the top of the stairs. When she reached the kitchen landing, the demented woman screamed, "Bitch, you're mine! God can't even save your ass!!!"

She slammed the door not a second too soon. Natasha hurled a machete through the air with unnatural strength. The sharp blade pierced the wooden door like a hunter's spear, protruding six inches through the frame. The Thai model stared in shock as she realized the deadly blade came within an inch of ending her life. The crazy woman's words echoed in her head: "Bitch you're mine!!!" She quickly bolted the lock and then ran to the front door.

A look of sheer panic leaped across her face when she realized the dead bolt was locked and the key was missing.

The basement door rocked violently, rattling her already frayed nerves. She stood in the deserted foyer with her heart racing and her mind unraveling. A wave of nausea suddenly struck her. She clutched her stomach, doubling over in pain.

"Lord, help me," she cried out, grabbing her forehead. The sight of blood and mud smeared on her flesh horrified her. "No!!!" she screamed.

Thunder echoed from the kitchen, spurring her to move. She staggered through the vaulted archway leading toward the stairs. She lunged for the dark oak banister and heaved herself up the carpeted stairs.

The injured beauty queen collapsed in a heap at the top of the staircase. The sudden sound of the basement door crashing open resonated up the staircase.

She lay in shock, struggling through the pain. *Oh my God! She's coming!* She crawled down the hall toward the nearest open door.

Clad in a black skully, black hoodie, black sweats, black Timberlands and black gloves, Natasha looked menacing as she held a black crowbar in one hand and the glistening machete in the other. She was death coming to claim its next soul.

She stood at the top of the stairs scanning the long cavernous hallway, searching for her victim. Natasha's voice spoke chillingly, "Hey, Malaysia … I'm here to kill you, bitch!"

The sound of the crazed woman's voice made the Thai model tremble to the core. She froze for a moment on her hands and knees, then curled up in a fetal position inside a closet.

Like an evil spirit, Natasha drifted silently through the hallway.

"Why did you run from me?" Her voice was ominous. A dark silhouette appeared in the doorway and stared into the dark, cluttered interior. "All you've done is made your death that much more painful ... 'cause bitches that fuck married men don't deserve life."

The Thai beauty was terrified as she stared into the eyes of death. "No!" she declared through tear-flooded eyes. "What are you saying?"

"You're not only a freak, you're a lying whore!" Natasha hissed venomously, and brought her booted foot down on the woman's head. She stomped her unmercifully, crushing her nose and lips. When she finished, the woman's face was a gory mess of blood and mud.

While her victim lay in a daze, Natasha produced a transparent plastic bag from her pocket. She shoved the bag over her victim's head and dragged her kicking and choking out of the closet. She flopped down on the floor in the middle of the room, straining with both hands to hold the bag over the woman's head as she kicked and tussled with all her might.

Damn! This bitch won't give! Natasha said as she fought with every fiber in her to hold on to the bag. Her victim continued to kick, claw and twist all over the floor. Natasha managed to hold the bag over her head while she pulled the struggling woman between her legs, wrapping them around her body to weigh her down.

After putting up a helluva fight, her body and soul finally submitted.

"Fucking bitch!" Natasha spat, out of breath. She glared at the dead woman's petrified face. The light had faded from her warm brown eyes, which were wide open, frozen in the grip of death.

Natasha rose to her feet in a trance. Her cold eyes were lifeless. Her movements seemed mechanical as she gripped the handle of the machete laying beside the closet door.

A Beautiful Satan

She lugged the corpse across the cream carpet, and propped the body nicely against the side of a black wrought-iron bed. She placed the machete on the raspberry comforter, kneeled beside the body to tie a particular knot in the plastic sheath covering. Her movements were slow and meticulous.

Natasha placed a hand on the dead woman's forehead, bowed and began to mumble fast and furiously under her breath.

The bizarre ritual was brief. The eerie séance ceased, and Natasha's head rose suddenly. Her apparent exhilaration had worn off, but the lurid craving had returned.

Her head was pounding, tiny voices playing a tug-of-war inside her mind. The muscles in her neck pulsated with rage. She needed to appease the voices. Her eyes glittered dangerously as she rose slowly to her feet. Natasha snatched the machete off the bed. "Whore!" she screamed suddenly, her voice simmering with rage. She gripped the plastic sheath with her left hand while her right hand brought the machete down in a powerful swooping arc, beheading the corpse with a single swing of the blade.

Then suddenly, like a crowd dispersed by a single shot, the voices in her head were gone.

Chapter 29

Malaysia arrived home early Monday morning after spending an erotic, sex-filled weekend with Jovan at The Gaylord, a swanky resort just across the Potomac.

When she stepped through the front door, she knew instantly something was terribly wrong. She sat her black overnight Coach bag at her feet.

"Mariah," Malaysia called out for her sister. "You still here?" Silence greeted her. She pushed the front door shut and locked the bottom lock. There was an uncomfortable coldness in the air, which she noticed right away, and she didn't like it. She looked around, grabbed the Coach bag off the floor and headed upstairs.

Malaysia hesitated when she reached the top of the stairs. Her instincts rattled. She sensed a caustic presence radiating along the empty corridor. Reaching inside her Coach bag, she retrieved her Glock-21.

Brandishing the pistol, Malaysia proceeded with caution. As she approached the open doorway to the first bedroom, her eyes began to squint. She noticed a number of

A Beautiful Satan

dark splotches scattered on the carpet just outside the bedroom.

"What's this on my rug?" Malaysia mumbled. She stepped in the doorway. The grisly sight inside rocked her body like a hard blow to the gut, knocking the wind out of her. She dropped the bag and staggered backwards, her eyes glassy and filled with tears. An indecipherable wail of pain and agony erupted from the deepest core of her being.

****

Malaysia Tomay, despite working in law enforcement, had never found herself in such a predicament. It was utterly incomprehensible to her sane mind how such a draconian act of violence was inflicted upon her younger sister, Mariah, especially at this milestone juncture in her young life. She had just received her graduate degree in broadcasting from Howard University. Today was to be her broadcast news debut. But instead of reporting the current events of the day, Mariah's brutal murder was the top story on every area newscast.

Malaysia couldn't for the life of her imagine who or what would want to bring harm to either her or Mariah. Although Malaysia's career was in law enforcement, she had never been put in a position to draw her gun on anyone.

Looking totally withdrawn, Malaysia sat in the living room on her chaise lounge in front of the warm fireplace. She was wrapped in her leather coat, arms folded, holding herself. She rocked back and forth, gazing into the fire.

One of Malaysia's co-workers, a dirty blonde by the name of Susan, walked over and sat down beside her. She hugged Malaysia, consoling her very distraught friend. "Everything will be okay. You just have to keep it together," Susan said.

Malaysia shook her head vigorously. "No, it's not, Sue," she replied, her voice filled with pain. "It'll never be okay. They took my baby sister from me. They did more than just take her life. They left me a headless corpse to bury. Where I'm from that's a grave travesty against the deceased. Her soul resides in limbo now. My sister can't rest in harmony with a partial burial. Unless I find her head, Mariah's soul will forever be banished into purgatory." Her dark emerald irises brimmed painfully with tears as she fought to control her emotions. A vision of her sister's decapitated body propped leisurely against the side of the bed flashed in Malaysia's mind. She broke down and dropped to her knees, hunched over the sofa like she was preparing to pray. With pain and agony etched deep in her face, Malaysia cried out for Mariah.

D.C. homicide cops swarmed the brownstone, scouring the crime scene for evidence. This case was labeled top priority for the department. Not only had the killer encroached upon the life of a fellow colleague, but the killer's barbarous act of decapitation sent a wave of panic throughout the city. The citizens of Washington and its surrounding jurisdictions were on edge, and they were demanding answers to why the public had not been put on alert concerning a dangerous serial predator walking the streets.

Those in the loop could feel the pressure. D.C.'s mayor and the chief of police were in an uproar and demanded answers. A rumor that was circulating at police headquarters claimed a list of names was floating around, hinting that whoever's name was on the list was headed for the chopping block.

Something had to be done soon. The serial predator had become more brazen and dastardly with his acts of violence. The situation had moved beyond the urgency stage. Homicide was in dire need of a major break in the case or a viable suspect, and the Dynamic Duo was in panic mode.

Chapter 30

It was sometime around noon when sunlight was finally able to break through the overcast. The clouds had been lingering for the past few days, causing a cold and dreary funk in the region. The sudden appearance of the sun's brilliant rays cascading from the heavens was a welcoming sight, especially along the clogged traffic-jammed artery of Georgia Avenue.

The rush-hour traffic commenced on Georgia Avenue just beyond the city limits in Silver Spring, Maryland. This was the norm for this heavily traveled gateway leading into the upper northwest section of the city, referred to by Washingtonians as "Uptown."

The lunchtime rush had a tendency to make drivers edgier than any other rush hour. This was probably due to the small amount of time most workers were allotted for their lunch break and the daunting task of traveling to their desired lunch destination and back before time expired.

No wonder why at this time of the day a number of Fourth District police cruisers had taken up position at different intervals along Georgia Avenue. Officers needing to make ticket quota for the month were apt to gravitate to this busy road, posting up anywhere, from the front gates of Walter Reed Army Medical Center to thirty-something blocks away at the intersection of Georgia and Florida to just beyond the entrance to Howard University Hospital.

The man at the helm of a black Dodge Charger sped along Georgia Avenue into the District without a care. The swarthy-looking muscle car dipped from left to right, cutting fellow drivers off with no regard for his or anyone else's safety.

The hefty green-eyed driver with the black Redskins fitted cap cocked to the side was doing him. At a glance you could see the bamma Mike toking on a fat blunt of Purple. The car swayed in rhythm to Rick Ross' "Spendin' Money Fast." Mike was bobbin' his head and pumpin' his foot on the accelerator in rhythm to the beat.

He was in a groove, flowing down the avenue without a worry in the world until he spotted the first cruiser pulled over with a traffic violator. The short uniformed officer was busy scribbling on his citation pad. Mike pumped the brakes twice as he passed.

Then he stomped on the gas pedal. The Charger responded instantly, the low-profile tires gripping the black asphalt and propelling the vehicle along the road like a rocket on wheels.

At the intersection of Georgia and Missouri, the traffic signal flashed. Mike had the Charger boucin', and the lane ahead was clear. He watched the light turn red, and then he punched it.

The muscle car roared through the intersection. Fat Mike was grinning from ear to ear as he gripped the wheel. His expression turned grim when flashing lights exploded across the rearview mirror. "Mutha-fuck!" he groaned. Slowing down, he tossed the smoking blunt of weed out of the passenger window before pulling to a stop directly opposite the rolling grass hills of Emery Park.

A Beautiful Satan

Surprise registered on Mike's chubby face when a petite chocolate honey with long braids and dark lip gloss atop a set of luscious lips appeared at his window. Mike went giddy over the hot-looking police woman.

He lowered the window just enough for her to see a pair of red-tinted bug-looking eyes gazing at her. He slouched heavily behind the wheel, trying to look cool. "Hey there, miss lady. How can I help you today?" He was trying hard to sound smooth but was faltering badly.

She lowered the dark shades from her eyes. "Excuse me, sir," she voiced with an attitude, her index finger tapping the gold nameplate pinned to her uniform. "My name is Officer McPhee. You can save your comments because I'm not for the games. You ran a red light back there. I need to see your license and registration."

Mike smirked. "Oh, it's like that, huh?" He flipped down the visor. "Here you are, Ms. Police Lady," he complied, rolling his eyes. "I was gonna treat you to a steak dinner at Ruth Chris, but you blew that now."

"Sir, is that marijuana I'm detecting in your car?" she questioned after taking his credentials. Officer McPhee eyed him skeptically before walking away.

As soon as she left, Mike popped a handful of Ice Breaker mints in his mouth. He then adjusted the driver's side mirror so he could keep a close eye on what the police broad was up to. Mike had to do some quick thinking. He was riding dirty and couldn't afford to get hemmed up on some bullshit. Besides, he was already out on one felony bond in D.C. and another bond out in Maryland. One more charge would put him out of commission.

Mike was getting antsy. His leg trembled on the accelerator pedal as he peered at the mirror. *Like I'm gonna tell you, Yeah bitch, I just finished puffin'. Dumb bitch!*

The whites of Mike's eyes expanded suddenly when he watched another police cruiser roll up. Instinctively, his hand gripped the gear shift. He cringed as the cruiser drove by and eased into the empty space in front of the Charger. Mike cursed himself silently for not seeing this coming. He felt sick all of a sudden.

Usually backup arriving was an indication that authorities had more in store than just a written citation.

A black Incredible Hulk-looking cat emerged from the red, white and blue police cruiser. He shot Mike a hard mug as he moved toward him. A wave of panic struck him as the mountain-sized man stopped and hovered outside his window. He felt as if a dark cloud had settled over him.

The gold nameplate on the Hulk's uniform read Officer Davis. Mike smiled slightly and asked, "Is there a problem, Officer Davis?"

Davis held his eyes on Mike until the smaller man dropped his eyes. "Yeah, buddy, you gotta big-ass problem," he said in a hostile tone. More cruisers arrived on the scene.

"Man, what's going on? What's this all about?" Mike asked the officer.

Davis snatched open the door and drew his service weapon. "Put your hands in the air and step out of the vehicle, slowly," he ordered.

He pushed Mike's heavy frame against the side of the car and kicked his legs wide. "You know the drill. Spread 'em!" he said, holstering his service weapon. He began to frisk the suspect.

"Hey, look what I found," Officer McPhee called out from the passenger seat. She pulled a fully loaded P-94 gun from the glove compartment and held the pistol in the air. "Might get lucky and find some one-eight-sevens on it," she said with a hopeful look.

Davis grabbed Mike's arm and twisted it behind his back until he had to stand on his tiptoes. He put his lips an inch from the suspect's ear and asked with ice in his voice, "So what's the deal with the burner? I know you ain't dumb enough to roll around with the murder weapon from that triple over in the Farms. Then again, your ass might be that dumb."

A Beautiful Satan

He yanked him off the car and pushed him toward his cruiser. "You are under arrest for weapons violation, buddy. That's just for starters. Homicide would like to have a few words with you. That's okay with you, isn't it?" Davis chuckled loudly.

Mike was transported a couple blocks north on Georgia Ave. to the Fourth District police station. He was charged with a weapons violation and booked into the system.

For the next hour Mike spent his time pacing back and forth in a four-by-six steel gray box. His eyes roamed the cell walls reading the jailhouse scriptures of those who were there before him. For a second Mike thought about adding his name and a few words to the wall's history until he remembered what an old head had warned: "Write on a jailhouse wall, you're sure to come back and read those same words one day." The thought repulsed him and eventually drifted from his mind.

A raspy voice yelled aloud, "Mike Lewis! Your ride's here. You're going downtown to meet with the big dawgs."

The thought of going downtown filled Mike with apprehension. Police headquarters was a place reserved for the most serious offenders. They had nothing on him that would warrant a ride downtown. *The gat they confiscated was clean, so what are they trying to pull? That cop Davis mentioned Barry Farms. But shit, they can't tie me to that joint,* he tried to convince himself.

Mike flopped his rear end on the cold steel bench. *Or can they?* he silently questioned, heaving a frustrated sigh before burying his face in his hands.

The interrogation room was empty, except for a wooden table with a black ashtray in the center. There were two matching chairs. The office space was spotless, and the mirror on the wall looked freshly polished.

The heavy oak door opened abruptly. Detective Clark stepped in the room. The air inside was cool, as expected.

"C'mon in here," Clark waved Mike in.

Mike's hefty frame slinked through the doorway. He looked timidly around the room. "I dunno what you think you doing by bringing me down here," he muttered with a withering look. "But you're wasting your time." Before Mike sat down, he stuffed the bottom of his navy We R One hoodie in his pants and pulled the deep hood over his head, covering his ears.

Clark unloaded his trench and slung it over the back of the chair. "Have a seat there," he ordered. "I'll be the judge on whether or not someone's time gets wasted." A creaking sound echoed around the room when Clark propped his wide buttocks on the table's edge. He retrieved a fresh pack of Newports from his shirt pocket. The cancer sticks were nothing but interrogations props used as an icebreaker, a way to calm the suspects' nerves right before detectives pounced on them with their psychological barrage of questions.

Interrogations were the only time Clark would dare light up a cigarette. He quit the disgusting habit more than ten years ago.

Clark offered politely, "Here, wanna smoke? Go 'head, take a few of them. I know how these situations can weigh on a person's nerves," he said with a fake smile, fishing a lighter from his pants pocket. Clark waited. He watched Mike light up and take a few puffs on the cancer stick. The suspect leaned back in his seat, making himself comfortable.

"Well, Mike, why don't you tell me what part you played in that triple shooting over there in the Barry Farms project? You were there, right?" A raised eyebrow accompanied Clark's insinuating question. Mike thought long and hard.

"Hold on," he said flicking the ash. "You think I played a part in a triple murder?"

A Beautiful Satan

Clark folded his arms across his chest, glaring with a look of disdain. "I didn't say anything about any triple homicide. I said triple shooting."

"Triple shooting, triple murder. What's the difference? They both the same to me, and I ain't got shit to do with either one," he said nervously.

Clark leaned over. "If that's the case, Mike," he said gritting his teeth, "then why are you riding around in the getaway car? A heavy-set male was identified driving the getaway vehicle. You know how this is looking for you right about now?" He paused to examine the effects of his words on the suspect.

Mike sat stone-faced. "I don't know what you talking about. Ain't nobody see me nowhere. Your full of shit."

The detective surprised him. "Look at me, " he said, palming the back of his head so they were eye to eye. "We know you were there. We know you were the getaway driver. We don't really give a fuck about the getaway driver. You're the small fry. We've got bigger fish to fry. I want the two shooters. Who are they, and where can we find 'em?"

Three hours into the interrogation, Mike was tired and his nerves were shot. He was struggling to hold strong. So far, so good. But the detectives weren't letting up; they continued to put the press on.

Detective Louis worked his angle by playing the good cop role. "Now, Mike, you know we're offering you a free pass on this. Our main objective is to get the killers off the street," he said casually, circling the table while flipping through Mike's rap sheet. Then something caught his eye. The detective changed gears suddenly. "Hey, I see you got a big drug trial coming up soon in Prince George's County."

Mike groaned and shook his head.

"A kilogram of cocaine, huh?" Louis uttered, eyeing him suspiciously. "So you aren't the small fry after all. Or is that what you're trying to portray?" he asked in a condescending manner. "Hey!" Louis shouted, then paused in mid-step. "Ray Leone was on this charge with you? You cut him loose? Damn, Mike, how much you get paid for being the fall guy?"

At the mention of Ray Leone, Louis saw that Mike was visibly shaken. He continued reading. "What do we have here?" he grinned, tapping his chin. "You were transporting in a gold BMW. Well, I'll be damn. What a fucking coincidence ... a BMW was seen fleeing the scene of the shooting." Louis tossed the folder on the table. Fat boy's ass was in a tight squeeze now, his bubble ready to burst. Louis walked around the table and kneeled beside Mike.

Louis rested a hand on Mike's shoulder. His composure faded. "Listen here, Mike. We know you weren't the trigger man. I'm not saying Ray was the trigger man either. I know that's highly unlikely. He rarely gets his hands dirty. But what I need from you is for you to fill in the blanks. There were two shooters, and two people were seen fleeing the scene in that BMW. That's four blanks that I need filled. You help me out, and I'll see what kind of strings I can pull out there in Maryland on your behalf." Louis' comment was a thin veneer for the truth.

The earnest concern in his eyes felt like the warmth of a father. Mike rubbed his head in frustration. He trembled, wringing his hands together. He hated himself for what he was about to do. His life would change from this day forward.

Chapter 31

Seated on the leather sofa in front of the fireplace, Jovan sipped bubbly and ate Oysters Rockefeller, feeling the intoxicating effects of alcohol permeate his senses.

The sounds of Maxwell greeted Angel as she walked through the front door. She beamed when she entered the family room, which was basking in the glow of soft candlelight.

"How is my lovely Angel this evening?" Jovan asked smoothly, standing. He looked suave in his black Prada suit. "Come over here, precious, and show your Daddy some love." He spread his arms wide, welcoming her.

Angel dropped her Nordstrom shopping bags at her feet. When her man beckoned for her, she could not resist. No matter what discord they may be experiencing, Angel had a profound weakness for Jovan. All he had to do was shower her with a little love and affection and her head would be floating in the clouds.

Angel melted in Jovan's arms. She gazed up at him. "This is such a romantic setting," she voiced softly, taking in the enticing arrangement of tasty aphrodisiacs displayed on the gold marble coffee table. "I was beginning to wonder how long it would be before this man right here decided to show up again. He needs to show up a bit more often, wouldn't you say?"

"I know, precious. There's a lot that I need to be doing that I've been slacking on," Jovan said, then kissed her sweetly. "Why don't you have a seat on the sofa? I've got a surprise for you."

This moment seems surreal, Angel thought as she draped her Bebe shearling across the ottoman. She was sensual and chic; her tan-colored suede dress hugged her curves with a sensational effect.

She took a seat and began to sample the Oysters Rockefeller, Oyster Royal and the oyster bisque. Angel was feeling this. *That's the man I married right there,* she silently told herself, leaning back with a glass of pink champagne. *This is how every evening is supposed to be.*

Jovan appeared behind the sofa and smiled down on his wife. "Look what I have for my baby," he said lovingly. The necklace he produced and placed around her neck was laden with quarter-carat rocks.

Angel couldn't believe her husband. Jovan was so unpredictable. Just one of the many traits that made him so attractive, she conceded. Angel was tickled pink, her eyes dancing jubilantly as she hopped up and rushed around the sofa to show her appreciation.

"Thank you," she said with a hot, passionate kiss. "This necklace is beautiful!" she expressed with heartfelt emotions.

Moments later the sound of R. Kelly breezed through the room, and emotions escalated. Jovan and Angel melded into a sensually erotic dance, intertwined in a salacious mating ritual.

"Step, step, side to side ... everybody do the love slide ..." The song "Step In the Name of Love" set the tone for the remainder of the evening.

A Beautiful Satan

For a week straight, Jovan remained monogamous. It was a major task, no doubt. But he deserved an "A" for effort, if nothing else.

He sat on the edge of the bed and took her by the hand. "Angel, I love you, and I want nothing more than for our life together to work. It's not gonna be easy, I know. But that's what I want."

Angel sighed but remained quiet. She came to the conclusion long ago that Jovan's mind is a divided one. He craves his wife and home life one minute; he craves the streets and its whores the next.

She smiled, covering his hand with hers. "I love you too. You know that, and there is nothing more in this world that I want more than to make it work with you. You have to make the choice. You know what you're doing, so it's up to you. It's not who you are underneath, it's what you do that defines you."

Jovan looked at his wife with love in his eyes. At that moment, nothing else mattered. This was his world right now. He knew within himself he was a man divided. What he craved one minute, he rejected the next. He wanted to do right by his wife, he truly did. But when his urges got the better of him, all rationale went out the window.

Angel kept a close eye on him. She knew it was only a matter of time before Jovan dipped out, so she figured she might as well make the best of this time they were having together. Because there was no telling when it would all come to an end.

Chapter 32

It had been more than a week since Ray got the call tipping him off there was a snitch in his crew. He had retired to his ritzy Potomac estate, seeking refuge and peace of mind as he devised a plan of action to counteract the unexpected revelation.

The wintry gray sky darkened as Jovan climbed out of his Benz truck. He saw Dank hand Ray a pistol. He shoved the gun down in his waistband, turned and trotted up the concrete steps and disappeared through the smoked-glass entrance.

"Move your ass now!" Psycho yelled, and put a foot up Fat Mike's ass. "Bitch-ass nigga! Get your ass up them steps!" he commanded. Mike shot him a harsh look, like he wanted to buck. Psycho reached for his burner. Fat boy turned and dragged his feet up the steps.

Jovan reached across the seat. He wore a heavy white leather jacket with the Washington Redskins logos embroidered all over the back and sleeves. He pulled his matching leather cap low, just above his eyes, before heading inside to find out what was going on with Fat Mike.

A Beautiful Satan

Jovan stood in the vacant marble foyer, listening. He heard voices drifting from the stairwell leading to the lower level and the pool house.

Ray strolled into the room, his hands waving in the air clutching an aluminum Louisville Slugger.

"But Ray ..." Mike began.

Ray shot him a piercing look, and he immediately shut up.

His body stiffened, preparing for the blow.

Ray had a crazed look in his eyes. "Fucking rat!" he growled, and slammed a hard blow to Mike's chest.

Jovan stopped abruptly and cringed. He watched the fat boy cry out like a wounded puppy. Dank bellowed with laughter at the top of his lungs as Mike stumbled backwards and tripped over a lounge chair. All 300-plus pounds smacked hard against the floor.

"You son of a bitch!" Ray spat heatedly. "I lay down my life for this shit, nigga! I breathed life into your ass, muthafucka! And this is how you repay me?!"

Jovan walked into the pool house. The air was full of menace. Ray, Psycho and Dank watched him silently as he strolled across the floor with his hands in his jacket pocket. He stopped. His sharp eyes covered all the men in the room. "Who this nigga snitch on?" he asked, glaring at the hurt man.

"My crew," Ray sneered.

"Your crew," Jovan retorted sharply, his mind reeling. "You mention my name, nigga?" He stared at Mike, his contempt for the snitch was barely concealed.

Mike rose to a sitting position, groaning in pain. "Nah, man," he stammered weakly. "I ain't do nothing like that."

Ray's face distorted with a heated look. "You can't believe shit that fat fucker says." He threw him a murderous look. "I got the lowdown on everything."

Fat Mike hauled his heavy 300-plus ass off the floor.

Psycho suddenly became furious. "You ready for me to squash this fat piece of shit?" he asked with a smug grin, drawing a .50 caliber from the small of his back. He rushed Mike. "How you want it?" he asked, raising the gun. Psycho placed the hammer at the base of his skull.

"Yeah, that's it!" Dank smiled coldly. "Blow his fucking head off!" He laughed ruthlessly.

There was no humor on Psycho's face. His finger was poised on the trigger. Mike was shivering visibly, his eyes full of unconcealed pain. Ray made his familiar gesture of impatience. His hand cut down with a swift, chopping motion. His eyes glittered dangerously.

A twisted smile rolled across Psycho's lips as he nodded. He turned to Mike with a demented look in his eye.

"C'mon, J." Ray whirled on his heels. "Let's go up and have a drink. We can talk business while the brothers have their fun."

Mike looked to Jovan. He was pleading silently.

Jovan hesitated briefly, then fell in step behind Ray. Fat boy had made his bed, now he had to lay in it. Wasn't nothing he could do. Snitches got their shit pushed back. That was an unwritten rule.

When they got to the top of the staircase, three consecutive gunshots rang out from the pool house.

Ray gloated happily. "Hey," he began, throwing his arm around Jovan's shoulder, "you and me cut from the same cloth," he said, smiling. "I lay down my life for this shit. And so do you."

Jovan managed a smile, and they both laughed good-naturedly. He felt his strength, his conviction and his faith were being tested at the moment.

Four Hours Later...

A polished white Mercedes Benz rolled off the beltway exit ramp, veered right, then cut across four lanes of traffic like a bat out of hell.

Natasha kept driving, cursing the entire length of Wisconsin Avenue as she fumbled with her laptop. She tapped in her access code and up popped a D.C. street map and the surrounding jurisdictions. She punched in a few more keys and the GPS recalibrated. A satisfied expression appeared on her face. She could now see the exact location of Jovan's vehicle.

Inside the seductive confines of the exclusive Paramour Bar and Grill, behind a sheer silk veil of a coveted VIP booth, Malaysia's captivating emerald eyes twinkled in the candlelight as she spoke.

Jovan sat feasting on her loveliness with his eyes. She was a vision of carnal pleasure, and he couldn't get enough of her.

Malaysia glanced at Jovan, uncertain whether he was really listening to her pour out her feelings about her sister's murder or if he was daydreaming.

"Is there something on your mind that you'd like to say to me?" she asked smartly.

"I would love to," Jovan said. The moment he spoke he realized his mistake.

The lines in Malaysia's brow grew deep. "You mean to tell me that you haven't heard a word I was saying about my sister's murder?" Her eyes narrowed sharply.

Jovan offered an easy smile. "Precious, c'mon now, I deserve more credit than that. Of course I'm listening to you. And I'm so sorry about the tragedy involving your sister."
He drew close, gently he took her hand and lowered his head. "I just wanna do whatever you need to help soothe you and take away the pain that you're feeling." Jovan moved his lips to the nape of her neck, breathing heavily. He kissed her. "Whatever you need for me to do," he whispered, "just say the word and it's done."

"Anything?" she breathily whispered in his ear.

"Whatever your heart desires," he said, placing a trail of kisses along the crease of her exposed bosom.

"I wanna have your baby." She smiled devilishly. "You said anything. So let's have a little girl. We can name her Mariah, after my sister. That would mean the world to me." Malaysia caressed the back of Jovan's head, caringly stroking his head and neck in an attempt to stroke his male ego.

After the word "baby," Malaysia might as well have been wasting her breath. The air was ridiculously hot all of a sudden. His vision was blurred, but he quickly brought it back in focus.

Jovan exhaled and forced a balmy smile. He tried to swallow but couldn't. "You want a baby?" he managed to say evenly. "Right now?"

"Why wait?" she replied frankly. "We've already committed to being together. And that would make your precious so happy." Malaysia batted her eyes and smiled.

Her mega-watt smile touched his heart. *But a baby? She's going overboard with that.* Jovan's slick persona kicked into gear.

"Precious, I would love for us to have a baby. That would be wonderful," he said as quietly and collected as he could. "But I don't want to complicate your life. Baby, I'm still married."

Malaysia's jubilation waned when he mentioned the "M" word. She countered by softly outlining his lips with her forefinger. "I've given you the most precious gift that I can give to a man: my heart and my body. Baby, I expressed this clearly to you once we took that step to consummate our souls as one. Once we crossed that threshold, which we've done, under the laws and religion for which my life abides, we are now bound as one. You betray me now, you will be breaking a universal law." She hesitated. Her expression grew dark. "The consequences and repercussions behind an act of betrayal would be disastrous for all parties involved."

A Beautiful Satan

The look in Malaysia's eyes and the cryptic tone in her voice aroused a sudden and unexpected wariness deep inside Jovan.

He chose his words carefully. "I understand that, precious. But the fact still remains: My present situation hasn't changed yet." Jovan eased his arm around her. Malaysia was stiff with unconcealed anger. "But it'll be coming to a close soon," he said smoothly, trying to muster confidence in his words. His free hand disappeared inside his white leather jacket, which lay on the seat beside him. "I got a surprise for you. You want it now or later?"

Malaysia smirked, then made an impatient gesture. Jovan's hand appeared before her eyes. When he released his hold, a string of glittering rocks dangled in front of her. It was the identical necklace he had given Angel last week. Instantly, he could feel the tension in her body subside.

"Thank you, love," she said quietly, as Jovan strung the exquisite piece around her neck. "This is a lovely necklace," she added, admiring the jewelry. "But it does little to change how I'm feeling."

Her response made Jovan grimace. "Then perhaps we could indulge in something that would be more fulfilling for the both of us. You look pretty thirsty, baby." He grinned mischievously. "Why don't you quench your body's thirst with a drink of me." His lewd gesture brought a vision to his mind of Malaysia's moist, honey-dipped lips wrapping themselves around his throbbing dick.

Malaysia took pleasure in nipping that thought right in the bud. "Thanks, but no thanks," she answered concretely. "I'll take a rain check. I need to get home and prepare for tomorrow. I've got an early meeting to attend in the morning." When she stood, Malaysia was a vision in hot-pink couture. She eased her arms into her matching leather trench. While fastening the belt around her waist, she added with a friendly kiss on the cheek, "Thank you for the dinner, drinks and the company tonight. I needed some relief."

After some hesitation, Jovan conceded. "Oh, okay, baby." He flashed a plastic smile, snatched his leather and stepped out of the booth. "I'll walk you to your car," he offered, tossing his jacket on.

She placed a hand on his shoulder. "There's no need for you do that. I'm valet."

He smirked. "I know that. Everybody in here is valet. I was walking you out to your car to see you off."

Her head lowered. "That's okay," she replied dejectedly as she started walking away. "I'll call you tomorrow," she added with a wave.

Sucking his teeth, Jovan grumbled incoherently under his breath as he watched her walk away. He eased back into the private enclosure. Just as she left his phone rang.

Jovan looked down at the screen and saw that it was Tina calling. He smiled with a devious gleam in his eye. *Fuck it, I gotta enough time to swing her crib, break her off and then hit the club afterwards.*

ⱷⱷⱷⱷ

The bright white leather jacket and cap made Jovan an easy target to spot. He got up to leave and strode past a clean-cut majordomo dressed in a crisp gray Armani suit. A broad, welcoming smile broke out on Victor's face. "Have a good night, Mr. Rising. Please come again soon," he said in a tone that was unmistakably German.

A polite Hispanic doorman with a long ponytail smiled and waved as he opened the door for Jovan.

"Later, José," Jovan muttered quickly in passing. He stepped outside when he saw his black SUV pull to the curb. A frosty breath of wind smacked him in the face as soon as he moved away from the building. Jovan pulled up the collar on his jacket and hurried around to the driver's side of the car. He pushed a twenty in the parking attendant's hand as he got behind the wheel.

A Beautiful Satan

"Thank you, and have a good night, Mr. Rising," the Frenchman Adrian said as he pushed the door shut after him. He turned, adjusted the hood and rushed off to retrieve the next car.

A white Mercedes sedan pulled slowly away from the curb. Natasha allowed two cars to go ahead of her before she merged into the oncoming traffic. The glowing automobile accelerated into the traffic flow without drawing so much as a glance.

Her look was shrewd as she steered the sedan. "Let's see where you're off to now, Mr. Street Runner," she said, glaring intently through the windshield. She looked over at the laptop and noticed Jovan's position was right on target. "I can feel it in the air. There's going to be bloodshed tonight, and that person's spirit is going to haunt you for their death." Natasha was looking forward to killing her next victim. There was bloodlust in her soul.

ⓌⓌⓌⓌ

A teardrop hovered for a split second on the tip of Natasha's eyelid before rolling down her cheek. Her bottom lip quivered as she peered from a small opening in the doorway of the stairwell.

The beige door to unit 1206 opened. Jovan appeared with his white leather slung over his shoulder, and a half-naked Tina draped on his arm with his white leather Redskins cap cocked on her head.

"You sure you can't stay a while longer? I promise I'll make it well worth your time," Tina offered desperately, her mind and body exhibiting withdrawal symptoms. "Please, I'll do whatever you want."

The sound of Tina's whining made Jovan wince. He shook his head and peeled her paws from his arm. "You can't handle 'whatever.' Besides, I can't. Not tonight, shorty," he protested, plucking his cap from her head. "Maybe we can hook up tomorrow," he lied, attempting to take the sting out of the situation and get her off his back. "Alright, so give me a holla sometime tomorrow evening and I'll slide through."

When he looked back at her, he swore she was on the verge of having an all-out tantrum. Tina's bottom lip was poked out and her arms were folded defiantly across her chest. Her pouting didn't faze him one way or the other. There was no love lost for him. Baby girl was nothing more than a good acrobatic fuck partner.

Jovan leaned down, kissed Tina on the forehead, then spun around and marched toward the elevator. *I'm gonna have to cut that freak bitch off,* he confirmed to himself.

ⓌⓌⓌⓌ

Five minutes hadn't passed before Natasha emerged from the stairwell. She looked around and felt as if the long, deserted corridor was closing in on her. Her entire being was about to explode as she walked toward unit 1206.

She stood at the door breathing heavily as her trembling fingers moved along the door frame. She drew a long, serrated blade from inside her black North Face and rang the doorbell.

Tina walked out of the bedroom combing her hair. She smiled knowingly before she answered the door. "Yeah, I knew you wanted—" Her smile vanished when she saw a blonde, blue-eyed Angel framed in her doorway. Tina was shocked.

"Girl, what the hell have you done to yourself?" she asked, amazed.

Natasha's eyes glittered with an unholy light that made her tremble uncontrollably. "Whore!" she snarled between clinched teeth. Then with the fury of a demon's tempest, she began stabbing Tina.

A blood-curdling scream reverberated along the vacant hall for a chilling second before the loud slam of a door drowned it out. Silence rang out through the deserted corridor, leaving an ominous chill in the air.

Chapter 33

The ceiling fan whirled noiselessly overhead, pushing the sweet fragrance of expensive perfume around the room.

A noise sounded in the distance, causing Jovan's eyes to pop open. The bright morning sun greeted him. Its warm beams streamed through the window and felt good on his face as a thick white cloud of smoke began to roll across the floor.

A rash of goose bumps broke out along Jovan's exposed limbs. Worried, he sprang upright and saw a pair of manicured hands appear from the frosty cloud. They were surprisingly warm to the touch as they gently caressed his face. An eerie voice whispered from the smoky mist. "I want to have your baby, my love." The pair of manicured hands then slipped around Jovan's throat, gradually applying pressure, cutting off his air.

Malaysia floated from the mist like a ghost, her emerald eyes now devoid of color except for the ghostly white irises that cast a deadpan look upon Jovan. Her lips curled into a menacing sneer, like a soul possessed. Malaysia growled, "Put your seed in me!" Her hands locked around his throat with the strength of five men.

Jovan awoke coughing and chocking. He sat up, grabbing at his throat, struggling to breathe. His eyes swept across the empty bedroom, searching for his wife. Where was Angel when he needed her, he wondered. He jumped out the bed. He could hear the shower running. That's odd; she usually took bubble baths in the morning, he thought.

Staggering naked into the bathroom, he still was holding his throat, like a fish out of water straining to breathe.

"Angel!" Jovan called out in a raspy voice. "Angel, help me." When he snatched open the gold shower curtain in frustration, his expression was one of absolute shock when his eyes fell upon the bloodied, disemboweled corpse of Tina lying in his tub with cold water raining down on her lifeless body.

Suddenly Tina's eyes sprang open. "You said you were coming back!" she hissed, leaping from the tub like a hungry lioness.

"No!!!" Jovan shrieked.

The phone rang in Jovan's ear. "Oh my God!" he blurted, looking traumatized. The phone rang again. He groaned while rubbing his temple. He felt like shit, and he had himself to blame. All that overindulging he had done the night before.

He remembered starting the night with a Bone Crusher, then a Zombie, then a Tequila Sunrise. All that before taking two bottles of Cristal to the dome. Jovan reached over on the nightstand and fumbled with the cordless phone. "Hello. Who's this?" he grumbled. "Yeah, this is he. What? She's in the hospital? A car wreck? Yes, yes. I'm on my way," he said, talking fast, worried. He bounced out the bed. "Angel's in the fucking hospital!" Jovan said as he rushed to get ready.

A Beautiful Satan

When the maintenance crew found Tina's bloodied, naked corpse days later, she was lying on the kitchen floor, spread-eagle, with the body of her 18-month-old daughter curled up beside her. Both bodies lay in a mess of blood, shit and piss.

Immediately, the men could see the deep gash in the woman's throat. She had been slashed from ear and ear. The horrendous scene was too much for the trio of workers. They were so hysterical after seeing the bloody carnage that by the time homicide arrived on the scene to interview them, the men had to be whisked away in an ambulance.

Tina and her daughter were covered in so much blood the maintenance crew assumed the little girl was dead. The trio hightailed it out of there without looking back. Later, the maintenance crews were overjoyed to hear the good news: The little girl had survived. She was barely holding on, but she was alive.

It was a miracle the little girl lasted as long as she had. The medical tech was surprised and relieved when she detected the baby's slight pulse. The little girl could barely open her eyes or move any of her limbs. Immediately, they rushed the blood-soaked baby from the apartment via Medivac.

From the moment Louis and Clark stepped foot off the elevator, they knew right away from the horrid stench permeating the air that a decomposing body was nearby. Tony Woo stepped into the hallway covered from head to toe in a translucent plastic suit. He carefully peeled the latex from his chunky hands as he eyed the two characters moving along the carpeted corridor.

Clark walked with a purpose, his hands in their usual position: behind his back. His always stylish hat was placed perfectly on his shiny dome.

Louis was twirling his handlebar mustache, his baby blues constantly shifting to and fro as he absorbed every possible angle leading to the crime scene. Tony took an extra liking to the Canadian. His integrity was questionable, but Tony knew how powerfully persuasive a man his partner could be. He was the kind of intense personality capable of making a totally straight man doubt his own manhood. Tony had seen him in action on many occasions, and the man was definitely a master at his craft.

Tony Woo greeted the duo. "So how are my two favorite homicide detectives doing on this cold winter day?" he said, his slanted eyes peering over the top of his wire frames.

Clark sucked his teeth and replied tartly, "Cut the bull, Woo, and bring us up to speed on this crime scene. What'cha got so far?"

Tony snickered. "Mighty testy today, aren't we there, Clark?"
Sensing the tension tighten between the men, Louis disrupted the exchange. "Okay, guys," he said, gesturing with his hands. "Look, we're here to do a job, so the both of you need to chill out."

A humorous whistle sounded from Clark. "I heard that, Rich," he said, smiling. "My man here says cut the bull, Woo, and let's get down to work." He finished with a friendly pat on his partner's back.

Tony brushed the remark off with a look of discord. "It's our boy," he remarked grimly. "Slashed the lady in there from ear to ear."

"Any notable body parts missing?" Louis asked bluntly.

Tony hesitated before saying, "Well, I wouldn't say that it's a notable body part." His look hardened. "But it's extremely vital. The bastard sliced her clitoris from her vagina."

Clark cut in, "Is that the reason P.G. County requested our assistance?"

A Beautiful Satan

"Well of course," Tony smirked with disdain. "Why else would they want you out here in their jurisdiction? Your bubbly, outgoing personality and good looks?" He laughed at his own remark.

Captain Hill emerged from the elevator. He was a tall, strapping fellow who demanded attention. He cast a stern look down the corridor and descended upon the trio. "Gentlemen," the captain said, extending a welcoming hand. "I'm glad to see you were all able to make it here on such short notice. From the look of this crime scene, it's evident that we're dealing with an individual with an extremely dangerous mind and—"

"Captain Hill, I have some pertinent information for you and our visitors here," a uniformed sergeant interrupted. "It concerns two eyewitnesses." Once he had their undivided attention, the sergeant provided them with the eyewitness accounts of the desk clerk and a neighbor down the hall.

The desk clerk remembered seeing a man come into the lobby around 10:30 p.m. She had a distinct memory of him because of his nonchalant attitude. He was wearing an expensive white leather jacket and matching cap with the Washington Redskins football logo all over it. The neighbor's account backed up the desk clerk's description.

The desk clerk was an attractive young lady in her early twenties. She said the man looked like he could be a model and that he had piercing gray eyes. She remembered the hypnotic effect the man's eyes held over her when he waved and blew her a kiss. When he left around midnight, she attempted to get his phone before he left. She noticed his demeanor had changed. He rushed through the lobby and disappeared out the door without so much as a glance her way.

Louis and Clark recorded the witnesses' information. They would do a follow-up, but they weren't holding their breath. They doubted very seriously that a desk clerk would've seen the suspect they were looking for. They doubted that he even came in the front at all. In the words of their CSI counterpart, Ben Gordon, they were searching for a "chameleon." The pair was leaning more and more towards Ben's explanation. The description of a male model didn't go unnoticed by Tony Woo, however. Ben had also mentioned a ladies' man in his brief profile.

Tony Woo's assessment of the murder scene was really no different from all the rest. All pertinent forensic evidence had been wiped clean. He informed the men that he believed their break in the case world come from a public murder. Their serial predator was too crafty with the aspects of a controlled murder scene and was able to set the stage easily on a closed environment. He left what he wanted to leave, took what he wanted to take and allowed them to find what he wanted them to find.

There were a couple of significant details about the case that Woo wasn't being totally forthcoming about. For starters, he realized the killer was setting a stage with the bodies after slaying them, though the significance of the staged crime scene wasn't yet apparent to Woo. Secondly, the forensic guru had discovered a unique chemical element at each crime scene. The concentration and form of that specific chemical indicated that someone in high places may have direct involvement with these vicious murders.

Too Woo was leading a separate covert operation, investigating the serial case from an entirely different angle all together.

"Woo, why do you think our break will come from a public slaying, huh?" Louis inquired, skeptical.

Tony paused, studying his Canadian counterpart before stating plainly, "One of the book's golden rules, my friend: Haste leaves behind evidence."

Chapter 34

The constant blip on the EKG monitor seemed to have a certain calming effect over the hospital room and its resting patient once the room was totally devoid of any other disruptions. Suddenly light spilled across the white tiled floor, along the bed frame and across Angel's sleeping face.

She clenched her eyes tight to the invading light. She recoiled, startled. "What are you doing here?" Angel sat up, rubbing her stiff muscles. Her emotional state was a bundle of nervous energy.

Dr. Alverez seemed to have stopped breathing as he stared across the room at her. He whispered with fearful exhilaration, "I was just checking up on some of my favorite patients, that's all."

He approached the bed when she smiled. He loved the way she smiled. At the moment, he was fantasizing about her naked body intertwined with his.

"Is there anything that I could get you before I retire for the evening? Anything at all—food, drinks, myself? It wouldn't be a problem for me to pull up a chair and keep you company all night if you'd like. Not a problem at all. A crooked grin parted his dry, thin lips.

Angel shook her head, tickled by his flirtatious comment. "Now, Dr. Alverez," she said, "you know that I'm a married woman." She stopped and looked down at his ring finger. Angel added quietly, "And you're a married man, I can see. You know better than that. Your wife would be very disappointed in you, I'm sure."

Dr. Alvarez felt a wild excitement surge through his body from standing so close to this gorgeous creature. "You know your stay here with us is just about up, don't you, Mrs. Rising?" It was apparent he wasn't paying any attention to the comment she just made. He went on to say, "Your recovery was remarkable. But I was wondering … the place where your car was towed … my cousin owns the yard, and I have a few of your personal belongings that I'm sure you'd want back. Matter of fact, I'm certain of it."

Angel shot him a cautious look. She sensed something deceptive in his demeanor. *What is he hiding?* she wondered.

"Well," he continued, as he moved to the door and proceeded to push it shut and turn the lock, "I have your belongings with me now." He turned and flashed a devious grin. "Right downstairs in the trunk of my car. There's your overnight bag with your blonde wig, contacts, gloves, scarf … and a big machete? Oh, I can't forget I also have your laptop, and only God knows what's on it." He was hovering over her now, sexually perverse illusions swirling in his head.

Dr. Alverez traced his fingertips along the white linen. "I also found something very peculiar." He gazed down at her with spit forming in the corner of his mouth and surprised Angel when he stopped abruptly and grabbed her brutally by the wrist.

"I also found a bloody vial inside your bag with a woman's clitoris floating around inside, so don't play games with me, bitch! Give me what I want, or I'll have the whole fuckin' D.C. police department crawling up your ass faster than you can scream 'daddy,'" he hissed with lust brewing in his eyes.

Angel's lips trembled with contempt. "I don't know what the hell you're talking about, but you better get your dirty-ass hands off me!" Angel cringed when she felt his onion-tainted breath on her face. The dirty grin on his face made her want to vomit.

Dr. Alverez leaned in closer. I don't have time for this shit," he hissed bitterly and ripped the iPhone from his waist. "Let D.C. police handle your ass." He pressed the screen icon marked "security."

The phone speaker came to life. "Corporal Monroe. How can I assist you?" a voice answered.

Two seconds later a knock sounded on the door.

"Dr. Alvarez? Nurse Lewis. Are you in there?"

Beads of perspiration broke out on Angel's forehead. She shuddered when she felt that clammy sensation saturate both her palms. It was already too late. The nausea and butterflies were churning in her stomach, and the light in her hazel eyes grew dim.

Angel was claustrophobic all of a sudden as she watched the pitch-black shadow engulf her mind. Angel's conscious faded as the wicked nature that is Natasha emerged.

About The Author

R.J. Champ is a self-taught author. His passion and creativity for writing has given him the drive and vision to enlighten the urban genre and its readers with compelling new story lines, plots, and characters that will take the realm of urban street lit to unchartered territories and exciting new regions that have yet to be explored.

Contact Info:
R.J.Champ@gmail.com

I love feedback. Please be sure to post your reviews at dcbookdiva.com, amazon, b&n, and goodreads.com.

In Stock Now!

In Stock Now!

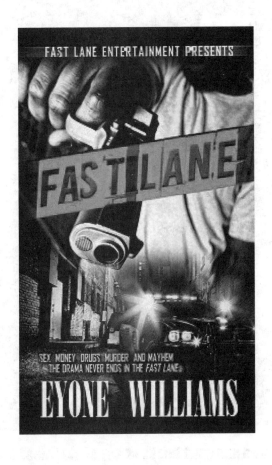

In Stock Now

DC BOOKDIVA PRESENTS

TRINA

THE HYDRO KILLER

DARRELL DEBREW

In Stock Now

DC BOOKDIVA PRESENTS

LORTON LEGENDS

EYONE WILLIAMS

COMING SOON

NOVEL BY
FRAZIER BOY

Order Form

DC Bookdiva Publications
#245 4401-A Connecticut Avenue, NW
Washington, DC 20008
dcbookdiva.com

Name: _____

Inmate ID _____

Address: _____

City/State: _____ **Zip:** _____

QUANTITY	TITLES	PRICE	TOTAL
	Up The Way, Ben	15.00	
	Dynasty By Dutch	15.00	
	Dynasty 2 By Dutch	15.00	
	Trina, Darrell Debrew	15.00	
	A Killer'z Ambition, Nathan Welch	15.00	
	Lorton Legends, Eyone Williams	15.00	
	A Beautiful Satan, RJ Champ	15.00	
	Coming Soon		
	The Hustle	15.00	
	A Hustler's Daughter	15.00	
	Q, Dutch	15.00	

Sub-Total $_____

Shipping/Handling (Via US Media Mail) $3.95 1-2 Books, $7.95 1-3 Books, 4 or more titles-Free Shipping

Shipping $ _____
Total Enclosed $ _____

Certified or government issued checks and money orders, all mail in orders take 5-7 Business days to be delivered. Books can also be purchased on our website at dcbookdiva.com and by credit card at 1866-928-9990. Incarcerated readers receive 25% discount. Please pay $11.25 per book and apply the same shipping terms as stated above.